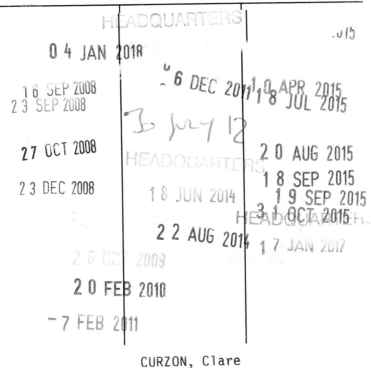

Off Track

Off Track

CLARE CURZON

First published in Great Britain in 2008 by
Allison & Busby Limited
13 Charlotte Mews
London W1T 4EJ
www.allisonandbusby.com

10 9 8 7 6 5 4 3 2 1

13-ISBN 978-0-7490-7946-8

Typeset in 13/16.5 pt Goudy Old Style by
Allison & Busby Ltd

Printed and bound in Great Britain by
MPG Books Ltd, Bodmin, Cornwall

CLARE CURZON began writing in the 1960s and has published over forty novels under a variety of pseudonyms. She studied French and Psychology at King's College, London, and much of her work is concerned with the dynamics within closely knit communities. A grandmother to seven, in her free time she enjoys travel and painting. Clare lives in Buckinghamshire.

Acknowledgements

The Misbourne Line is a fictitious railway company, but readers in Thames Valley who travel to Marylebone will recognise routes, stations and trains of the Chiltern Line. While all characters and incidents in this story are also fictitious, I wish to thank members of the Chiltern Line management for help they have given, including Naomi Simmons of Public Relations who referred me to DSM Mark Edlington for several technical questions on driving standards.

Again I am grateful to Ex-DCI Laurie Fray of Thames Valley Force, this time for introduction to members of British Transport Police, principally Albert Ryan, now retired, and Robin Tamplin with whom I enjoyed exploring sidings and locations. As ever, I thank my son John Curzon for generous advice on technical matters, and Louise Watson for her care in editing.

Chapter One

Piers Egerton carefully carried the two overfilled glasses of pina colada across, but Professor Clara Foulkes had turned her attention to a small, immaculately dinner-jacketed man with a white goatee beard. More than the force of her argument had crowded him into a corner, where he cowered under the hoisted spinnaker of her formidable bust.

Intervention was not only unwise but physically impossible. Piers retired to find some other recipient for the drink. Turning, he encountered a blonde young woman in black taffeta. 'Hello-o-o-o,' she cooed at him. 'We've not met. I'm Melissa. Tell me about yourself.'

'Piers Egerton. I'm a microbiologist.' He handed her one glass.

'And I'm a brain surgeon, a neuro-whatsit,' she claimed outrageously, half-flirting. She flung her shoulder-length hair and handed him her empty champagne flute. 'No, seriously, what do you do?'

That was the billion-dollar question: what *did* he do?

He considered this. 'You could say I destroy things,' he told her simply.

'What, in a demolition gang?' She sounded incredulous, by now taking him more for a bit of rough scrubbed-up for the evening. Rather, in fact, like her, tagging along as trophy girlfriend to a boring little fart from University College.

He nodded. 'Something like that.'

She struck a pose, weight on one jutting hip balanced by the out-flung arm, cocktail glass rotating between silver fingernails. 'So what? You're the bloke up in the crane cab swinging the big ball?' She looked at him with mock innocent eyes. 'I adore big balls.'

She was more than a little squiffy, he saw. It hardly mattered what he told her. 'I'm not let loose with such heavy stuff. I work on a very small scale.' He heard his own voice tinged with bitterness. So what? If she thought him pathetic, she might let him go. He could pretend he recognised someone over her shoulder, give a little wave, excuse himself and move on.

But no need: she'd beaten him to it, vaguely drifted away, finding him tedious. And that, as it happened, was his opinion of this whole academic social setup. There were more urgent, soul-searing subjects to bedevil his mind. He'd had enough here.

He dumped the untasted drink and the empty flute, went down by the grand staircase, collected his briefcase and went out into the street. It was a balmy evening; a slight coolness stirring the air after another torrid day. It smelt of London summer, something quite different from what he was used to: a blend of old, sun-dried stone and dusty leaves with a lingering hint of spicy food.

Sitting in the car, in comparative darkness, he watched the socialising figures move across the brightly lit, long windows, mingling and regrouping to seek fresh audiences for their competitive brilliance. All those robust egos; preening, everyone talking at high pitch, nobody listening: so much intellectual froth. For him, these academic gatherings had never been more than an embarrassing diversion from his work. It was fitting now to be the outsider looking in, because at this crossroads in his life, he was finished with it.

Professor Clara could stay on, boring and bossing her way round the roomful of colleagues, until the last bottle was empty and the last learned academic equally wrung dry of counters to her proposals.

He would catch her as eventually she left vexed at his disappearance – once she noticed it. He'd do this last escort duty, an ironic courtesy. And once he'd deposited her on her doorstep, that would be the end: the end of his career and of any deserved honours in his chosen field. Even, perhaps, the beginning of persecution.

Martyrdom: his mouth twisted bitterly. He knew he was no hero.

After almost a decade of compromising with his conscience, Piers had been considering alternative paths his studies might have taken him: genetic engineering; organising and developing new saprotrophs and yeasts into fresh areas of food production to save the starving hordes of Africa and Asia. Even the humbler posts of sewage-farm manager or coordinator of the nation's refuse dumps might have been more palatable than his present researches, the culture and proliferation of viruses capable of turning a human's frame and innards into sludge. The academic challenge had once excited him beyond considering the outcome to either humanity or himself, but it no longer excused what he now found himself immersed in.

At the time of the Cold War, when the project was conceived, it had been necessary to build up defences to counter the USSR's enormous outlay on military strength with nuclear and space research. He had assumed that when the Curtain finally came down, the project would be set aside, grind to a halt, and then he could turn his mind to beneficial medicine.

The Curtain fell and the Soviet Empire fragmented, but the project rolled unassailably on. Yearly he expected that the Financial Review would kill it off, but the damn thing had developed a hideous life of its own. Now, with it past the animal-testing stage, visible suffering had a power to move him that he could never have imagined while all was theoretical and at lab-experimental level. And its instigators marched on like zombies, robots manipulated and enslaved by the study itself. Only he seemed aware of the almighty obscenity it was becoming. Never attracted to religion, he now was held transfixed by an image of men's souls themselves turned to slush inside by the evil he had sold himself into.

And so, in revolt, he must finally summon what little was left to him of decency and human dignity: turn his face away, become a traitor to his lifetime's work.

They were expecting him at Beaconsfield, but it wasn't MoD Intelligence he'd be talking to. Instead there would be someone waiting to whisk him away to a safe house while they worked together on an acceptable way to make this available to the gulled British public. He'd left no trail. Long after anyone missed him, they might find his car in the underground garage to Professor Clara's apartment block.

Chapter Two

A week earlier

Lee Barber gently pulled the control handle towards him through four power notches to the wide open position. As the engines picked up, the Turbostar accelerated smoothly past the end of the platform ramp at Denham Station. At once the bright pools of sodium lighting were gone, and Lee rubbed his eyes, straining to adjust against the wall of darkness enveloping the cab.

He considered the irony that the headlights weren't for his benefit, but to warn anyone on the track of the train's approach. The beams spread too thinly to light up the route ahead. It might be the twenty-first century but as far as rail progress went, that hadn't changed since the 1850s.

A driver had to know where he was without needing to look. Even in a pea-soup fog, he was expected to run at full line speed, so long as the signals were green. But then, night driving was a skill that Lee enjoyed. There was something primeval about the way that, once you lost vision, your other senses were stimulated and you fell back on instinct – almost became a hunter.

Even though you drove this route every day, you were now 'flying blind'. Once in the country and away from the town lights, although your eyes were of little use, you heard the changing rhythm of the rails, the whoosh of structures that the cab passed by; you felt the jolts and the swaying; you counted the signals and you could smell the different crops in the fields. It took time to pick up on the sensory map, but once cracked, it was a skill that set you apart.

Lee smiled, wondering how long it would take him to forget this local lore once he'd escaped to join the Big Boys. He silently thanked the Misbourne Line for his training, but any debt would be paid after his probation and two years of productive driving. Then he'd be off like a greyhound from the traps to something bigger and better.

It was the European Express he would go for. On the Continent they had fantastic routes and all the latest technology; no more being held up for lost backpackers stowing camping junk and bicycles, and doddery old grandads limping the length of the train for a favourite carriage. No, he'd be carrying the elite – senior government officials and captains of industry. On silky smooth rails he'd whisk them at 180 mph between Europe's capitals. International train cabs were air conditioned, with state-of-the-art electronics and in-cab signalling, more like the Space Shuttle rather than a train.

Beside all this there'd be an enhanced lifestyle with improved status, a higher salary and private health

care. As often as they wished, he could take the kids
to Euro Disney. They'd be really chuffed with that;
and later it would be cool for them to trail their friends
round Europe for free. Also, he could sweep Kathy off
to candlelit dinners in exotic places where the famous
were on show. She wouldn't then say that train-driving
had destroyed what little romance her husband ever
possessed.

She'd never understood the domestic problem that
the shift system played on drivers forever catching up
with their body rhythms. You started on a week of the
rarer night shifts, and just when your body had settled
into them, learning to sleep in the daylight, your roster
changed you to Earlies. Then, as you were adjusting to
those and going home to sleep afternoons, you were
moved over to Lates. And so the cycle went on and on,
alternating and wearing you down to a frazzle.

When Lee had passed his entry assessment, his mate
Justin, a lifetime train driver, had congratulated him.
Then he said, 'So now you've joined the ranks of the
Permanently Knackered. You've yet to learn that sleep
is for girls, old son. It's a good life, but remember this –
strangers will become your family, and your family get to
be strangers.'

Justin had raised his tankard and laughed when he
said it, but Lee knew him well enough to pick up on the
bitterness. He'd been there when Justin's family tore
itself apart.

* * *

Lee grunted and turned to look at the track maintenance engineer who had joined him in the cab at West Ruislip. Raising an eyebrow, he said, 'Well, it doesn't feel bumpy to me.'

Frank Morton smiled. 'Yeah, it's pretty smooth. Actually, it was one of your guys who called in the "Rough Ride", but that was at midday when the sun was cooking the ballast. The rail would have been tightening up in the expansion joints. Now that the sun's down everything has cooled off and slackened back to normal. I really wasn't expecting to find it so late in the day, but I was overdue a ride down to GX anyway, and it gets me out of the office.'

Lee nodded. 'Well, it's always good to have company on the Graveyard Run.'

'You been long on the night shift then?'

Lee nodded. 'Three days down; four to go after this one.'

'Do they come round often?'

'No, but never would be enough. It isn't the Nights themselves; the work's really easy: late trains, and then shunting and next-day preparations. The hard part is at the end of the run, when you're struggling to get your body rhythm back on to the early shift – that's the killer.'

Drizzle misted the windscreen. Lee turned the wiper control to 'intermittent' and squirted a couple of jets of screenwash. After early June's torrid heat this was the first rain in several weeks. By now the rails were contaminated with oil and brake dust. Not a problem while the weather stayed dry, but with a few drops of rain a fine greasy film would form on the railhead. This would be as slippery as a buttered frying pan.

Stopping at Denham Golf Club could prove a little tricky. He usually started his braking sequence as the train rattled over the Home Farm foot crossing but, with the drizzle, that would be too late tonight. He might need as much as thirty per cent extra braking distance.

He considered how much earlier he should start. His eyes had now adjusted to the dark and he made out the silhouette of Fletchers' Wood to his right, like a pile of cumulus cloud.

Yes, putting the brake in Step One when passing the field of pig pens would bleed the speed off gently, giving control space if she started to slide.

He drove on in silence. The engineer, thumbing through a bunch of papers under his clipboard light, raised his head to complain. 'You know, this job's gone to shit. We spend half our time filling in forms to explain why we're only half as productive as we should be. If we threw away all the bureaucracy we could be *fully* productive. Then the nit-pickers and accountants would have to find proper, honest jobs – which has to be good.' He grinned wryly. 'Would you believe that I started out reading for a Law degree?'

'No kidding?' said Lee. 'Just think of the money you gave up on!'

'Stuff that. Actually, I get all the courtroom contention I can handle in *this* job. Besides, I sometimes like to get my hands dirty and feel the rain on my face.'

'*Rain!* Oh God,' shouted Lee. By now they were past

the pig-pen field. He'd missed the early braking. Already the foot crossing rattled underneath. Lee knew he had no choice. He must go for the usual full brake pressure; not the light application he'd planned.

He pushed the control handle forward into Step Two and checked the brake pressure gauge. The needle rose boldly to display the expected two bars, but began to quiver, and then dance crazily between zero and two bars. The speedometer, which seconds earlier had shown a steady 70 mph, was now also performing a drunken wobble.

'No, *no!*' he growled.

'She's sliding!' The engineer braced himself in his seat as the bogie below him shimmied between the rails with the wheels fighting for a grip.

The train had Wheel Slide Protection, like ABS on a car. Whenever the wheels started to lock, it released the brakes, and then once the wheels were turning again, reapplied them. There was hissing as the air brakes released.

'Nothing you can do? I can't feel we're slowing.'

'I've pressed Emergency Sanding, so we're laying a trail of grit to give more friction. All we can do now is hope.'

The bright lights of Denham Golf Club station flashed into distant view. OK, there was an optical illusion, Lee told himself. Stations always look closer at night, brilliant against the dark.

But DGC *was* coming up fast. He knew the train couldn't stop within the length of the platform.

'Nothing for it, but to go into Emergency,' Lee groaned. He slapped the plunger by his left elbow and the whole train juddered as the braking force dramatically increased.

'Won't hard braking make the slide worse?' Morton protested.

Lee grunted. 'Sure, but it's required company procedure for a station overrun. Either way, I'm damned if I do and damned if I don't.'

The hissing rose in intensity, but now both of them could feel the train lurching each time the brakes were applied. Carriages were slamming into each other and bouncing around as each of them braked.

The train *was* slowing, but not enough. A lump grew in Lee's throat as the platform rolled past his window. It was like a cliffhanging nightmare where you felt your grip slipping helplessly away. The far ramp of the platform slid past, leaving the cab once more in darkness, and then mercifully the train ground to a halt.

Lee opened his cab door and leant out to see by how much he'd overshot the station. 'Thank God,' he said, squinting back. 'With luck, I reckon I've got the last set of doors against the platform.'

He reached in his bag for his orange hi-viz jacket and Bardic lamp. Then, lifting the public address handset, he counted to three to steady his voice and keyed up the mike.

'Good evening, ladies and gentlemen, this is your driver speaking. We've just arrived at Denham Golf Club station. Due to a temporary technical fault on this train,

I can only release the doors on the rear coach, so would any passengers wishing to alight at Denham Golf Club please go to the rear end of the train where I will release the doors manually. Thank you.'

Lee passed through into the carriage behind him and hurried down the train. The few passengers were either asleep, listening to personal stereos or chatting quietly among themselves. Nobody looked up to enquire what the problem was. In the last carriage only a middle-aged lady was waiting for him, smiling as he inserted his carriage key into the release on the doors.

He followed her outside and glanced the length of the platform. At the far end, a single figure waved uncertainly and began to walk down to meet the passenger.

Nobody was waiting to get on. Lee boarded the train and closed the doors.

'Everything OK?' Frank Morton asked as he returned.

'Yeah, a piece of cake. Nobody's the wiser.'

Lee drove on in silence, but uneasy. With hindsight he knew he should have called the signaller for permission to change to the rear cab, and then back the train into the station. That way, all the doors could be opened properly. This was written in stone in the *Drivers' Rulebook*, and he had played it his own way, gone maverick.

But then, if he'd stuck to the rules and kept it official, not only would he have lost time but his licence would have been marked with a 'Safety of the Line Incident'.

A flipping minor overrun that he'd rapidly sorted without anyone being the worse off!

As with a road driver's licence, railway incidents remained on record for years, but a helluva lot longer, hanging like an albatross round your neck. It would have counted against him at every job application and promotions board he put in for. The recruiters – office-bred twits who wouldn't know one end of a train from the other – didn't want 'dodgy drivers', so it was the sort who kept their records clean by wriggling out of the hard stuff or going sick on their occasional week of Nights – *they* would be the ones to get to the top.

It's ironic, thought Lee, that experience gained from mistakes could deny you advancement. It seemed that initiative never scored against iron-bound regulations. I guess that would have been my chance for the European Express well and truly stuffed. Well bollocks, I'd just better stay shut about tonight's little lark.

Right now, though, keep my mind on track: can't risk another mistake tonight.

Across the cab, Frank Morton could appreciate Lee was in no mood for talking. He felt bad, conscious that his rabbiting had contributed to the overrun. He always lectured new graduate recruits on the importance of not distracting the driver when out on cab rides. Tonight he should have held his tongue, not gone ranting on about his ruddy paperwork. He was relieved when they pulled into Gerrards Cross station where he was to pick up his car.

Out on the platform, he leant in the cab's open side

window. 'Listen, Lee, I hate the Safety Taliban as much as you do. So I never rode on this train tonight. I didn't see anything amiss, OK?'

'Cheers, Frank. Every minute that goes by without me receiving a complaint improves my chance of getting away with it.'

'Yup, so good luck.'

Lee waved, pulled open the power controller, and the train rolled off into the night.

All went well until Beaconsfield station, when the signaller called him on the radio.

He picked up the handset. 'Hello, Signaller, this is the driver of 2C34, just pulling into Beaconsfield on the Down.'

'Hello there, Driver. Signaller on panel 5 at Marylebone here. Listen mate, this doesn't come from me, but I've just had your Control Centre on the phone. They're screaming blue murder because they've had a report that you overran Denham Golf Club, although there's nothing here on our signalling log.' He paused. 'What do you want me to tell them?'

Briefly Lee thought of claiming they were wrong. How could they possibly know what happened? But, after any allegation, the train's data recorder would be analysed, showing every detail of moves made. He would face an additional disciplinary charge for lying, after already failing to report an incident. And since all radio conversations were recorded, whatever he said now could later be checked for consistency.

He'd just have to bluff it.

'Oh God, yes. I meant to call that in, but I was so involved with the passengers that I missed out. I'm really sorry, mate.'

There was a brief pause at the other end, as the signaller considered this. 'OK, Driver, I'll pass that on. Panel 5 out.'

As Lee replaced the handset he thought he'd sensed sympathy in the signaller's voice. No railwayman liked to see another involved in an operating incident. Still, thought Lee, he's sitting pretty in his cosy signal box, whilst I'm up to my neck in ravening alligators. How the hell does he know the pressures?

From then on everything seemed to pass in slow motion, leaving Lee to puzzle over how the overrun had been detected. The track engineer wouldn't have reported him and the signaller had claimed ignorance. Denham Golf Club station was unmanned at night, so it couldn't have been platform staff there. Had a railway manager been on the train? Or was an ordinary passenger making trouble? How would he know who to report an incident to? Only one passenger had needed DGC, and he'd seen her off OK.

The rest of the trip took forever, until finally he pulled into Aylesbury. There, waiting at the far end of the platform, a figure in a bright orange anorak waited, a laptop case slung over his shoulder.

Thank God it's my own DSM, old Bascombe, Lee thought. He'll give me a decent hearing, unlike some of the younger managers out for fame through hanging a few drivers.

As the platform emptied of the last bleary passengers, Bascombe quietly walked up to the cab. 'Now, Lee, as you probably know, there's been an allegation that you missed Denham Golf Club tonight. Has some dozy passenger got it wrong?'

Lee looked at him evenly. 'No, boss; it's down to me. I screwed up. It was an overrun.'

Bascombe straightened. 'Oh, pity! Right then, you'd better go over to my office and start filling out a report form. And try not to have a pee if you can avoid it: we have to get a Drugs and Alcohol Sample from you. I'll put your train away myself because I'll need to download the data recorder.'

Lee trudged along to the depot office, which was empty at this late hour.

So it actually was a passenger who'd done the dirty on him. The bastard! What harm had it done anyone? The lost time was made up. Nobody was inconvenienced or put at risk.

Some bloody little Hitler with a mobile phone has marked my card! I'll bloody wring his neck if ever I get hold of him.

The missing piece of the puzzle wasn't long in coming. A few minutes after Lee sat down at the desk in the DSM's office the fax machine sprang to life, spewing out several pages. With a quick glance at the open door, Lee walked across and read the top sheet. It was a Control Log report for the night, and his own name leapt out at him.

Reference 1187658
*Alleged failure to call at Denham Golf Club. Derby
Control Centre contacted by Network Rail Enquiries.
Passenger Mr Donald Ince enquired why the train had missed
Denham Golf Club Station. Train Operating Company
unaware of this incident.*
Driver L Barber to provide a report ASAP.

Lee scribbled the name *Ince* into his diary. The flaming
idiot had got it wrong: I *did* stop at Denham Golf –
though only just. Anyway, cheers, Mr Ince, for stuffing
my career. If I ever get the chance to return the favour
I'll happily oblige.

Boiling with resentment, he waited while Bascombe
walked back down the track from South Sidings. Then
the questions began.

At home, Kathy was deep asleep in bed, accustomed to
his creeping about in the early hours. But never this late,
he thought grimly.

He knew he couldn't settle to sleep. Too much
rancour was burning inside him. He wandered around
downstairs, careful to make no sound that would wake
the restless toddler.

Reaching for fruit juice from the fridge, his hand
slipped on the bottle. It fell, smashing on the ceramic
tiles. The crash brought Kathy down, alarmed and still
confused with sleep.

'Lee, are you all right?' Then she saw the time on
her kitchen clock. 'Where on earth have you been?'

Concern changed swiftly to accusation. 'You haven't been out *drinking?*'

He stared at her, baffled and furious. 'No, I bloody haven't.'

Any other time he would have opened up, poured it all out – the stupid mistake, the blot on his record. Then Kathy would have put her arms around him, rocked him gently in a big hug. And understood.

But not tonight. She thought he'd lied to her about the drink. He felt it like cold air rushing between the two of them. 'I'm bushed,' he said shortly. 'I'm going to turn in.'

He walked past her, but halfway upstairs he stopped and came down again. He felt worse now. He knew he could never settle in bed alongside her. Tossing and turning, burning with anger, there'd be no rest for either of them.

'I'll doss on the sofa,' he snarled, and made for the sitting room. There all the heat of the past day lingered with a shut-in mustiness. He opened a window, peeled off his clothes, dropping them on the carpet. His flesh felt clammy to the touch.

Sitting naked on the edge of the cushions, he was instantly shuddering with cold. He reached for the rug folded along the back of the sofa and wrapped it round his shoulders.

Tomorrow he'd be stood down. No, that was actually tonight. He couldn't drive a train again until the result of his urine test came through negative. He'd be sitting on his arse all night at the depot. The standby driver brought in to cover for him would be moaning about picking up an extra set of Nights, and word would go round what he'd done. It could even get back to Kathy. So he'd better soon come clean.

He curled up on one side, hugging his resentment and the scratchy rug to him, until eventually sleep came and wiped everything out.

Chapter Three

Early Saturday, 2nd June

The familiar rhythm of wheels on track should have soothed him, swaying with the home-going train, but he was too embittered to allow it. Anger, simmering all day, his Friday Rest Day, had to be given full throttle. The petty irritations – the kids' racket when he'd meant to lie in, and the new distance between himself and Kathy – scratched at the surface of the deeper, permanent sense of everything working against him.

It had been like this ever since the overrun, days of mounting frustration against the inevitable system that applied rules irrespective of circumstances. It still rankled that Bascombe had trotted out with his bloody clipboard ready to haul him over the coals the minute he knocked off that unfortunate night run. Thank God that Morton, the track inspector, hadn't still been on hand to witness his humiliation.

He knew he should snap out of it: this wasn't the end of the world. More than half the trouble at home was due to his own surliness and inability to unburden himself to Kathy about what had happened a week back. On top of all this was disgust at this present inability to make up his mind and stick with it. Were the rails so magnetic that he had to be here riding them again when off duty? He was a bloody poor fish, a sad sack.

Why had he agreed to turn up for Brenda's fortieth birthday bash in Soho? He was in no mood for a staff piss-up or to waste time on others from the depot, mostly no-hopers; even worse, the bright-eyed youngsters who were out to get somewhere, the way he'd been before this incident happened.

But, anyway, escaping the domestic fracas as Kathy prepared the kids for their half-term week at her mother's, he'd started out that afternoon for London, regretted the move halfway and ended up skulking on his own around the West End. The heatwave hadn't let up and there wasn't a breath of air stirring in the narrow streets. He was bored out of his rancid mind and uneasy with the mixture of greasy hamburger and fizzy beer lying heavy on his unaccustomed stomach. At Marylebone he'd caught the last six-carriage train home, unrecognised out of uniform, and used his BR1B key to slink into the rear cab of the leading three-car unit, like a hunted fox gone to earth. There, in an alcoholic haze, he hugged resentment to him until gassy disturbance boiling up in his gut overrode all else and forced him out.

He left the cab, checked that the lock had dropped in, and began walking forward. In the passenger section of this coach its single occupant sat by the window, an anonymous dark-suited shape bowed over a sheaf of official-looking papers. A scuffed black briefcase lay unlatched on the seat beside him, its faded silver monogram facing blankly upwards. In passing, Lee saw the inscription leap up at him: four equidistant capital letters, INCE.

It was beyond belief.

He stared, transfixed, a great pulse drumming under his skull. It was happening over again; this last train down; and Ince here – the very man who had wiped out his golden dream, wrecked his European ambitions – here, just as on that other night. His lips, suddenly dry, snarled against his teeth as his stomach convulsed and bile spurted over his chin. The whole carriage swung away as he clung to a seat back.

The name was seared into his brain: *Ince*. This dark-suited, rather undersized man was the bastard who'd destroyed him, cost him his clean licence, even upset his happy homelife; made a mockery of any efforts ever to get clear of the faceless crowd.

Ince, the pompous git who'd seen fit to slime him out like a slug underfoot, self-righteously looking for trouble, making an officious phone call, maybe in a crowded carriage; showing off how much he was in the know, how superior, how *un*-vulnerable.

Lurching on, Lee Barber made his way down the carriage; with a shaking hand reached for the lavatory door, went through, slammed it against the world and fell against the wall. His head felt like a balloon engorged with blood. He retched, managed to raise the seat before throwing up, again and again, until only a thin, acid trickle was left. His forehead was clammy and his throat seared. He shivered, still on his knees.

Ince on this train! The man was pursuing him, had caught up again. But now it was different. This time there was nothing left in Lee to destroy: just a seething hatred and the overwhelming passion for revenge.

Now the roles were reversed. The man Ince, totally unaware, was offered up to him. This enemy, never seen in the flesh until this moment, had materialised as an undersized minor official, a paperwork puppet, yielding itself up for settlement: no longer a menace, vulnerable in his turn. And he, Lee, wasn't officially here; had slunk in, unrecognised in civvies. Nobody would ever know he'd been here this night.

It was meant to be. There was a demonic force driving him, compelling him to act. And he knew he had to.

He got up, relieved himself, threw water over his face and wiped it off with a harsh paper towel. He scowled at his face in the mirror. He hardly knew himself. The consuming, crimson heat still powered him; but with the earlier shakiness controlled, every tense movement was deliberate now, focused; his only fear – that the man should leave the train too soon.

In the corridor, he stumbled against the Emergency Cupboard. Mesmerised, he stared at the words which seemed to come closer and recede as he swayed on unsteady legs.

No need to break the glass: he has his key. Robotically he opens up, surveys extending ladder, cable ties, saw, crowbar, nylon rope, short-circuiting bar, first aid kit – so often checked before on train 'preps'. This time they have a special meaning.

He takes a length of cord. It seems as though he has done this before. He feels the strength of it, taut between his hands. Unobserved, he returns through the almost empty coach to where the small man is still frowning over his papers. He stands close, ready, waiting to be seen.

Ince looks up. He sees the taut cord held out towards him, reads the intention in Lee's drunken face; is paralysed with fear.

Lee slips the loop over the creature's head. He can barely make out the man's features through a reddish haze. His hands cross over the exposed throat and they pull. There is barely a gurgle as the man's legs start kicking. His face is suffused with blood. Lee goes on and on, pulling until the body's convulsions cease. The frantically clutching hands fall away. The body goes slack.

Regaining the cab, with the slumped figure dragged in at his feet, he feels a brief surge of almost superman wellbeing. From the side window he watches the lights of Seer Green Station slide slowly past. No one alights; no one boards. The night is dark, moonless. He must stay on till the end of the line and the train is left in sidings.

In slow motion, it seems, the train makes its customary journey, calling at every station: Beaconsfield, High Wycombe, Saunderton, Princes Risborough, Monks Risborough, Little Kimble…

An eternity later, at 01.24, the final weekday train from Marylebone pulls into Aylesbury and the last few passengers leave. Silence. It is like the end of the world. There is nothing beyond.

Out of the void footsteps approach. One of the station staff is walking through to check that all carriages are empty. He completes the first section, glancing into the third carriage.

In the locked cab Lee crouches low, the body at his feet. Shocked, he remembers the briefcase with its worn, silver monogram lying to be discovered where the dead man had sat. But no, surely it had fallen to the floor in their struggle, so at a cursory glance into the carriage it may not have been noticed.

Was there a pause in the man's invisible progress? Hard to tell. All existence is suspended as Lee holds his breath. The steps recede. Double doors wheeze open, whoosh shut. The man has stepped out on the platform, goes past the cab towards the train's rear half, his boots echoing hollowly in the silent night.

In a new life, Lee breathes again. Something like reality begins to return. Minutes later the train slides quietly out of the station. Lee hears the familiar clunk as it passes over the points and enters South Sidings with a gentle swing; then the final slowing; a smooth stop; a pause as the driver collects his stuff to climb down. The last lights go out, the cab door slams up front.

Lee is left alone with the body, to wait for his shattered mind to catch up.

Luck is with him, because earlier that evening he'd

parked the car quite close to the spike-topped steel fencing. Tonight there are no graffiti artists tagging walls or trains; Transport Police have made a recent clean sweep of them. Lee enters the code and opens the electronically operated gate.

Ince was nothing like Lee's own weight, but it took four minutes, with a break halfway, to get him to the car, unlock the boot and heave him over the back sill. He found himself shivering despite the night's warmth. His mind was numbed and jumpy all at once.

Everything stayed quiet and he questioned if he should go back to check on the briefcase. But it could be too late. Cleaners could already be on the train's far side. The case would be docketed and sent on to Lost Property. Or someone might even fancy it and not hand it in. No way could it be traced back to an off-duty driver supposedly spending his evening at home.

What had he done? He sat behind the steering wheel, suddenly chilled, petrified. He couldn't believe it: that he had actually taken a man's life. Even if Ince wasn't a man, but a vindictive monster.

Surely, sooner or later, here or elsewhere, Nemesis would have caught up with the bastard, going through life with no thought for anyone, officiously, callously destroying other men's lives. It was only by chance that it had been his, Lee's, hand that finished the creature off. It just happened that it was tonight, when he was outside himself with drunken anger. Could that be excuse enough?

He found he couldn't remember the man's face; had

never properly looked at it. The small, suited figure had been a *thing*, not a man at all. His head throbbed. Misery, combined with a shift-free weekend, had led him to overdo the booze. The earlier vomiting hadn't settled that. Looking up-line now, he was aware how the rails appeared to be weaving, knotting like macramé. Glad he hadn't to pick his way on foot along them, he leant against the back of the driving seat, his ribs still sore from retching. It seemed the shuddering would never cease.

He re-ran the incident endlessly in his mind, as if he could rehearse it into some different outcome, edit out the bad bits, build himself into some more heroic figure. But no: it was gross.

The illuminated dial of his watch showed 01.39. Saturday already, and more than time he made for home. Home and normality. But could anything be normal any more, after what he'd done? Fresh panic struck with the thought that he had to cover his tracks. There was yet more to do. He groaned aloud, turned on the ignition and began shakily backing out.

Thank God Kathy and the kids were now safely away at Granny's. No one at home to see the state of him. By Monday's shift he'd have pulled himself together. The whole free weekend lay ahead, in which to sort himself out and face what he'd done. He must try and decide how to cope with the fallout. But not go to the police. That he couldn't do.

With his fury cooling, doubts began to creep in: a new shift of unreality. Driving on familiar roads towards home, he could almost believe it had been no more than a wild fantasy in his mind: a wishful dream about the man he detested. Befuddled, he could barely sort his mind to deal with gear change and steering. All the automatic, habitual actions had to be worked out again as if he were a novice, because of the intrusion of this other thing. He tried to persuade himself that the whole encounter was some monster illusion. It couldn't have happened.

Once he reached home he knew he must open up the car's boot and make sure. Was it no more than some imagined revenge he'd dreamt up about the despicable Ince?

But no; he knew he couldn't truly hope for that. However much he might long to believe it wasn't real, the impossible had happened.

But he wasn't like that. Not a bad man. Ask anyone who knew him; easygoing, amiable old Lee, the gentle giant, always willing to help a mate out. His hands clamped stiffly on the wheel, as they had on the murderous cord. Unthinkably, overwhelmed by some outer force, he, Lee Barber, had taken a man's life. And the law would demand he pay the price.

He must have been thinking aloud, for the words hung on, as if echoing from the closing-in sides of the car: *Pay the price!*

Yet that hopeful sliver of disbelief remained, and when he had garaged the car he had to go round to make sure.

He opened the boot and dared to look. The body lay folded as he'd packed it in, with the murderous rope tucked in beside it. Sickly he turned away. Best leave the lid open. Dead things soon start to smell.

He switched off the light, fumbled over double-locking the garage door, and stumbled blindly into the house.

Going through to the unlit kitchen, he drank water under the cold tap, drenching his face, and as he reached for the roller towel on the door, his boot caught against a solid, canvas-covered object on the floor.

Kathy had left it there as a reminder. This weekend, he was to remove the rotten limbs on the old apple tree. It wasn't enough that he'd taken down the children's swing. Protective as ever, she'd insisted branches could fall on them as they played below.

He rubbed his face dry, contemplating the shrouded chainsaw. It was more than providential. Like finding the loathsome Ince alone and defenceless tonight, this was surely meant to be. Sickly, he knew that tomorrow he would tackle the tree. And later, on a groundsheet in the garage, he must put the chainsaw to grimmer use.

Repellent as it was, in small parcels the body could be more easily disposed of. Not with the recyclable waste, but in plastic sacks dropped far out to sea, lost for ever.

Ben Hartley's boat was lying up unused at Newhaven while the old chap recovered from his hip replacement operation. He'd be happy for Lee to take it out on a Sunday fishing trip.

He'd intended going straight to bed. He was tired like he'd never been before in his life. But when, still dressed, he stretched out on the mattress, he knew sleep wouldn't

come. Terrible things were being re-enacted on the back
of his eyelids.

He had to finish the job. He went downstairs, lugged
the chainsaw into the garage and closed the door after
him. How much noise would the bloody thing make –
enough to wake old Godden next-door? How could he
explain if the man called round to complain later; or
even worse, got up and came poking his long nose in
while Lee was still at it? No, it wasn't on, not now the
shaking had come back. He wasn't in a fit state to tackle
it.

He put the heavy chainsaw down and groped in the
dark for the sill of the car boot. His hand fell on fabric:
the dead man's quality suiting. It was still warm to the
touch.

It moved under his fingers. There came a strangled
sound; strained croaking. '*No, no! For…God's sake, no!*'

Ince, not dead? – that or his ghost.

Lee staggered against the wall, reaching for the light
switch. When it came on, a feeble naked bulb, it still
dazzled his eyes adapted to the dark. Ince straddled the
edge of the car boot, one hand to his throat, the other
shielding his eyes.

'You don't…under…*stand.*' Ince made an effort to
swallow, pleading; putting out one hand to Lee to delay
him. 'We want the…same thing. I'm…on…your side.'

Anger flooded Lee, leaving no further room for fear.
How could this happen? It hadn't been meant to go like
this.

And then it struck like a blow to the solar plexus: *he*

wasn't a killer! Enormous relief surged through him, and then left him struggling with the enormity of the new situation. Ince still alive! Had he to do it again? How could he let the man survive, surely to tell of what had happened?

His whole body shuddered as fear repossessed him. The man was babbling, his words making no sense. He broke off in a prolonged fit of coughing and slumped against the car body, slithering towards the floor. 'Don't...don't!' he pleaded, his hands going again to his damaged throat.

Lee found he had already opened the driving door and reached in for his water bottle before the intention reached him. He stood looking at it in his hand, stupefied.

Ince appeared to have collapsed. It was instinctive then to unscrew the cap, pour water over the man's face and force his lips apart to drink. Ince made more choking noises and his eyes came open. He grasped Lee's hand on the bottle and began gulping thirstily.

'Thank...you,' he managed brokenly, and stopped to take breath. He tried to sit up. 'I've thrown...it in. You people are right; it's...hideous. Not just...the animals. Humans too. Well, even...worse. I...didn't re...a...lise, until I *saw*...what it does.'

What the hell was the man going on about? Animals, and then people. What was hideous? Did he mean Lee was hideous, trying to kill him? There were no animals involved. The man's wits had gone; he was raving.

If so, perhaps he'd have no memory of what Lee had

actually done to him – *tried to do* to him, and by almighty good fortune had failed. Did a chance remain that it could all be wiped out – as if it had never happened? Like they'd never met? Just vanish like a bad dream on waking?

Maybe that could happen for the moment; but later? Tomorrow – what would happen when the man recovered?

'Help me,' the man said.

'Why the hell should I?' Lee blazed, outrage returning. 'After what you did to me? You…you self-righteous little prick. Just a phone call to you; but for me – no, not the end: you don't get sacked for a station overrun, but it's gone on my record and I'd meant to do so much better. Listen, Ince, you fucking bastard, safe for life in your protected job…you've really fucked me up.'

'Ince?' the man faltered. 'Who's…Ince? My name's… Eger…ton. Piers Egerton. Look, I can…prove it.' One hand started fluttering towards an inner pocket in his jacket.

Going for a weapon, Lee thought and punched his hand away. A small wallet of credit cards fell to the garage floor. 'You can't fool me,' he threatened. 'Your name was on the briefcase for all to see. *Ince*; you can't deny it.'

'Ince, yes. Ince – I-N-C-E.' The man was again on the verge of choking. Lee watched while he tried to get the next words out.

'Initials, see? That's…the department I used…to work for. Immuno-neut…ralising…Combat Exercise.'

Lee stared. The man looked as though he meant it. In his present state, could he instantly have thought up such a preposterous name for any organisation?

'It was closed down...when our new...research department...was created.'

'No. You're Ince, the passenger a week back, on the last down train to Aylesbury. And I'm the driver you grassed on. How did you know to ring Network Rail Enquiries and complain? It was only Denham Golf Club, and nobody needed to get on or off there, except one woman. They never do at that hour.' His voice was getting hoarse with desperation.

'I don't...know...what you're talking about. I've never...travelled on the Misbourne Line...before tonight. That's...God's own truth. Tonight...I was meant to meet someone at...Beaconsfield; a newspaper man, to...to come clean.'

Lee picked up the wallet and examined the cards. They were all embossed with the name PT Egerton. He felt no wiser; just scared. If these were genuine, then he'd made a hideous mistake. This man was not who he'd thought him. He became conscious of his last words: *come clean.*

'Come clean about what?' It was Lee who was confused now. Was this Egerton some kind of crook?

'My research work. I can't...do it any more. I'm... chucking it in.'

Even in his befuddled state, Lee thought it was starting to make sense. He suddenly decided: 'Look, you'd better come into the house. We need to get things sorted.'

He reached down roughly and slid his hands under Egerton's armpits. 'Can you stand?'

They managed well enough through the narrow passage to the back door and into the kitchen, where Lee lowered him to Kathy's nursing chair by the window. Then he went for the Scotch and two glasses. He couldn't go as far as admitting how wrong he was, far less apologise. How do you say you're sorry for having on a tide of rage tried to commit murder? But he had to say something. Feeling cold sober now, he poured two good measures of the whisky and squatted on a kitchen chair opposite his victim. 'I'd better try and explain.'

But where should he begin? 'You see, I drive trains...' he said. It sounded limp, like a dragged-out confession.

'...on the line you travelled tonight. Only I meant to get ahead and do so much better...swot up my languages; get a cushy job on a trans-European service. Better pay and prospects. And free rides for the kids to Euro-Disney whenever they wanted. Shopping and sightseeing for Kathy in Paris. Maybe holidays on the Riviera. Not stuck on a suburban commuter line like here.

'Only there's not much hope of that unless you keep a clean record. That's why it was such hellish bad luck that you – no, all right, not you but this Ince – stirred up such a fuss about the overrun. Not that he needed the stop that I'd missed out. Nobody did, except a woman, and I saw her off OK. It all happened because I'd someone in the cab and we got talking.'

He realised he was sobbing over the words and

stopped in shame. He didn't need to make any more shitty admissions, but the man had to understand why it had all happened. Which was impossible with him in his present state: he could barely stay conscious.

'You attacked me,' Egerton managed to get out. He didn't seem to have taken in anything Lee had said. His hand reached out shakily for the tumbler of Scotch. As he tried to drink, some ran down over his chin. He winced as it reached his neck. There were vivid patches of crimson there, whether beaded blood or bruises starting to come up. Lee's eyes were drawn to them. He'd done that. It was past explaining. Past sane belief.

Egerton had given up on the drink. He pushed the tumbler back into Lee's hand

'I need...' he said feebly. '...to lie down.' His eyelids flickered. He slid gently from his chair on to the kitchen tiles.

Chapter Four

Lee lifted Egerton like a baby and carried him through to the sitting room. Being small, he fitted better to the sofa than Lee had done during his recent retreat from the marriage bed. Covered with a tartan rug, he slept on fitfully until woken by the blinds being raised to allow in the rheumy light of a new, cheerless day. It was going to be hot again, but cloud seemed to be pressing down like a felt cover.

'How are you?' Lee asked cautiously.

'Alive,' Egerton croaked. Gingerly he lowered his feet to the floor. 'Walking wounded, see?' He stood stiffly, one hand braced against the sofa's arm, and looked around a room strange to him, taking it all in.

'Saturday,' Lee announced unnecessarily. The man wasn't disoriented; appeared to account for his surroundings instantly on waking; mentally alert, even coolly ironic. With air suddenly cut off and unconscious so long, he could have suffered brain damage.

Alive, as he said, thank God; but acknowledging, as Lee did, that that fact was purely accidental. His survival was thanks to luck alone.

'Breakfast,' Lee told him, 'in the kitchen.' He didn't feel all that fit himself after yesterday's unaccustomed drinking, but the man needed building up.

Egerton ignored him, reaching for a framed photograph off the nearby side table. 'You're married then? You have children.'

Lee nodded, but the man wasn't watching him. He made an attempt to build bridges. 'That was taken last summer,' he admitted. *Last year*, when life had been so secure, relations with Kathy fine and his European ambitions still attainable.

'A girl and a baby boy. You're lucky.' Egerton spoke like someone who had nothing.

'Jenny's five now. Stevie's two.'

Egerton raised his head as if expecting to hear sounds from the room above.

'They're away. It's Jenny's half-term. Not back till next Saturday.' He wouldn't have explained so much, except that he owed the man. Maybe it could even make a difference, help him see he was ordinary, not a vicious assassin.

Egerton replaced the photograph, and one hand went to his throat. It came away tacky and he sniffed at his fingers, questioning the smell.

'Antiseptic balm,' Lee explained, almost obsequious. 'We use it on the kids: grazed knees, that sort of thing.'

'And on failed murder victims.' The man was cool, taunting him with black humour. 'Should I still be afraid of you, Lee Barber?'

So he remembered the name. He hadn't been so far gone as he'd appeared.

'God, no! Even if you really were Ince, it's all over. I was momentarily right out of my head.'

'Train Rage?'

The man was incredible. How could he stand there and remember nearly being killed and cynically just *take it*? Lee stared back at the clever, academic face drained of colour, the weak sag of the small, stooping body, and his mind filled with terrible suspicion. 'You wouldn't have cared, would you?'

Egerton stared him out. When he answered, his tone was sardonic: 'At the end, no one likes facing death. But, with hindsight, it might have been the best thing.'

A willing victim, a would-be suicide? Or maybe he'd not quite reached that point, Lee thought. But his own actions might have given the momentum towards Egerton making the choice. The man's desperation didn't absolve his attacker of responsibility. Somehow he felt bound more tightly.

'Breakfast?' he asked in embarrassment.

'I need to shower.'

A normal reaction; but could he be trusted in the bathroom, with razor blades in the cabinet?

'And if you could spare me a shirt?'

Lee's 17-inch neck would swamp him. Just as well, perhaps, allowing for some kind of dressing on the abrasions. Kathy still had a couple of her dad's silk cravats that she refused to believe would be totally naff these days. One of those could fill the space. 'I'll look something out.'

It gave them time apart so that, when Egerton came

down later, Lee had a firmer hold on himself. Something not unlike fatalism had taken over. He'd been spared killing the man. It rested with him now to move on from there: ensure Egerton didn't waste his remission.

He returned smelling of Lee's aftershave and shower gel. His walk, still stiff, was more assured. He accepted the plate of fried eggs, bacon and tomatoes, eating them in silence. At the end, 'I guess I was hungry,' he admitted.

'Toast?'

But he refused that. 'Perhaps more coffee?'

Lee drained the cafetière and fixed a new filter. They'd plenty of talk to get through this morning and the caffeine could help. By now there'd been time for resentment to stir in him. The man was altogether too cool.

'I've told you the truth about me,' he said levelly, while the kettle boiled anew. 'How I came to act as I did. But I still don't get what you meant by "coming clean". And who the devil did you think I was – someone *having reason* to attack you?'

Egerton leant over his elbows on the table. For a while he said nothing, staring at the formica top where Lee's sloppy pouring had left brown coffee rings from their mugs.

At length, he said, 'You think you have it hard. Believe me, you haven't been born. You have so much – your job, your family, your home. Your self-respect. Mine has all gone shit-side up. What I did have, that is.'

Lee waited. 'Your name's Egerton. Piers, wasn't it? That's all I know about you.'

'Except that I'm not Ince, the man you blame for ruining your life. That's my one virtue: hardly a positive one. Not worth inscribing on my gravestone. But anyway I hate the name Piers. I'm usually called Tim. Timothy's my second name.'

The kettle clicked off, allowing some distraction while Lee poured water into the cafetière and resettled the lid. Egerton appeared lost in thought.

'It all started a long way back, but rot's like that, insidious; takes its time, so you don't see it creeping in.' He frowned with the intensity of the recall.

'I was a student at Cambridge, serious enough and pretty solid: no Einstein, though. Not really planning ahead like you. In my final year I was expected to pull off a First, but ended with a 2:1.

'There was a girl, though I can't blame her. She seemed willing enough, but it was my fault she got pregnant. Those last months were desperate. She was too scared to tell her folks; threatened to kill herself. I said I'd see her right, marry her; anything she wanted. In the end she had a…a termination. Killed my child. She said life tied to me would be utterly abhorrent.

'Then she just disappeared, flunked out; never sat her finals. She'd been reading History. I heard much later that she'd gone out to Burundi as a Christian missionary, but at the time I was afraid she'd do as she'd threatened. I sat my last papers with her death like a sword hanging over my head, expecting the police to come at any moment with the news.'

He stayed silent, head bowed between hunched

shoulders, fingers pushing at loose breadcrumbs on the table top.

'When the offer came, it seemed an ideal way out: a government department looking for young blood on a microbiology research programme. My prof was pushing it, and I was flattered enough to grasp it with both hands. Not such good starting pay as with a commercial company, but there'd be enormous scope later; great kudos when the research was finally published. The sky, as they say, was the limit. And all that pensions stuff they sell you.

'My widowed mother had just been diagnosed with terminal cancer, though I never knew that at the time. She saw the career offer as a godsend.

'The mention of MoD didn't mean much to me. Later, if a few doubts slid in, I told myself I was doing my patriotic duty. So I kept my head down and beavered away like a good little boy; one of the faceless researchers of Porton Down.'

Lee looked up, startled. 'The nerve gas and poisons centre?'

'Yes. You see, the name means something to you. But whatever your misgivings, you've never been moved to do anything to stop it, have you?'

'It's not my bloody business…'

'It's done in your name, though…citizen.'

'But, surely, the work's defensive: they experiment with enemy chemical weapons to find the best ways of combating them.'

'You might ask "Who's the enemy?" These substances –

"enemy *agents*" we call them, and the terminology's ironically significant – have been employed experimentally since the late Thirties, covered by the excuse of the Second World War. Volunteers, all servicemen and women lured by money and perks, have been used ever since as guinea pigs, some now suffering suspected long-term health problems.'

Lee stirred in his seat, ready to argue. 'There are always wide boys who'll play the compensation card. It's part of modern culture. If they'd had a real case against the government, the papers would have been full of it. Like the Gulf War Syndrome.'

'Not for want of trying. You'd be amazed what can be suppressed in the name of patriotic duty. But sufficient fuss was made for an independent ethical assessor to be appointed by the government to look into questions raised. He found "serious departures from acceptable standards" involving the exposure of volunteers to agents found in German shells. And then in the 1950s came tests of the nerve agents known as VX and GD. He also raised "question marks" over the copycat use of sarin in which a Royal Air Force mechanic was killed; likewise the artificial inducement of the eye condition miosis.

'If you doubt my word, look back through copies of the *Daily Telegraph* for mid-July 2006. It's all there, albeit tucked away in a small side column and couched in cautious, non-litigious wording.

'About then I started on some new stuff. That was the year certain undercover changes came in. I discovered

I was now mysteriously employed by a "private-sector company" with an intriguingly innocent-sounding name, although all my pension rights continued unchanged and my salary had increased by 18%. My colleagues and I now work out of a private sanatorium in Essex. Or did until yesterday; which is when I jacked it in. Finally I'd had enough, after a grisly walk through the closed-ward section in the sanatorium. As I said, there have been accidents.'

He fell silent, looking up at last to face Lee, whose mind made the final leap. 'That's why you talked about Animal Rights activists. They'd be opposed to your experimentation. You thought I was one of them, who'd sussed you out and meant to attack you because of your work.'

'It seemed possible. They're obsessed, though they seem less concerned about the human subjects we employ.'

'But out there in the garage…I thought you were raving. You said, "Stop! I'm on your side." If you thought that I was one of them, how could you be on my side?'

'You haven't got it, have you? I'm sick to the back teeth with what I've been doing all these years. I've turned whistleblower. I'm selling it out to the press. That's why I was on that last train down from Marylebone. I was to meet a newspaper man called Max Harris at Beaconsfield, who would take me to a safe house until he had learnt all the details.'

'But you didn't get off at Beaconsfield.'

'You'd seen to that.'

Lee's jaw tightened. 'So what next?'

'That's what I have to decide. Or maybe *you* will, since it seems I'm in your hands for the present.'

The digital clock at her bedside showed 03.17 when Detective Sergeant Rosemary Zyczynski awoke and guessed that she'd picked up on quiet sounds outside: a car approaching on gravel. No sound of a dropped garage door followed. That was Max playing low key, back from his overnight meeting. He'd warned her that he might not return alone, so wouldn't be joining her.

She switched on the light and listened for him coming upstairs. Only one person on the treads, she thought. Maybe he would let himself in here after all. But the footsteps halted and she heard his key in his own lock across the landing. Disappointed, she put out the light, turned her pillow to the cool side and settled to sleep again. Saturday – delicious thought – so no need to stir until the paper was delivered about 8.30.

Max's knock came as she was sliding two slices of bread into the toaster. She sang out to him and reached to put in another two. He came up behind her, rested his hands on her shoulders and kissed the back of her neck.

'You didn't get much sleep,' she said. 'It was after three when you got in.'

'God, were you waiting behind the door with a rolling pin?'

'The frying pan, more likely. Are you hungry?'

'I could eat a horse. I missed out on dinner, and then the person I was meant to meet failed to show up. I hung around on the off-chance, until I concluded he'd had second thoughts on handing me the dope.'

'Not dope as in…?'

'As in drugs? No: spilling the beans, providing the copy. I'd hopes of some interesting revelations. But it was not to be.' He made it sound final and she didn't enquire further.

'Another fish that got away. I know the feeling well,' she consoled him. 'I lost my case at Amersham court yesterday. We thought CPS had it all sewn up, and then chummy turned up with Paula Musto to plead for him. Boy, she's good. Angus'll go mad when he sees the report. At least she has the decency to keep to her maiden name. It wouldn't look good in the local paper to reveal a couple of Motts at loggerheads.'

Max slid into an empty chair by the window, nodding as Z waved a pack of bacon rashers in his direction. 'Yes please, and a couple of eggs if you can spare them. Actually I never believed she'd go through with it, or at least not before the baby had arrived.'

'Well, it's as a defence barrister that she made herself a name in London. Now that she's marooned out here, I guess she'd feel odd playing for the opposition.'

'Then there's the considerable money difference, which must count against joining Crown Prosecution, and she's tough enough to fight her corner in a court where her husband's pushing a case through. Awkward, but it's her life, her choice.'

Z paused to look at him directly, wondering if they'd ever face a similar dilemma: Max making copy from some professional failure of her own. Not that it could be so personal, because, as a mere DS, her name didn't get bandied about when the police issued a press statement. But even as a team thing, it would be something she'd resent.

'Max,' she suggested, 'don't you sometimes find that pursuing your own job can let other people down?'

He played with the fork at his place setting, idly prodding at the folded napkin. 'Actually, that is what exercises me somewhat at the moment. Whose is the greater good? That sort of question. I thank my stars that I'm a columnist and not an investigative journalist.'

'Sometimes you stray near the dividing line.'

'Dally there, on the sideline. But mostly I enjoy writing the lighter stuff.'

'Like last week's article: "Loofahs, their Acquisition, Use and Loss". I loved that.'

He smiled. 'You should see the stacks of the things that arrived at the office from my fans. We're inundated with them now. I could start a bathroom shop.' He grinned. 'But what's on your programme for today, Poppet?'

'That depends.'

'On?'

'How tired you are.'

'Ah.' He pushed his spectacles up the bridge of his nose with a forefinger and looked profound. 'That is something we must look into seriously. I'm quite prepared for a demonstration.'

'Don't you have loose ends to follow up – because of last night's fiasco?'

He considered. 'That depends,' he said again. 'I'm not sure what my missing contact has in mind: whether his wobbly conscience has persuaded him to withdraw, or whether – and there's a slim chance of this – he's been prevented by external influences. In which case I can only wait and see if he manages to get in touch again. So no, I shan't be taking it any further for the moment. I'm entirely yours to command.'

'Then let's go to the zoo,' she said impulsively, 'and feed buns to the bears. That's what Nan Yeadings accuses us of doing with the Boss; and today I fancy a spot of the real thing.'

Chapter Five

Kathy had left a list of instructions for running the house. Lee read them through over the breakfast table before clearing it. You could tell from the detail that Kathy had been an infant school teacher. Every task was explicitly described, the necessary gear bracketed alongside with clear directions where to find everything.

As if the washing machine might fox me, Lee marvelled; or I couldn't rummage through the sink cupboard for a refill bag for the vacuum cleaner. Or read manufacturers' instructions, for that matter.

Maybe she really did think he was four years old. Though just being a man didn't rate all that highly with her when it came to the grey matter. Women, these days!

No, he mustn't go there. She was a sweetie in her own way, and he couldn't imagine life without her. It was just that sometimes… The quote from *My Fair Lady* came into his head: *Why can't a woman be more like a man?* Only he wouldn't fancy Kathy with a hairy chest and size eleven feet. Better the way she was, bless her.

'Anything I can do?' Egerton enquired. He was bent on being useful.

'Housekeeping instructions,' Lee said, actually welcoming the normality of it all. He gestured with the densely written pages. 'Small beer: little here that can't be left for tomorrow. More important is what we're to do about you. I should get you to a hospital.'

'Not easy to explain the marks on my neck,' Egerton said shortly. 'They might feel compelled to inform the police. As for the rest, there's nothing much that's new. My blood pressure's low. Just recently, two or three times, I've passed out for a few minutes. Low haemoglobin levels. Probably stress. Maybe that's partly what happened back on the train, and you thought I'd gone for good.'

'Well, shouldn't you do something about that?'

'I have medication. I'm basically a medic, able to cope with most things.'

Lee stared at him.

'What I need is a couple of days to think things out. By Monday someone's going to miss me and alarm bells could start ringing. By then I have to decide how to act.

'If I could stay here with you... I mean, I'll pay my way; only I need a stretch of normality to calm me down.'

Normality, that word again: what we both crave after the nightmare, Lee thought. Neither of us is Stallone or Schwarzenegger.

'No one would look for me here. We've no traceable connection.'

True; except for his mistake over Ince, Lee thought bitterly. And by now memory of the man had faded, become almost irrelevant – a bogeyman in the past who for a matter of days had made a vindictive idiot of him.

Egerton was waiting. Lee closed his eyes: this is unreal. One day I'm trying to squeeze the life out of him, and now he's asking for asylum. But I owe him, if only for his silence. And while everyone's away, why not?

'I'll make up a bed in the spare room,' he offered gruffly. 'Take your time. Sort yourself.'

'Thanks, Lee. Just show me where the sheets are and I'll fix the bed myself. And if you'll risk it, I'll do lunch. I'd invite you out somewhere, only I don't yet feel up to facing other people.'

In the event they found fridge and freezer well packed, ready meals wrapped in foil and labelled with instructions for thawing and preparation.

'Your wife's amazing.'

'She is that.' Lee wondered what she'd been feeling as she wrote out her instructions for him. Still resentful? God, he'd been a surly bugger; given her a hard time, snapped at her and she'd done nothing to deserve it. It had been his own fault he'd got in such a bloody stew over the incident at work blackening his record. He still had the job, after all. Nothing lost but his dreams.

Since the enormity of his attack on the imagined Ince, the overrun too had faded in significance. He could see now he'd blown it out of all proportion. Everyone at the depot picked up these incidents. When the story about him got around, there'd been a ragged cheer, half sympathy, half congratulation at his losing his professional virginity. He should have taken it in better part; not with such dog-in-the-manger sulking. As for his hopes of the European line, well, maybe he'd sunk his chances, but maybe not. If he stuck where he was, the local runs didn't seem so bad really; it was his highfalutin' ambition that had made him undervalue the present job. And he did enjoy the driving most days.

Foremost in his mind now was shame over attacking Egerton, overshadowing anxiety about the track incident. Offering a temporary roof over the man's head was the least he could do. Almost relieved, he started working through some of the household jobs, performed the ritual weekend washing of the car; filled the dishwasher after Egerton's well-presented lunch of cheese and ham omelettes with mixed salad, followed by a reheated jam sponge from Kathy's stash.

He'd intended starting work on the apple tree, but Egerton had gone to lie down and the row would have disturbed him. The chainsaw must stay in the garage meanwhile. Later, maybe Tim would lend a hand with some of the smaller branches, help keep his mind off what was troubling him about his work.

Lee recalled the kerfuffle over Kathy's demands about the apple tree. Not satisfied with his removing the kiddy swing, she had decreed that the children shouldn't play in the back garden until all rotten branches had been safely removed. Roars of protest had had no effect on her, and he guessed the kids were still miffed as she tucked them into her green Mini Cooper to set off for Granny's.

For the present he needed to go into town. There

were things to buy, and while he was there he'd lay in some stuff for Tim: a couple of casual shirts; spare string vest and pants; razor and toothbrush. For the rest, he could borrow a pair of Lee's over-large jeans, a cardigan and the less ratty pair of indoor slippers.

A brisk wind from the south-west had been breaking up the cloud cover. Frisky, Lee thought, surveying the sky. If he'd been alone he'd have headed for Newhaven and taken out Ben Hartley's boat, staying down there overnight. He wondered if Egerton sailed. It might be something a toff like him had done at boarding school.

Maybe he'd suggest they spend Sunday that way. Out on the choppy water Tim would get a chance to clear his mind of all that soul-searching over his research work. Ironic thought; when yesterday he'd insanely expected to take the poor devil to sea in plastic rubbish sacks!

He put the suggestion to Tim when he got back and the other man had come downstairs looking slightly more rested. Egerton grinned wryly. 'Sorry. Can't do. I get seasick just looking at holiday posters. Not a good sailor at all; didn't even do rowing at school. I took the lazy way out with sports and chose the only one you can do lying down. With the school shooting team, competing at Bisley.'

'You're a marksman?'

They talked guns for a while, airing the usual complaints against the government ban on handguns, leaving as competent shooters only a few cops and the inner city crooks gunning each other down in the drug trade.

Lee was taught to use a gun by an uncle who ran a small stock farm near Tenterden and took him rabbiting as a boy. That and searching for mushrooms in the dewy dawn had been among the happiest memories of his early orphaned years. Later, at eighteen, he'd joined a gun club, and after marrying would have continued except that it meant regular weekly attendance, which left Kathy alone at home and critical of anything possibly lethal.

'Don't let me spoil your weekend,' Egerton offered. 'You go fishing tomorrow. I'll stay on here if that's all right with you. I guarantee not to do anything you wouldn't approve of.'

It would have been surly to refuse, besides possibly implying that he didn't yet trust the man to be left alone at the house.

'I might do that. It'll give you some peace on your own.' He collected his seagoing stuff from the garden shed and packed the car ready for an early start next morning. The Internet provided all he needed on the state of the tides. Meanwhile, Egerton was sorting things in the fridge for their dinner.

Lee unearthed the I, *Claudius* videos which Kathy had requested for her last birthday and they watched the first volume before turning in early for bed.

Saturday's zoo visit was sheer tourism. By the penguin pond Z slipped her arm round Max's waist. She pointed to a plump, complacent-looking bird at the top of the water chute. 'Deputy Chief Constable Dench to the last impeccably turned out feather. And, over there, morosely regarding his feet, DI Salmon.'

'Yes, I get that one.' Max nibbled at the last of an ice cream cone and wiped his hands on a handkerchief. 'Rosebud, your mind's still on work. It was even the thought of your Boss that suggested we came here. I feel slighted. Doesn't my vibrant company swamp all else?'

'Not entirely at the moment.' She turned to face him. 'And how about you? I can see something's bothering you, Max. A minute ago you were miles away.'

'Sorry, love. Would it be too rude if I do some phoning, in case my last night's stand-up is trying to contact me elsewhere?' He reached for his mobile and moved a little apart. She watched him twice punch in numbers, with an interval of brief conversation between. He snapped the phone shut and returned looking thoughtful.

'He's lying low,' she guessed.

'Let's hope it's voluntarily. There's a chance he could be in trouble.'

'Trouble, how?'

'Possibly with some very powerful people, or some really nasty ones.'

It sounded intriguing, but his tone of finality prevented further questions. He started walking on again.

So whose mind is still at work level? she asked herself, catching him up.

'Camels,' he decided abruptly. 'Let's check whether the foul-mouthed beast that bit me last year in Egypt has met its full desserts and become incarcerated here.'

'Incarcerated? Are you really against animals kept in zoos? You should have told me. We could have gone someplace else.'

'No, this is great. It's true I prefer them in the wild, but I'm really enjoying myself here with you, hair let down and all that. We should have brought along a small brood of children to make it a grand occasion. But then I may have mentioned them before.

She punched his arm. 'There are enough of them here without our contributing.'

'Tell you what: forget the disgruntled camels. I'll race you to the Mappin Terraces. Last one's a dodo.' He loped off and Zyczynski, loftily disregarding the challenge, took her time following. At a little after midday it was too hot for childish games.

They exchanged indifferent stares with the mountain goats. 'It makes you wonder,' she said, 'who are the exhibits and who the spectators.'

'It's evens,' he decided. 'Another thing we all share in common is a need for sustenance. Let's look for somewhere to have lunch.'

They found a table free under a striped canopy, ordered fruit juice and salmon salads. Max removed his glasses to polish them and winked at a small boy faced by a Knickerbocker Glory at the next table. 'Bet you can't finish it,' he mouthed across.

The child waved the over-long spoon and grinned back.

'Fraternising with the ankle-biters,' Rosemary warned him, 'can get you into trouble these days.'

'You have a crime-bound mind, my love. It's deprivation in my case. Just one little cherub of my own and I might lay off making overtures to other people's.'

The second time within minutes he's brought the subject up, Z reflected. And this time it's more than a hint. Maybe it was my mentioning Paula Mott set him off thinking babies again. She'd hoped that subject had been put on the back burner.

Max had enough of the feminine in him to be aware of an instant shift in atmosphere. His Rosebud had mentally drawn apart. He left her to it, making his own tactical withdrawal. They ate their lunch more or less in silence and he kept his attention off the adjacent table, not noticing that the Knickerbocker Glory had eventually been surrendered to the little boy's father to finish.

The family concluded their meal, paid their bill and prepared to leave. Zyczynski saw the child get down from the table and dart a hard glance in their direction. She tapped Max's hand and he looked across.

'I did,' the boy said defiantly, 'well, nearly.'

And then the mobile started to vibrate in Max's pocket. He waved at the child, grinned and looked for the caller's ID.

Z watched him stiffen. He listened for a while, and then asked, 'So where would that be?'

The answer clearly wasn't what he'd wanted. 'I see, yes. Well, thank you for letting me know.' He shut off the mobile, his face thoughtful.

'Your missing contact?' Z assumed.

'Apologising,' said Max. 'He's polite, if uncertain of his next move. Says he's staying with a friend. I may have lost him.'

She moved her chair slightly to watch the departing family. Next time she glanced back at Max he was asleep, like an old man after a heavy lunch, slumped and with his head fallen towards his chest, soft fair hair flopping forward over his eyes.

The waiter approached but she waved him away. He nodded. Visitors were thinning at the tables: no need to hurry this pair on.

Max awoke as suddenly and as quietly as he'd dropped off. 'Sorry, love. Not scintillating, am I?' He rubbed at his stiff neck.

'You had a long night.'

He grinned. 'I was dreaming about a camel. Not the savage beast that bit me. Rather a pretty little thing; bodywise, that is. You can't do much for a camel's face, even in a dream.

'Whereas yours…' He bent forward and kissed her.

Z was aware of the waiter watching. 'You need a haircut,' she told Max. 'It's starting to fall in your eyes.'

Max had said he'd cook dinner that night, but Rosemary could see he'd something else on his mind. Maybe his next column for the *Spectator* was already fermenting in his head: something called up by the zoo visit, most likely.

Arriving home, he went off to his own flat, and she knew that once he sat at his computer he could be gone for hours. So she must conjure up a makeshift meal for when he returned. She looked through the freezer and decided on pizzas with salad. Not quite in the same league as a Max Harris home-bake. Still, that was the way it was, and she could at least open some wine and lay the table.

Her own telephone's red light was winking: two messages. She heard them out, sipping a chilled Californian Chardonnay. Nan Yeadings announced a garden picnic for next day. Just a few friends, twelve-thirty for one. She apologised for the short notice but hoped Z would bring Max along. Angus and Paula would be there. Beaumont had cried off under pressure of family commitments.

Going fishing with his son to keep out of Audrey's way, Rosemary guessed. She hoped the invitation wasn't a thin veil for a sorting-out of the Mott couple's present tension.

The second message was proof that her misgivings were shared. 'Z, it's Paula. Angus has let us in for a short-notice lunch party tomorrow at the Boss's. I hope to God you're accepting, else I'll be compelled to cry off with a headache, and I hate having to lie. Don't fancy a grilling, unless there's someone there to back me up. Do ring me this evening if you can, there's a sweetie.'

'Sweetie,' Z echoed. Why did Paula have to do that? – treat her as from a dowager height. They were about the same age. The difference, of course, was in their jobs. How could a mere sergeant in CID compare with a barrister who'd already made a name for herself in the capital's law courts?

She wasn't sure she wanted to be dragged into any contretemps between Angus and his very pregnant wife, particularly in Superintendent Yeadings' presence. On the other hand, she hadn't seen Nan and the children for some time, and Max always enjoyed hobnobbing with the Boss: two different worlds finding common ground. So she'd leave it to him to make the decision.

He wasn't gone as long as she'd expected. 'Tomorrow?' he queried when she told him. 'Just pencil me in. There's a chance I may have to drop out at the last minute.'

'So, provisionally, I tell Nan yes?'

'That's fine with me. For the present, is it too late for me to produce a rabbit out of the hat? A risotto, I thought.'

'Lovely. I'll look out some background music. What do you fancy – bracing or smooch?'

'Digestive. And you can leave the smooching to me for later.'

All the same, she thought, he's distracted. Something's still bugging him about the missing contact from Friday night. If he keeps it to himself, it could mean that it's borderline dodgy.

He was involved with the cooking, a tea towel tucked round his waist, when his mobile vibrated. 'Can you reach in my pocket and see what that is?' he called across, raising his arms out of her way.

'Pardon me while I grope,' she warned.

It was Lloyd Fairchild, a PI Max sometimes used to chase up information. 'Oh, hello Ro'mary,' he greeted her when she answered. 'I've got the address Max wanted. Chased up a car licence number as well, while I was on it.'

Oh, did you; she silently disapproved. Maybe Lloyd enjoyed involving a policewoman to pass on the message.

'I'll just get a pen.' She found one and tried to write with it on a piece of kitchen tissue. She read it back to him. 'Have I got that right?'

'Nothing you couldn't have found out for him yourself. If you so wished, of course.'

'As you say. Don't worry. I'll pass it on.' She cut the call.

'Max, that was Lloyd Fairchild, leaving a message.'

Max had picked up on her chilly tone. He stood at the ready, wooden spoon raised above the sputtering saucepan. 'Sorry, love, he should know better.'

'You probably can't decipher it anyway.' She sounded offhand, but the address was still in her mind. A house in Thame; the resident's name Lee Barber. That, Lloyd had said, was where Max's earlier call had come from.

Maybe newspapers and PIs had access to a reverse telephone directory, but obtaining a car's licence number could mean somebody breaking into the national police computer, or access to a bent copper. She didn't care to be colluding in that. She stuffed the paper in Max's trouser pocket along with the mobile.

Max continued with the cooking. 'Fruit salad for afters?' he suggested.

Later, while Z filled the dishwasher, Max went to turn on the television, stretched out on the sofa and read the message off the screwed-up kitchen tissue. It was unlucky that Lloyd's call had come while he was preoccupied with the cooking. Reasonably enough, Z wasn't happy about the way his informant worked. Normally he took care to keep his professional researches private when they might involve police contacts, though she must guess at these occasional peccadilloes. He'd need to tread a cautious line with her. She wasn't the sort you could win over with flowers, chocolates and sweet words.

When she came back in, he patted the cushions beside him. She hesitated a moment and then came across. 'Am I forgiven?' he asked.

'It's not for me to forgive. I appreciate you didn't try to get the information through me.' She still sounded cool, a trifle schoolmarm.

'Right; so can we forget it?'

'I guess so.' She wasn't sure she would; because it had come too soon after wondering whether she and Max could ever find themselves on opposite sides, as Paula and Angus had been.

'I'm having a few doubts about this lunch party at the Boss's,' she admitted, 'in case there's any mention of Paula having squashed the prosecution's case.'

Max considered this. 'I think Yeadings would avoid an inquest. And anyway, Nan would mediate.'

'Maybe the subject won't come up, but it's a suspiciously sudden invitation just after Paula's win.'

'More likely they simply want to check that the Mott domestic boat's not rocking. My money's on Angus being broadminded enough to accept he's been outsmarted this time and be extra careful in future. You win some, you lose some.'

Z frowned. 'Perhaps; but since his stint in Bosnia Angus has changed. He's tougher; quick to get touchy.'

'Well, tomorrow we'll see. And maybe we can help things along.'

Chapter Six

Sunday dawned still fine, and wind was rolling the tops of the firs at the end of the garden. There'd be no call to waste any of Ben Hartley's fuel: Lee could go out under sail, anchor, and spend two or three hours fishing before running the boat in again on the tide and setting her up on blocks.

Egerton handed him a foil-wrapped package. 'Cheese and onion quiche with some salad,' he explained. The dressing's separate in a little pot.'

Lee had expected to pick up something in Newhaven, but this was more convenient. Tim was quite the little housewife. No wonder he ran his nerves to shreds, always bedevilled by details.

For the first time Lee wondered idly about the man's sexual preference. If he'd ever married, it hadn't been important enough for him to mention.

At that early hour there was little or no traffic and he made good time to the coast. The key to the hut was where Ben always left it hidden, and the boat, although weighty, ran smoothly down the slipway and onto the shingle. Lee got his shoulder behind the stern for the last heavy yards; and then he was plunging, thigh-high in shatteringly cold water, laughed in delight and scrambled aboard.

Busy with the sails, he set the course across wind. Then with one hand took over at the tiller, using the other to unfasten his belt and shed his jeans, later pulling on fresh dry ones. He hadn't felt so good in weeks, months. He filled his lungs with the good sea air, relishing the tangy tar and rope scents of the old boat. The horrors of what he'd done – attempted to do – just a day or two back became impossibility as he settled to deal with choppy waves offshore.

The wind, ideal for sailing, had sent the fish deeper. It didn't bother him that nothing came to his line for some time. He left it fixed while he tucked into the lunch Egerton had given him, swilling it down with mineral water. Then he lay flat on his back, staring at the sky until the streaming clouds were replaced by a strange sequence of faces and muddled events. At one point, he and an unknown but almost familiar man were arguing over a bag of tomatoes; and then his head was resting on Kathy's breast and he was trying to tell her how right it all was and how they had to stay like that forever.

But a whirring started and his line was reeling out fast: something biggish on the end. He struggled up, stiff from the boards, and took over his line, playing the thing in. It wasn't as large as he'd expected, but the fish was lively, a good-sized plaice. A few minutes later, he pulled in a smaller one. That would do them both for tonight: wasteful to take more.

He decided to stow the tackle, turn and make back

for the shore, riding the flow tide. His face was rough with salt and felt leathery under his hands. When he got to the depot tomorrow there'd be sarky remarks about sunbeds.

There was the usual stripping-down of the boat and lashing the sails. He was glad of the winch to get her up the shingle and he left her there above the tidemark, on her blocks, while he went back to lock the hut and hide the key. Old Ben would be down here tomorrow, taking his practice walk on two sticks, and he'd know Lee had been out with her. When Lee reached home he'd phone him and say thanks.

After Lee left, Tim Egerton had emptied and refilled the dishwasher and made their beds. He sat for a while examining the bookshelves. It wasn't hard to see which were Lee's and which more likely Kathy's favourite reading. The books consisted of practical manuals; a clutch of maps; some poetry ranging from Donne to Auden, Betjeman and Hughes; then a selection of paperback fiction, mainly crime and historical; French and English dictionaries and a thesaurus. The rest were children's stories and colouring books, well thumbed and slightly grubby. He resisted diving into the novels and went out to the garage.

The chainsaw lay there in a canvas bag and he grunted as he lifted it. More than he could cope with unaided, but there were ways of dealing with it. He loaded it into Lee's wheelbarrow and hunted in the fruit nets slung under the roof for a suitable length of rope.

The apple tree was like the curate's oft-quoted egg:

perfect in parts. Lee had been wise not to condemn the thing out of hand. Cut back carefully, it could yet bear good fruit, and, apart from the peripheral firs, would provide the only garden shade on hot days. One side of the tree, however, was definitely a hazard. He could see the worn part where the children's swing had caused chafing. That branch, and two other thick boughs, would have to go.

He chose a solid horizontal branch and flung one end of the rope up and over. This he attached to the handle of the chainsaw and hauled it up to hang swinging in an arc, allowing approach to the first rotten branch. With most of the weight taken up, he thought he could manage to operate the saw without too much difficulty. It started up throatily and he shoved it at the rotten wood. The note changed as it bit in. A few seconds of snarling and the branch fell. A piece of cake, Egerton told himself smugly.

He made a swing at the second rotten limb but the rope was too short. With the arc lengthened, the chainsaw was unsteady. It meant finding another suitable branch to hang the contraption from.

The effort to re-hang the chainsaw left him panting and he knew that in his present state he wasn't up to anything more strenuous. He hunkered on the ground by the tree's base until his heartbeat steadied, and then took the job up again. It took longer than he had hoped, and all the time his energy was draining. All the same, he was determined to have the lopping finished before Lee returned.

The saw was biting away at the final branch when he became conscious of being watched. He cut the power and turned. A whiskery old face had appeared above the garden fence shared with Lee's neighbour. Its expression was one of concentrated disgust.

Egerton couldn't be bothered with small-minded interference when he was so near exhaustion. He switched back the power and resumed sawing. Beyond the swearing as metal bit into gnarled wood, he thought he heard a voice raised in angry protest, but the competition was unequal. When he had finished and again looked across, the face had disappeared.

He rested before reloading the chainsaw in the wheelbarrow and trundling it back into the garage. He'd done enough for now and he couldn't leave the saw outside, risking a sudden shower. The branches still needed cutting into logs easier to handle, but that must wait for another day. Just now he needed to stretch out and take it easy. He slipped off his shoes and went wearily upstairs to bed. To ease his muscles he swallowed two Co-proxamol tablets and went out like a light.

He had no idea how much later he came suddenly awake. Downstairs, sounds of breakages and furniture being dragged about brought on a sweat. Daylight still showed between the curtains he'd pulled across before sleeping.

He didn't think it could be Lee returned already. He was a big man but not clumsy, and he wouldn't trash his own home.

Someone had broken in. Egerton slid his feet to the floor and steadied himself against the door to listen. There was no telephone upstairs, and anyway, calling the police was out of the question: there'd be too much to explain about his own presence and condition.

He had to do something, but was helpless. So much depended on who it was down below. Could he have been followed here by someone out to get him? God knew he'd be in danger from the department once colleagues got wind of what he intended doing. But surely they couldn't yet have raised an alarm. And anyway, they weren't vandals.

More likely this was some vagrant breaking in; a random search for anything of value to turn into cash. Egerton edged towards the top of the stairs. He needed something to threaten him with, to make him turn tail and run.

In his sock soles, he stole down towards the hall. The noises were coming from the sitting room. It sounded as though the little writing desk in the window recess was being forced. Something heavy was thrown on the floor. Cautiously Egerton inched closer.

Then there were footsteps, and suddenly the intruder was there, towering in the doorway; a tall, rough-looking man in black sweater and jeans.

Because he'd decided to garage the car, Lee went in by the front door. Everything was quiet inside the house. 'Egerton?' he called. There was no answer.

Asleep? Did the man ever do anything else? Or lying low, just in case…

Lee went through to the kitchen, dropped his fishing bag on the floor and went to the fridge for chilled water. Then he saw the blood. It clung stickily to the edge of the steel door in a clot of red-brown, dangling long dribbles like the legs of some obscene spider.

What the hell had the man been up to? How had he got hurt?

Or was this someone else?

He wheeled, feeling the draught, saw the outer door unlatched, the frame splintered beside the lock. God, there'd been a break-in.

'Tim!' he called, urgently.

A swift run through the downstairs rooms found everything there in disarray; desk, sideboard and cupboards ransacked, his computer switched on, but blank-screened; even pictures removed from the walls.

Had Egerton gone mad and ransacked the house? Was that his blood on the fridge door? Or was there an intruder?

Steady, he warned himself. He reached for the frying pan still left out from the breakfast fry-up. He started for the stairs, moving silently on his rubber soles, taking care to avoid the centre of each tread and their warning creaks.

No sound came from any of the rooms. The strong pulse hammering in his head must surely give warning of his approach.

On the landing every door stood ajar. Any of the four could have someone standing behind, ready to attack. His fingers tightened on the frying pan handle.

He knew just how he'd swing it – fast, at crotch level: a Wimbledon backhander, leaving no time for the other, lurking, to bring a weapon down. But which door?

He waited, listening for another's breath, his own painfully suppressed. And heard the slow drip, drip of water from the leaky cold tap: not hitting the bath's floor, but a filled tub. Egerton, he knew then, was taking a bath.

He walked straight in. The man was submerged, fully clothed, the water crimson, but the swarthy, bearded face staring up was a total stranger's. The mouth stretched wide, revealing a row of crooked, tombstone teeth in the lower, prognathous jaw.

Lee sank to his knees. He'd expected Egerton. But the bastard, the treacherous, stinking bastard, he'd done this, killed this intruder and fled, leaving Lee to face the music.

Time passed as he knelt, head in hands, fighting nausea and panic. How could he ever account for what had happened? – ever prove Egerton had been here to do this? He'd accepted him too readily, shielded him from publicity. Nobody knew of the man's recent moves, not even his newspaper contact, Max Harris. There was nothing to prove that he, Lee, hadn't made up the whole unlikely story of their meeting.

He would have to ring the police. But he could never tell the true version: that he'd tried to kill the man he thought was Ince. When they questioned him, what a crazy story he'd be giving them: that Egerton was running from his past and intended exposing some evil government project.

The *drip, drip* continued. When he dared look up

again his eyes were drawn to the leaking tap and the submerged, bloodless, bearded face staring up through crimson water. Dead, murdered! How could Egerton have done that, a man so moved by compassion for humanity that he'd been ready to sacrifice his livelihood? A rather puny, unwell bit of a wimp in some ways – actually *kill* a man?

But, only two days back, half-drunk and in a furious frenzy, he'd attempted that himself. It had been too easy to lose control with all that build-up of despair and loathing inside. And God knows what terror had possessed Egerton in his damaged state and faced by this brutal-looking intruder. It must be true what he'd once read: anyone can kill if pushed to the limit.

So what was this unknown man to Egerton; and what had he intended by breaking in? He seemed to have been searching for something. He couldn't be an Animal Rights activist. There was nothing here to draw him. Only Egerton himself, and nobody knew about him.

Lee shuddered. Security Services. *They* could be involved. Who else would have had the need and the resources to track the whistleblower down to put an end to the threat he presented?

MI5, wasn't it? Spooks. They'd followed Tim here, sent their undercover man to break in and kill him, to prevent the damning truth coming out.

But somehow Egerton had got the better of him, which left this stranger dead. And Lee himself at risk. *They* would know he was involved, because obviously they'd traced where he lived. He could equally be their intended victim.

Perhaps this address had been accessed through Max Harris. While Lee was away, Tim had all day to contact the newspaper man and reveal where he'd gone to earth.

When their man failed to return, they'd wait for Egerton to meet up with Harris, arrest them both; finally come here for him.

And since they couldn't risk the full truth getting out, they'd find some way to silence them all.

Did such far-fetched things really happen? Surely not in England, in quiet Thames Valley. It was too much like some overdone spy drama on television, or something that you read about in the news, happening to other people.

Lee, mainly law-abiding, hadn't given much credence to the recent tide of conspiracy theories, seeing them as an expression of anti-Establishment spleen. But, even rejecting them, you were left with a certain unease, a sliver of doubt: that maybe the authorities could get over-confident, exceeding their legal powers when it came to self-protection.

Since hearing Egerton's account of the work he'd been engaged on, his confidence was shaken. By now he totally believed him. It was generally accepted that scientific research was underway which involved cultivating dangerous viruses, but surely only to discover the means of preventing their spread? Now, he must face the possibility that the government in London had authorised one step further, planning for future warfare that covered wiping out whole areas of civilian population in some enemy land. It was no better than Saddam with his cruder gassing of the Kurds. Mass destruction. At first it was unbelievable that the government should even contemplate fighting at that level. But, having listened to Egerton, he was forced to face such a possibility. Unless he was a nutter.

And now this man was here, dead in the bath. That was real enough.

But had he to be a government agent? Lee's mind swung back to his earlier suspicion. Hadn't Egerton other enemies? Colleagues at the lab had received death threats, and once letter bombs. Whether there'd been a mole inside the organisation or these vicious maniacs had hacked into confidential data, they had already identified where the secret work was being carried out, forcing the project to relocate. That was the point at which Egerton had become disturbed, starting to feel shame over what he was engaged in; and ultimately decided to sell out.

Sell? Had Max Harris promised him a fortune for a newspaper scoop; more than just protection? And, fearing that Egerton was on the point of withdrawing, had he sent someone to get the information direct?

No, Harris was supposedly a columnist, not an investigative hack for the gutter press. But, in any case, Harris was out of it now. The meeting he'd set up for Beaconsfield had been prevented by Lee's own actions. Unless Egerton had phoned him since, there was nothing that could lead back here.

Yet this man had broken in. Somehow he'd made the connection, following Egerton's trail. If that hadn't been through Harris, how else?

Get a grip, Lee told himself: your mind's going in circles. Nothing is for certain.

He was pretty sure that, driving back from Aylesbury with Egerton unconscious in the car's boot, he hadn't been followed. Drink and relapse after the surcharge of adrenalin as he attacked the supposed Ince hadn't left him in the brightest of states – the writhing railway lines flashed back in his mind – but at that time of night there'd been practically no other traffic on the roads. OK, he'd been well over the drink-drive limit, but the glare of headlights in his driving mirror would have burnt itself into his foggy brain.

So was this last incident simply random after all? The man could be a tramp assuming that the house was empty and breaking in on the off-chance of something worth stealing. And certainly the downstairs rooms had been ransacked. He looked scruffy enough to be someone used to sleeping rough – or, for that matter, one of the Animal Rights terrorists; even a member of Security, undercover and in disguise. Or was he a foreign spy primed to get his hands on Egerton's research findings?

Again, Lee saw, he'd come full circle. So far, there was no way of knowing. And guessing got you nowhere.

Meanwhile, there was a dead body to be dealt with; either to be officially reported or kept concealed. And that was left to him, since Egerton had done a runner. But how far had he got, if he'd been the one injured in the kitchen? Had some third party bundled him into a car and made off with him?

Must he notify the police of a possible kidnap?

Chapter Seven

Lee reached over and lifted the chain securing the bath bung. Slowly the water level started dropping. Madly chortling, it swirled down the drain, carrying a man's lifeblood to distant sewers.

Something clattered as he got to his feet. The bloodstained bathmat was rucked up beside his shoe, but something gleamed inside its folds. He straightened it, and saw one of Kathy's cherished Sabatier knives from the kitchen rack. Blood was congealing on the steel, already granular in the join between blade and handle.

God, Kathy! What would happen to her after this – to the kids? No way would the police believe he wasn't implicated. He had to make sure the body was never recovered.

In a surge of nausea, he couldn't handle the knife; went downstairs and rummaged for a freezer bag to seal it away.

He must think, and he knew alcohol wasn't the answer, but his hands were shaking and he needed to dispel the chill in his bones. Bitterly he recalled the hot passion of his attack on the supposed Ince in the train. He could do with some of that now. God, that was a lifetime away. And now Ince-Egerton was a killer himself, leaving Lee as the only suspect.

He sat on in the kitchen, a half-full tumbler of Scotch clasped in both hands, staring out at the twilit garden and the dim outline of the apple tree with its rotten branches. Kathy would expect him to have dealt with that before she came back from her mother's. Oh God, Kathy!

The apple tree had to wait. Now he had something far more urgent to get rid of.

And instantly it was plain what he must do. He took another slug at the whisky; then, in anger at himself, poured the rest down the sink.

Since the early summer's heatwave the ground in neighbouring woods was too hard for him to dig even a shallow grave, but he had the hired chainsaw. Two nights back he'd madly intended using it to dismember the supposed Ince, disposing of the body in plastic rubbish bags. It wasn't so crazy an idea now, in his desperation. He thought he could best do it where the body was, with a minimum of mess, but it could be hellish difficult not damaging the surface of the bath.

To bring himself to face it he must see it as dead wood: anything but human flesh and bone. Rotten branches; not a murder victim killed by someone he'd got to know and exchanged confessions with; someone now even more in the shit than himself.

No, that was no path to take. Forget the treacherous Egerton and his enemies, whoever they were. There was the body. No; think *a dead tree*: something to be disposed of skilfully and carefully; a practical job. That way he believed he could do it. He just *must* do it.

He needed to fetch the chainsaw and some plastic sheeting from the garage. Leaving by the splintered kitchen door, he turned into the narrow passage between his and the Goddens' house, and in the fading light saw the body ahead, slumped beside the trellised gate.

Egerton hadn't run far. He was conscious but his eyes were hooded, his pulse feeble, and his head was bleeding into the wooden gatepost.

Lee had carried him before and could do it again. He lifted him by the armpits and the man's eyes flickered open, recognition in them. 'Have to...' he managed weakly.

'You'll be all right,' Lee promised, knowing it a lie. 'I'll just get you indoors. Then we'll sort it all.'

Sort it how? he asked himself, staggering back the way he'd come. In the kitchen he laid the flaccid body on the ceramic tiles. Egerton's eyes closed again.

Lee heard himself sob, and repressed it.

He stared at the deathly pale face, staunching the blood with a length of paper towelling. Egerton's eyes remained closed.

Had he to do the thing twice over? Saw up *two* bodies now, not one? This was more than he could stomach.

No, he couldn't let the man die. He owed it to him. None of this would have happened if, mistakenly and almost fatally, he hadn't attacked him on the train.

For the third time he must carry him, get him to bed; try to care for him until he was fit enough to leave, taking his troubles with him.

The man had more guts than he'd thought, and he struggled to come round. Almost an hour later, when Lee had patched him up in the kitchen, fed him the last of the Scotch and then a bacon sandwich, the story began to filter out.

Tim had been asleep upstairs and hadn't heard the man break in, but noises downstairs startled him awake: sounds of breakages and furniture being dragged about. Lee couldn't have returned so early, and he wouldn't trash his own house.

It meant someone had broken in.

Egerton had steadied himself against the door to listen. There was no telephone upstairs, and anyway, calling the police was out of the question: there'd be too much to explain about himself. No good trying to contact the neighbours. That whiskered old face watching him over the fence hadn't inspired confidence.

It had taken him minutes to summon up the courage to go and face what was happening downstairs. Had he been followed here by someone out to get him? God knew he'd be in danger once news got out of what he'd intended doing. But surely it was too soon. He wouldn't be missed until tomorrow.

Which left outsiders. Animal Rights activists had been making a nuisance of themselves for months, getting ever more vindictive. But how could they have traced him out here?

Lee listened and nodded. It was much how he'd been thinking himself.

Eventually Egerton had forced himself to believe it

was a tramp or some delinquent youngster robbing the house for what he could get. Surely he could deal with that sort of thing, bluffing that he owned the house and would send for the police…

Lee let Egerton babble on, relieving earlier stress in a torrent of words. He followed his cautious movements down the stairs in search of some defensive weapon, hoping maybe the intruder would turn tail and run.

The noises were coming from the sitting room. In his sock soles Egerton had stolen across the hall to look in. He heard wood splitting as if a lock were being forced, followed by the thud of something flung on the carpet.

Then there were footsteps, and suddenly he was there, looming in the doorway: a tall, unkempt man in dark sweater and jeans.

'He must have thought the house was empty. He was as startled as I was when we came face to face,' Egerton said. 'God knows who I thought he could be, in my panic.'

'Someone out to get you?'

'Well, you saw what he was like: so fierce. I nearly wet myself.'

Lee let that go, waiting for the rest of the story.

'It was no tramp, though. You see, he knew who I was. He demanded the briefcase. To gain time I said it was hidden in the kitchen cooker. I followed him in. I thought I could get one of those knives from the rack to threaten him with, but he was too quick, lunged at me and I fell, knocking my head on the corner of the fridge. For a few seconds I didn't know where I was. Then I think I heard the front doorbell. The man swore and went to look out through the sitting room curtains.

'I managed to get to my knees, but by then he was back and into the cooker. At once he discovered I'd lied, and went for a knife himself. I got as far as the staircase before he could rush me.

'I dragged myself up, hand over hand on the banister rail, and he came after me; but not too close, in case I kicked out. And then, on the landing I lunged at him and somehow managed to wrench the knife from his hand. He recovered his balance and threw himself on me. I was driven back against the wall, and...'

Egerton closed his eyes and was silent a moment. Then, 'The knife went into his chest. It just happened. I swear to it. I didn't aim. There wasn't time. He staggered, went limp and fell to the floor, right by the bathroom door.

'So I dragged him in – he was so heavy – and I heaved him over the side and ran some water on him.

'Oh God, the next bit was horrible. He started to pull the knife out, staring at me and with blood trickling from the side of his mouth. I don't know why, but I took the knife out of his hands and it dropped on the floor. And then he just slid down while the blood started gushing from his chest, and the water went crimson, running over his face. And when he didn't choke I realised...

'So I put the bung in and when he was quite covered I turned off the tap. And I thought, what in God's name do I have to do next?

'Then I remembered the plastic sheeting in the car boot, so I was making for the garage when I guess I just passed out. That must be where you found me.'

The plastic sheeting I'd once meant to wrap you in, Lee thought in silence. 'Which is where I found you,' he agreed. 'But I'd seen the body just before, and I thought you'd run off, leaving me to carry the can.'

'You thought I was that much of a shit.'

'The truth is, I'm not thinking straight; right out of my depth. All I know is that we have to get rid of the body. And quick.'

'You mean you'll help me?'

Lee stared at him. 'We're both in this. If I hadn't mistaken you for Ince... If I hadn't tried to strangle you...'

'Tomorrow,' Egerton insisted. 'We can't do anything till morning.'

'I'm on Earlies,' Lee said. 'No. I'll call in sick. You can't manage it alone, and anyway, I couldn't take a shift because I've already been drinking. In case the neighbours get curious, we'll make it look like we're dealing with the apple tree. Then if we take the felled boughs into the garage to finish off...'

'You mean...use the chainsaw on...'

'Think of it as scrap timber,' Lee said doggedly. 'And remember why he came. It was either you or him.' Bile filled his throat as he realised the irony of it. Egerton must never know he himself could have ended that way. In black plastic rubbish bags.

'Bed for you,' he said shortly. 'You're on your last legs, and we'll need an early start in the morning.'

At the door Egerton turned. 'One thing. Wherever

you hid the briefcase, it foxed him all right.'

Lee felt his face drain. 'The briefcase? I don't have it.'

Alarmed, Egerton came back in and stood over him as he sat. 'Where is it then?'

'Well, if everything's been done by the book, by now it's in Railways Lost Property.'

Sunday lunch at the Yeadings' had been *al fresco*. A table was set for six on the patio and a rug spread for the children under the mulberry tree whose umbrella shape had long established it as campsite, Indian reservation and refuge from imagined adult persecution.

Not that today was other than sunny in every sense when Max and Zyczynski came round the side of the house. Nan greeted them in casual jeans and sun-top. The Boss, in rolled-up shirtsleeves, was partially visible among the raspberry canes. When he became aware of the visitors, he waved and invited them down. 'Come and help yourselves.

'Sally, be an angel and fetch a couple more basins, will you?'

The little girl appeared from indoors and ran to hug Z, giggling when Max swooped to swing her in the air. 'Swishers,' she cried. 'Do it again!' Her blunt little face was freckled and puckered with pleasure. She looked like a happy puppy.

'Hat,' Nan reminded her from the kitchen door, waving a floppy scrap of pink cotton. Good, Z thought: everything relaxed and informal. Let's hope it stays that way when the other two arrive. They both joined

Yeadings, to start filling the bowls.

Little Luke marched out from the farther canes with a mouth stained red, and solemnly offered his sticky hand to be shaken. 'I've got a new go-kart,' he confided to Max. 'But you'd be a bit too big to fit in.' It sounded alarming, but proved to be only pedal-powered. He dragged Max away as audience while he demonstrated it over the lawn.

'Front doorbell; that'll be Angus and Paula,' Nan called, and went back to let them in. When they came out from the house a few minutes later, they were carrying salad dishes for the first course and an ice bucket with the wine.

'Wash hands,' Sally instructed her little brother, and they disappeared into the house with their mother.

By previous arrangement, Z thought. The suspicion came across that this was all a trifle too well choreographed, leaving the CID team members and their partners to greet each other and set the atmosphere.

'Are we late?' Paula asked. 'I'm never quite sure what time people have Sunday lunch.'

'A moveable feast,' Yeadings assured her. 'Plenty of time for a drink first. What'll you have?'

He took their orders and went indoors to fetch them.

'So,' Paula demanded of Z, 'which way's the wind blowing?'

'Oh, gently, I think. From the south-west.' She was conscious of Angus's sharp glance at his wife. He would obviously have preferred to ignore the delicate situation, but she wanted their differences out in the open.

'You heard I'm in the doghouse, I suppose?' Paula demanded of Max.

'Your baptism of fire on Friday? Yes. Congratulations. Keep 'em on their feet and running.'

'That's uncommonly civil of you. I warned Angus: somebody has to lose in court. God knows I've been sorely reminded of that often enough. Anyway, it wasn't through any slipshod preparation of the case. Z had it nailed. Blame that blabbermouth uniform who drove my client to the station. He'd no right to interrogate a suspect like that.'

'It's done now,' decided Angus. 'Case closed.'

But it's not the case that's rankling, is it? Z thought. His objection is to the opposition stance. Paula must be very sure of her marriage to risk so much.

'It's what I do,' she said, sensitive to the unspoken comment 'Defence; I've no experience in prosecution. Not that it was a terribly important case this time.'

Her words hung in the air. Every case is important, Z argued silently. Why else do we slog at it so? And before it reaches court we've already beaten Crown Prosecution.

Angus had squared his jaw and walked off to inspect the go-kart. Max wandered after him.

'This business of setting herself up to oppose me in court...' Mott snarled, pushed to the limit. 'What the hell does she think she's doing?' He stopped, shook his head as if trying to distance himself from the outburst. 'Paula is the most rational, level-headed woman I've come across in my life. Then she does this.'

'This what – disruption? Maybe she feels disrupted

too – the baby, changed hormones.' Max frowned.

Mott shrugged. 'No advice to offer? Aren't you the columnist with all the answers?'

Max turned away. He said over his shoulder, 'Comfort her?' He was on his way to find Z. They'd been long enough apart.

'How are you bearing up in this heat?' Z asked Paula sympathetically.

'More sagging than bearing up. The bulge is very lively, especially at night. I expect it'll turn out to be the wild, clubbing type.'

'Boy or girl?'

Paula smiled. 'Yes, one or the other,' she said vaguely. She turned as Yeadings came up behind, carrying a tray with the drinks. 'The garden's looking wonderful, sir. How do you manage now a hose ban's been imposed?'

'Oh, *Mike*, please. We do our best with watering cans, concentrating on the neediest plants. It drives the slugs into ghettos. And our arms must be steadily elongating. We'll end up as apes.'

They discussed generally what an organic garden really involved. Sally, listening from her place under the tree, shrieked across. 'Frogs. You've gotta have frogs.'

'And ladybirds,' Luke explained knowledgeably.

'Which means a pond,' Nan added, waving them to their seats. 'We did some soul-searching over that, because of the dangers, but now that Luke's four he's grown-up enough to be careful.'

'Stout fellow,' Max complimented him, and the child grinned.

The meal was delicious and the conversation remained on a safe level, far from the subject of work. They lingered on until evening drinks, after which the Motts were the first couple to depart. After a final tour of the garden, Z and Max retired too, laden with their berries and a basket of runner beans.

'So,' Max said, as he eased the car out of the driveway into the returning Sunday evening traffic, 'all is peace on the professional front.'

'It looks like it,' Z granted cautiously. But under the surface? She hoped Max was right. If Angus was still touchy about Paula's decision to continue as defence barrister locally, there could be repercussions at work.

Chapter Eight

Early on Monday Lee Barber stood over the body of the stabbed man sprawled on the sheet of pvc. His pockets had furnished no clue to his identity, which in itself seemed suspicious.

'I'd give a lot,' Egerton said grimly, 'to know who the poor devil is.'

'And how he found out where you were. Could it be through Max Harris?' Lee demanded. 'Did you contact him while I was out?'

'On Saturday, but only to put him off. I didn't say where I was, or who I was with.'

'Using the landline?'

'Your house phone, yes. I hadn't anything else. My mobile was in my briefcase, and God knows where that is by now. The contact number he'd given me was a mobile's.'

Lee scowled. 'He could have logged my number. Newspapers probably have ways of tracing calls. That could have given him time to send someone after you.'

'You think this was Harris's man? But he attacked me.'

'He was looking for your briefcase. And he didn't

bring a weapon, did he? The knife was from our kitchen. You would have scared him, turning up when he thought the house was empty. He was on the defensive.'

'You didn't see him, coming after me with that knife. I was sure then he was going to kill me; but now…maybe he meant just to force me to tell him where the papers were he wanted.'

'Which you'd promised to Harris and then reneged on the offer. Newspapers use all sorts of dirty methods to get what will hit the headlines and increase circulation.'

'I still don't believe Harris would do that.' Egerton was beginning to sound ruffled at Lee's persistence.

'Did you ever meet the man? Or are you going by the image of him that he trots out in print? I think you're being bloody naïve, Tim. You shouldn't have rung him from here.'

Fear flickered in Egerton's eyes again. 'Look, we can't know anything for sure, but I'm convinced this is something more scary than an attempt to get a story for the press. Someone's out to get me, Lee.'

Almost eyeball to eyeball, the big man stared down at him and had to accept that Egerton's fear was infectious. For himself, he was more worried about what lay immediately ahead.

'Whatever,' he granted. 'For the present let's sort this lot. We'll have to start on the tree to cover what we do later, in case there are neighbours on the prowl.'

'I've done it,' Egerton claimed. 'The apple tree: yesterday, while you were at the coast. I took all the dead branches off. And the old man over your fence took good notice; shouted at me for breaking the hallowed Sunday quiet.'

'You used the chainsaw? On your own?'

'It wasn't that hard. I hoisted it on a rope from a healthy branch. Then I left the sawn-off stuff where it lay. You wouldn't have seen it from the house because it was dusk when you got back. With all that happened later I had no chance to tell you.'

Lee stared at him. Such a complex man. But that Egerton had meant to kill the intruder didn't fit with the rest of him. It had to be the accident he claimed. And now the apple tree. He'd taken on this last job like the rest of the chores: laying the table, cooking a meal, emptying out the rubbish. Trying to pay his way, poor sod. He might be puny but there was nothing wrong with his heart; it was in the right place.

'Well, thanks, Tim. That gives us a good start. Now we can lug the timber into the garage for show, and get on with the other thing in there.' His face twisted. 'I guess it'll be my turn to carve.'

Egerton looked sickly at him, recognised the black humour and managed a weak smile. 'Chainsaw gang,' he offered.

It was butchery. Messy, but with dead meat there's no great blood-flow. For all that, nauseated, neither could face the other. Lee worked taut-lipped, unable to believe what he was doing. Egerton, seated on an upturned oil drum, head in hands, was tortured by the rasping sounds and abattoir smells.

There were black plastic sacks left over from when the council had changed to providing wheelie bins. Four, double-thick, filled and corded shut, were lined up inside the garage's raised door.

As a finale, Lee sawed up the rotten limbs from the apple tree and finally the sawhorse he'd used for the dismemberment. Together they lugged all the timber down to the end of the garden and piled it behind the rockery.

They returned to find old Godden from next-door peering over the front fence. He gave an inimical glare at Egerton and then turned a wintry smile on Lee. 'You've been busy.'

'It had to be done. That old tree was getting dangerous. I couldn't risk the children playing underneath.'

'Pity your friend had to pick on a Sunday afternoon to make such a racket yesterday. I suppose you're taking advantage of young Kathy being away. Gone to her mother's, Freda tells me.'

'For Jenny's half-term week.'

'Yes, a schoolgirl now. How fast they grow up. Seems only yesterday she…'

'Look, Mr Godden, I've still some clearing up to do. Must get along.'

'Right; well, don't forget, if there's anything I can do…You only have to ask: Neighbourhood Watch, and all that. Like when that strange man was hanging around, coupla days back. Could have been up to mischief. I thought he was showing interest in your house, but then he disappeared. I went and rang your doorbell in case he'd broken in. Maybe scare him away, see? Anyway, seems no harm done.'

'None at all. Thanks.'

'Well, goodbye then, Lee. Nice to meet you, Mr…'

'Johnson,' said Egerton hurriedly.

Godden wrinkled his whiskery old face in semblance of a smile and tottered off.

The two men looked at each other. 'Why Johnson?' Lee demanded under his breath.

'No idea.'

'There must be some kind of association.'

'Maybe. Son of John; Johnson over Jordan; President Johnson; even Amy Johnson. It just came out of the air. Anyway, what now?'

'We load the stuff into the car boot and I drive down to the coast again.'

Egerton hesitated. 'Can I come along?'

Lee straightened over lifting one of the bags. 'If you want. Sure; glad of the company.'

'Thanks. Fact is, I don't fancy staying in the house alone. I'll find someone to fix the back door for you tomorrow.'

Lee glanced at him; put a hand on his shoulder. He couldn't blame the poor devil, scared shitless as he must have been over the past few days. At least he had the courage to admit it.

'Shouldn't we hose out the garage first?' Tim suggested.

'There's still a hosepipe ban. Godden's just the sort of

good citizen who'd grass on me to the Drought Police. We'll clean it all tonight with bleach. I'll lay in some cans when we get to Newhaven. We'll get everything straight when we get back.'

He wrapped the chainsaw inside the plastic sheet from the floor and carried it out to the car. They loaded up and drove in silence until Lee put in a tape, which was an old Bowie recording Kathy had liked. The rest of the collection was all kiddy stuff, so then he switched to Classic FM, guessing it would suit the other man best.

'Your neighbour…' Tim began.

'Old Godden.'

'He mentioned a stranger hanging around "a coupla days back". But it was only yesterday the man broke in. So, if it was Saturday when he first turned up, it couldn't have been Harris who sent him. It wasn't until then that I phoned, early afternoon.'

'You really want to trust Harris, don't you? It's more likely the old fellow's got it wrong. Yesterday or two days back, it's all the same to old dodderers like him. You can't go by anything he says.'

'He sounded well on the ball to me.'

'Good at poking his nose in, but he's pretty senile. If it bothers you, we can check with him when we get back. Or, better still, ask his wife. Freda still has all her marbles.'

At Cuckfield they took on petrol. 'Let me do this,' Tim insisted.

'Not with a credit card,' Lee warned. 'You could be traced.'

'I've plenty of cash. I stocked up because I knew I might have to lie low for a while. While I settle, can you pick up some coffee and sandwiches from the kiosk?' He thrust a twenty into Lee's hands.

An hour back, neither would have felt like eating. They had given breakfast a miss, but now Lee discovered he was famished. 'Another thirty miles,' he promised, 'and we'll be getting a sniff of the sea.'

Ben's boat was how he'd left it. They hefted the bags on board, pushed off with Tim at the tiller and Lee scrambled in after. 'I thought you couldn't face sailing,' he accused as they changed places. 'If you're going to puke, make sure it's over the side.'

'I've done enough of that these last few days. Maybe that's the end. ' His face was taut, but by now some of the colour was coming back.

There was a slight swell on, but nothing alarming. To save time Lee fired the outboard motor as soon as they were away from the river mouth, risking the pungent stench of two-stroke upsetting Tim's stomach. Then he set a course towards the horizon. 'It's lucky,' he said, 'that Customs are keener about boats coming in than going out, or we might have to cope with visitors.'

Egerton gripped the seat to either side of him, trying to predict the irregular movement of the waves slapping the bows.

Lee suddenly grunted. 'Do you know what?' he demanded.

'What?'

'Yesterday's fish. I just remembered. I dumped my bag on the kitchen floor when I got back. They'll still be there, stinking the place out.'

'No; I found them. They're in the fridge. They'll do for tonight.'

Lee scowled, irked that at that point Tim had been the better one at keeping his cool. 'There's nothing like eating them straight out of the sea. Still, inlanders can't be choosers.' It sounded ungracious.

He reached in the back pocket of his jeans for a knife and began to slit open the tops of the black plastic bags. Egerton turned his face away.

'Did you notice?' Lee asked. 'He'd been circumcised.'

Egerton stared at him. 'No. Does that make him Jewish?'

Not necessarily. 'My dad was nearly done as a baby, only the doctor wouldn't have any of it. Grandad had been a warrant officer in the Second World War; Eighth Army in the Western Desert, until he got a foot blown off by a landmine. He said those who'd been done didn't have half the trouble of the others when the weather got stinking hot. Circumcision's common practice in the Middle East. So Muslims too, I guess.'

Egerton continued staring. 'Terrorists? Do you think I haven't been afraid of that? – someone searching for a weapon to kill millions with a disease I'd a major part in cultivating? That's been scaring the daylight out of me, thinking that someone crazy might catch up and get hold of those research notes. God, I wish we had all that stuff with us here, to drop in the sea with the body.'

'Time for man overboard,' Lee prompted him grimly.

'Grab the bags as I empty them out. Then the plastic goes in at the end, slashed up.'

They worked together, out of sight of land.

'So that's it,' Tim said eventually, almost as a question. 'It's over.'

'Not quite. There's the chainsaw. It can't go back to the hire shop as it is. I'll dismantle it in the fish hut, use bleach and make sure there are no traces left.' He loosed the mainsail, turned the boat on the wind and set course due north.

Egerton sat hunched in the bows. Disposal of the body had brought no real relief. There were other issues to face now.

Lee watched him stand, uncertain, facing towards where the shoreline began to show blue through a light sea mist. He bent, reaching for the boat's side, and his knuckles whitened as he gripped the gunwale.

'Tim!' Lee shouted. The other man turned an agonised face. This was more than seasickness; much more. Lee uncoiled in a single leap and had the man pinioned by the elbows. Released, the tiller swung and the boat heeled over.

'Not on my watch!' Lee snarled, rocking to steady himself. Later he had no idea why those words came out, but they worked. Egerton crumpled, shamefaced, in his arms. He slid onto the deck, covered his face with his hands, shoulders shaking. At last controlling himself, he turned his face away. 'God, I'm sorry. That was bloody stupid. I didn't think how it could rebound on you.'

Rebound? Lee asked himself. What kind of remorse

was that? The man had meant to go overboard, drown himself. All along there'd been that possibility in the background – a depressive's intention to self-destruct.

It could still happen. Tim hadn't overcome the urge. He just regretted trying it on here, at this moment. He was *apologising* to Lee, because of possible backlash: the implication – two of them seen putting out to sea and only one coming back! Yes, there was that risk. He should have seen that himself, because wasn't he in shit enough, without being suspected of drowning Egerton as well? For the future, he must be more wary how he treated the man.

'Tim, forget it. You can't get out of things that way. Drop the whole idea. You don't need to blow the whistle. It's not too late for you to return to work, wait a decent while and hand in your notice. You'd no longer be responsible. You'd be free of the guilt without exposure.'

'Leaving someone else to continue my work? That's no solution. And I've taken a man's life. Whoever he was and whatever he meant to do to me, that was…so wrong.'

'But it was an accident, self-defence. And what good could killing yourself do?'

He looked uncertain, searching for an answer. 'Maybe the scandal would stir things up, bring some of the evils out in the open. Like it almost did after WMDs and Dr David Kelly.'

'There are still other options. Weren't you expecting Max Harris would do that for you?'

Egerton was silent. They hit a choppy patch of water,

and while Lee's hands were busied keeping the boat on course he was ever conscious of Egerton slumped in the bows, quietly despairing, still suicidal, preferring oblivion to falling foul of Official Secrets, and his career in ruins. Wasn't that the coward's way out when, like a soldier, he'd meant to take some of the enemy down with him?

Much the same thoughts were in Egerton's mind. He looked across and said wretchedly, 'If only I hadn't lost the briefcase. It had all I needed in it.'

My fault again, Lee thought wryly: can't get it right killing him, and then I make a pig's arse of clearing up afterwards.

'Twenty minutes till we make the shore,' he promised. 'I'll deal with the chainsaw in the fish hut, and by then we'll be more than ready for a meal. Get some food down you and you'll feel a different man.' Even to himself the cliché sounded false.

They made shore and Lee swung over the side, splashing through the shallows to fix the cable from the winch. Egerton gave a hand to beaching the boat above tideline and watched while Lee, tools spread around the hut's floor, began to take the chainsaw apart.

'Tim, there's a bucket under the bench. Can you pour some bleach in and start on the bits? You'll find another pair of heavy duty gloves in my bag.'

It took longer than Lee had expected, the reassembling being tricky. When he had the thing together again he wrapped it in one of Ben's dried-out plastic bags that he used to store iced fish. With it stowed safely in the car's boot, he threw an arm across Egerton's shoulders.

'So now let's eat, drink and – *be angry*,' he said.

He saw the sardonic quiver return to the end of Egerton's lips.

Yes, he thought with unaccustomed insight, that's what we have in common – a whole lot of pent-up anger. But it takes us in different ways. I get belligerent. He turns it in on himself.

Not that he felt the same rage about the real Ince that he had a week ago. He still felt contempt for the unknown man who'd pettily grassed on his overrun, but all the fire had gone out of it, dowsed in the shock of his own appalling attack on Egerton and the aftermath. He knew that he had turned a corner. There was a new perspective overall. Everything that had happened in these last few days had changed the way he saw things, perhaps for ever. And the other man's weakness had the effect of reaffirming his own strength. He felt hopeful enough to believe that by now the whole grisly business might be done with.

Chapter Nine

Next morning Egerton was asleep when Lee left the house to pick up the 04.59 up-train from Aylesbury via High Wycombe. He had been quiet all the previous evening, and before turning in apologised again to Lee for his suicide scare in the boat. He'd said he would take sleeping pills, which should see him through the night. When Lee looked in on him before leaving, he was breathing normally, his features relaxed.

With a conscience like his, Lee guessed, no way would he risk embarrassing his host by doing anything desperate in the house. Which didn't guarantee he'd not make another attempt elsewhere. Well, he must take his chance on that. Lee had no intention of nannying him, however dodgy the risk. He had a life of his own to take care of and, once at work, there was enough to demand his total concentration.

The first run was uneventful. On the return journey from Marylebone there was a delay at South Ruislip while a wheelchair invalid was loaded in by station staff. Nothing crucial in that, since it had been officially booked in, unlike the bunch of student types with bicycles getting on at Seer Green. However, he had made up the lost minutes by the time he reached Beaconsfield.

After that, he was driving on the longer runs, which he found more challenging. At the end of the last one, he phoned home. Tim answered cautiously on the fifth ring. He sounded breathless and explained he'd been letting himself in when he heard the phone, after a walk into town for some shopping.

'I bought a couple of steaks for tonight,' he offered. 'And a roasting chicken for tomorrow. We shouldn't run your wife's stocks too low. She'll need something for you all when she gets back. Oh, and your man came to mend the back door. He's made a neat job of it. I paid him and he receipted the bill for your insurance claim.'

Right, Lee thought; no mention of how long Tim intended staying on; nor of what he intended to do about Max Harris. 'Look,' he said, 'I've one or two things to do myself, so don't expect me back until about six.'

'Fine,' Tim said. 'We'll eat then.' Totally the dutiful little house-husband. It sounded as though domesticity had taken over, and for the moment panic stations weren't on the cards.

Lee filled in a form for Lost Property, pausing over what signature to use. The briefcase had the initials INCE clearly marked, but he couldn't remember whether there had been full stops between the letters. Better not use that. He doubted whether anyone would pick up on his own name, but you never could be sure, and anyway, the contents of the case would probably include correspondence, so Egerton it must be.

The first name had been Piers, he remembered,

signing the form PT Egerton in an almost illegible scrawl, with the same neatly underneath in block capitals. For address and contact number he could only add his own. Now it rested in the lap of the gods whether anything came of it.

Three ongoing cases were keeping CID Serious Crimes on their toes at present, but at Angus Mott's briefing that morning Superintendent Yeadings was notably absent. Zyczynski saw the reason later when she saw him ushering out a familiar craggy figure from his office. Linked with the sudden movement of filing cabinets and electronic equipment into the room next to their own CID office, this could mean only one thing. Special Branch was moving in on them.

So what was up that had to be kept under wraps?

There were obvious spheres of risk on their patch, such as the royals at Windsor or foreign VIPs' meetings with the Prime Minister at Chequers. And since a terrorist hotbed was unearthed at Wycombe, no part of Thames Valley could safely be ruled out as free of international intrigue. Proximity to the capital and fast motorways made Bucks and Berks ideal for lying up in rural peace while plans were refined and weapons training carried out.

In some outlying police areas there was an almost wartime paranoia about strangers taking over isolated properties and vans operating by night. Most reports produced innocent explanations, and some had led to clearing up run-of-the-mill criminal activity. In one case a zealous young probationer on a personal crusade of opening car boots had happened on a gagged and bound figure. His luck ran out when the driver winged him with an illegally owned handgun and tried to make off over the fields. He had disappeared into thick woodland. The wounded officer's partner had phoned for ambulance and back-up, but it took the Chiltern helicopter with thermal-seeking cameras to run the gunman down.

As far as Z could recall there were no planned special occasions demanding unusual security. So either something important had already happened or intelligence had been received of a threat to national security. If Yeadings had been let in on the act, how long would it be before Special Branch, notoriously exclusive, would call on her own local knowledge?

Meanwhile, she must report to Maidenhead Coroner's Court to give evidence in a motoring death. This would have been outside her remit, but she had been parked nearby and had noted down other witnesses' names before Traffic division arrived.

The case dragged on all morning before the inevitable conclusion of accidental death. A text message on her mobile informed her of a meeting with the Boss at twelve-thirty.

She was almost an hour late and the team had been dismissed when she knocked at Yeadings' door.

'Ah, Z, come in,' the Boss greeted her. 'The RTC case covered?'

'Accidental,' she told him. 'It dawdled rather.'

'Well, Ashbourne has always taken his time, and he

must be nearing retirement by now.'

As ever, Yeadings appeared to have even minor matters at his fingertips. She waited for him to let her in on the Special Branch presence.

'It seems,' he said, 'that a rather important research scientist has gone missing, possibly on our patch. Only twenty-four hours so far, but the immediate reaction suggests it could be a serious security breach. He was working at a research institute in Essex, but was last seen at Marylebone station near midnight on Friday. Indications are that he was making in this direction, but intended destination unknown. MI5 are onto it and Special Branch are keen to get there first. So, for once, they're not above calling on local knowledge.'

He paused. 'I queried how he came to be spotted at Marylebone, and was informed that he had seemed "unwell" of late and some doubts had been expressed as to his reliability. For that reason, his movements were under observation. Whoever was on surveillance, he managed to evade him. So, which train he took isn't known.'

'Could this be a voluntary disappearance, sir?'

'Possibly, or we may have a simple case of memory loss; but highly sensitive documents have been removed from a safe at the centre where he works. There's also a chance of abduction by a third party keen to acquire the information he holds, or by someone opposed to the direction the research has been taking.'

'A research scientist? So, as well as the terrorist possibility we have to consider Animal Rights activists?'

'It could be. We've been supplied with a physical description and a workplace photograph of the missing man. DCI Mott is organising visits to all possible stopping places on all routes departing from Marylebone that night. A considerable amount of questioning is involved, but of course not every station is staffed at that late hour. If he chose to leave the train at one of those unstaffed ones, he could have slipped away without being seen. This means we extend questioning to known passengers who may have seen the man. Altogether it's a very wide canvas.'

'Does he have any local connections?'

'None are known at present. Special Branch is looking into that. It falls to us to do the legwork, being familiar with the locality. You will be joining a DC Philpot from the Branch and he will give you the list of stations you're to visit together.'

'Right, sir.' Yoked to a Special Branch man, Z thought; it could be uncomfortable. Some of them were dour bastards; all of them superior and uncommunicative.

Yeadings handed her a clip of papers. She read them through: a short résumé of the career of Piers Timothy Egerton, aged thirty-eight, with the photograph of a fine-featured man with nondescript light brown hair and grey eyes. His height was five feet seven and a half inches; his weight one hundred and forty-three pounds.

'You'll find DC Philpot in the office next to your own, champing at the bit.'

Not a good beginning, Z warned herself. She doubted he would consider a road traffic death inquiry of sufficient importance to keep him waiting. One thing in her favour was that she did outrank him.

'DS Zyczynski,' she introduced herself briskly on confronting him.

'Philpot, Special Branch,' he responded slowly, eyeing her from top to toe.

Male chauvinist, she assumed. Or maybe he was silently condemning her, as a racist member of the public had actually voiced recently: 'Poles and Czechs, you lot get in everywhere these days.'

Well, he hadn't such a distinguished name himself. She caught herself smiling.

He surprised her by smiling back and it transformed the ferrety, dark-browed face into something quite interesting. She'd have to guard against prejudging the man.

'Your DCI has given us a route to cover.' He produced a clipboard and she read through the list of stations. They were all fairly close, probably because Angus knew she'd be hung up at court and starting late.

'My car. You drive,' Philpot ordered, producing a ring of keys.

'We'll take mine and start at Aylesbury, work up-line on the High Wycombe route, then back from Marylebone via Amersham. The trains are frequent enough, so we save time travelling that way.'

He hesitated. Clearly he'd have preferred to travel between stations by road.

'Maybe you've eaten,' she said. 'I haven't. I'll grab a baguette from the canteen and I'll get a chance to eat on the train.'

Again he hesitated, then, 'Fair enough.' But she knew he'd be pushing for his own way later. Well, let him. They could take it in turns to lay down the law.

He waited for her by the duty desk and she wasn't more than eight minutes getting back to him, with two sealed polystyrene beakers of coffee and her napkin-wrapped lunch in her shoulder bag.

'*Grazie. Andiamo*,' he said in a passable Italian accent, and airily waved her ahead.

Now she came to think of it he did have a rather Mediterranean look, although his surname was impeccably English. 'Your mother's Italian,' she guessed.

'She is, and then some,' he admitted. 'She makes us all speak the lingo at home, in case we forget it.'

'That's the best way to stay bilingual.' She forbore to admit that, although her father had been brought up to speak Polish, she had forgotten the little she knew, having been adopted by her mother's sister when both parents died in a car crash. Grandfather Zyczynski had been a fighter ace in an RAF Polish squadron during the Second World War.

She drove on in silence until they pulled into the parking lot at Aylesbury station, where they picked up a timetable and began questioning the staff on duty. None of them had been there late on the previous Friday night, but were able to produce names and addresses for those who were.

'Home visits,' Z said gloomily. There were four names, all men. A woman at the ticket office had gone off duty soon after the last up-train departed. Only a cleaner had seen the last train come in, on the down-line from Marylebone. He remembered four or five people getting out but was unable to describe them. He thought one had been a youngish girl a bit the worse for drink. Oh, and there was that man who wanted a taxi, and there wasn't one even when he rang through using the number in the kiosk.

'What was he like?' Philpot demanded.

'A bit rough,' he said, 'on his own. And he had a beard.'

Not the man they were looking for. Since they'd been obliged to go into town to follow up the four addresses it was pointless to go back for a train. 'We'll drive to the next station,' Z decided. 'It's going to take longer than I'd expected.'

They continued working through the list of stops without anything promising coming to light. By the time they reached Beaconsfield, a suspicion niggling in her head fully surfaced. She didn't like coincidences, although she'd grant that from time to time they did happen.

It was here, at Beaconsfield, that Max had waited for a man who'd failed to turn up. And this was possibly the line on which supposedly a man had travelled before going missing. Both occurrences were at some time after midnight on Friday/Saturday. So was there only one disappearance, rather than two? If so, it seemed horribly possible that the information Max had expected to glean could be contained in documents that the research scientist had removed from the safe at his workplace. So, had Max become involved in some subversive act that had sent alarm bells ringing in Whitehall?

He took risks, she knew. Although he wasn't an investigative journalist, his columns often dealt with facts he'd had to dig up in unsavoury places.

But surely she was adding two and two to make an idiotically large number. It wasn't even certain that the missing man had taken a train from Marylebone. If he'd been acute enough to shake off his shadow for even a few minutes, he could have led him there to fox him, and then slipped out of the station on foot. There was a taxi rank just outside.

Also, as Max had said himself, his failed contact could simply have changed his mind about handing over whatever information he had been offering. And hadn't he got in touch again on Saturday, phoning while they were at the zoo, to say he was staying with a friend? Then later, when Max was occupied making his risotto, she'd taken a message from one of his PI contacts. He had traced the man through his landline to somewhere in Thame. He'd even given the name of the householder but, unhappy at being used as an intermediary, she found by now she'd managed to forget what it was. Anyway, it seemed that Max's man wasn't missing at all. So she'd no need to confuse him with the one they were looking for now.

She and Philpot continued their questioning at every station to Marylebone, where they did a turnaround.

'Next we start on the loop we've missed out. That's from Harrow-on-the-Hill to Stoke Mandeville,' Philpot said, his nose in the Misbourne Line timetable. 'Your guv is covering all stations farther down the other line. He's lucky there's nothing running as far as Kidderminster in the early hours.'

'Has any thought been given to where this Egerton might have been heading once he left the train?' Z asked. 'Our job would be much simpler if we'd some idea of that. What had he intended to do?'

'Your guess is as good as mine, or the official one. To meet someone to give him the information? Or simply to get lost?'

Egerton rubbed at his eyes. Smoke from the bonfire had made them sore, but he felt compelled to stay on until every scrap of the sawhorse and the blood-soaked towels was turned to ash.

Mr Godden had walked down to the bottom of his garden to stare over the fence at him twice, but Tim had turned his back, making conversation impossible. No doubt the smoke had offended the old man, although the scent of apple wood burning alongside the other things struck Tim as quite pleasant.

Eventually he was satisfied, raking over the embers with a garden fork and dowsing the remains with several buckets of water to leave it safe overnight.

He let himself into the kitchen to rinse his hands and caught sight of his black-streaked face in the mirror over the sink. He had stripped off his shirt to plunge his face in the water when he heard the sound of a car drawing up outside. So, Lee was back earlier than expected. He went to let him in by the front door.

It opened on a small girl struggling with a suitcase. Behind her a woman had her head in the boot of a Mini Cooper, pulling out other cases. The toddler was in the car's rear, his wan face pressed against the window.

Lee's family, Tim realised in horror. And he was looking like a wild man escaped from a burning house.

The little girl shrieked. Her mother turned, was motionless a moment and then advanced on him, pulling the child away.

'You're Kathy Barber,' Egerton stammered.

'I most certainly am. And who, may I ask, are you?'

Chapter Ten

'I – I'm Tim, a friend of Lee's,' he heard himself babble. 'I've been staying over.'

Face to face with him in the hall, she was staring at his blackened face and hands, avoiding the bare chest. He tried to tell her about the bonfire; how he was getting rid of the rotten limbs from the apple tree, but she turned abruptly and ushered the little girl in. 'Upstairs,' she ordered her.

Then she faced the stranger again, her eyes angry. He felt like a young miscreant called before the headmaster.

'I have a sick child in the car,' she said shortly. 'I can't deal with this now.'

He followed her outside and picked up a case in each hand. She undid the seatbelt for the child to get out. He climbed down and instantly collapsed on the gravel driveway.

Kathy bent and lifted him. 'It's all right, lovey. We're home now.' She carried him in and Tim followed. He dumped the cases in the hall and stood feeling useless.

Kathy went through to the sitting room and laid the child on the sofa. She came back and faced up to Tim.

'Look, I'm sorry I was rude. I was already annoyed because I thought Lee had gone off to work and left all the upstairs windows open.'

Of course. It was to get rid of the stench of bleach. He tried to fix on the direction of her concern. 'Stevie's unwell. Of course you're worried. How can I help?'

'Get cleaned up and dressed first, while I see to the children.' She was still snappy, but she seemed to accept him for what he claimed to be.

He pointed to the cases. 'Do you want these upstairs?'

'On the landing will be fine.'

Dismissed, he made for the bathroom, where the smell of bleach was still noticeable. He'd have to think of an excuse to explain that away. He wished he'd had the number of Lee's mobile to warn him what he'd be walking back into.

When he came down, he was wearing his own clothes and had put a fresh dressing on his head wound. Kathy was kneeling by the sofa, trying to get the little boy to sip at some orange juice. Young Jenny had obediently stayed upstairs in her room, peeping out as Tim made for the bathroom, and then instantly shutting her bedroom door.

Kathy spoke over her shoulder. 'He vomited on the way home. We'd stopped off for some milk and vegetables. He just tottered over to the gutter and brought everything up. It was pinkish. I've never seen it like that before.'

'Did you have shellfish for lunch?'

This startled her. 'No; roast lamb.' She paused. 'But Mother had put out some frozen prawns to thaw for the evening. Maybe he helped himself. Could that account for the colour?'

'Possibly.' He sounded doubtful.

She got up off her knees. He saw her take in his changed appearance and she visibly softened. 'Look, I can't apologise enough for my rudeness. I was on edge about Stevie, and Lee hadn't warned me there'd be anyone here.

'It was good of you to help with the tree. He doesn't get a lot of free time, and then he's nearly always tired. It's the changing shifts that get him down. In his previous job we always knew where we were: eight to five.'

So she had taken in what he'd been telling her. 'How can I help? Are you going to ring the doctor?'

She stood undecided a moment. 'No, perhaps not. Children's sickness comes and goes so suddenly. And by the time we rushed him to the surgery it would be just on closing time. It could be difficult. He's had enough hassle today.' She looked rueful. 'Things didn't go all that well at Granny's. She's never been much good with small children.'

She glanced back at the little boy. 'I'll just pop him straight into bed. He'll probably be all right tomorrow, after a long rest. Come on, soldier, we're off upstairs.'

Stevie put his feet to the floor and took a few steps forwards, seemed to stumble, and fell forward, striking his head against the doorpost. Tim bounded across, but Kathy was there before him. Blood pouring from the child's nose spread across the cream linen of her jacket as she gathered him up. 'Paper towels from the kitchen,' she ordered.

He brought back a long strip and knelt to start staunching the flow. Wryly he thought he'd spent much of the weekend mopping up blood: first from his own head wound; then the dead man's; the gory mess after the dismemberment. It all seemed grotesquely impossible now in the presence of a family crisis.

Stevie grizzled a little, quietly, but seemed drowsy and Kathy had no trouble getting him to bed. As soon as she came downstairs again, without the stained jacket and trailing Jenny, there was a sound of a car on the gravel outside.

'That'll be Lee,' Kathy said. 'Would you mind letting him in? I must start fixing something to eat.'

Lee was already on the outer doormat, patting his pockets for his key. He took in at once Tim's slicked up appearance.

'Your wife's come home,' Tim told him tersely.

'I know. I saw her car. What's wrong?'

'She'll tell you.'

'What did she make of you being here?'

'I said I was a friend of yours, staying over. She was surprised at first…'

Lee pushed past him and entered the kitchen. 'Hello, love, what brought you back so early?' Tim heard the sound of a smacking kiss.

Kathy was flustered. 'Oh, I'll explain later. Actually, it's just as well we did come back, because Stevie's not very well. I've put him to bed.'

'What's wrong with him?'

Kathy explained, making light of it. Lee wanted to rush upstairs and see for himself but she wouldn't let him. 'He'll be asleep by now. Don't disturb him. Why don't you get your friend a drink, and I'll have one myself. It's been a trying day, one thing after another.'

'Look, I'm sorry about Tim.' He flicked a glance sideways to catch her reaction.

'You should have told me he was coming.'

'How the hell could I know?' Lee looked bewildered, but quickly recovered. 'I hadn't much choice.' That hadn't gone down well. Kathy's brows drew together. Desperately he tried for some plausible excuse.

'Look, he just happened to be lying by the roadside, mugged and too confused to tell me who he was. I was on my way back from the station. He'd had a crack over the head and was pretty groggy. It was so near home, I brought him here.'

'You should have taken him straight to hospital.'

'What? – A&E in the early hours of a Saturday morning? All hell breaks out then. They'd still be struggling with the drunks and beat-ups. Once he'd been patched up, all he needed was rest. So I let him have the spare room.'

'A complete stranger? In our home. He could have been anyone.'

'Well, you saw him. He's respectable enough. Bit of a toff, actually. Anyway, what would you have me do – pass by on the other side?'

She suddenly relented and gave him a hug. 'That's my

Good Samaritan. But you took a risk, Lee; for him and for us.'

'Well, he's paid me back by lopping the apple tree, and he's been cooking for us both.'

'He told me he was a friend of yours.' She still sounded doubtful.

'Well, that's what he is by now.'

She seemed to accept this. Tim, hovering within hearing distance, relaxed and slipped back into the sitting room. Jenny was now lounging in a chair by the window with a large book across her knees. 'Will you read me a story?' she asked.

When Lee came in to offer him a drink they were sharing the sofa and Tim was deep in the exploits of a heroic caterpillar called Sam.

Jenny looked up. 'Hello Daddy. We've come back.'

'I can just about see that.'

'Granny was grumpy with us.'

'Are you sure you and Stevie weren't being pests?' he teased, bending to kiss her. 'Anyway, why are you making Tim do all the work? You could manage that story on your own. Make her read alternate pages, Tim.' He stuck a chilled beer in the other man's hand.

'Should I tell your wife what we were going to have for dinner?'

'It'll keep. She's just fixing something for Jenny. I'm going up for a shower. Shan't be long.'

Jenny was ploughing through the next page, a finger following every word, when Kathy came in with a glass of white wine and seated herself opposite. 'Go on,' she urged when the little girl halted.

'…and so he – what's this word?'

'Curled,' Tim told her.

'…curled up in a lettuce – I know lettuce; we've had it before – leaf and went to sleep. The End.'

'Good,' Tim said. 'I thought that blackbird was going to get him.'

'No,' she said confidently. 'There's another story about him on the next page. He always wins.' She closed the book and went across to climb on her mother's lap.

'Do you have children?' Kathy asked Tim.

'I'm afraid not. I'm not even married.' He looked embarrassed. 'I guess no one would have me.'

'I can't imagine that.' She smiled, wondering if perhaps he didn't go for girls. In which case, what was behind this sudden attachment to Lee in her absence? No, that was an idiotic idea. Lee had explained how they'd only just met. Tim certainly had a sizable dressing on his head above the left temple. All the same, there was something a bit funny about the story she'd been given, although she couldn't say exactly what.

'Are you a driver too?' she probed.

'I have a car, but I left it in London.' He was starting to look uneasy at the questioning.

'Oh sorry, I meant a *train* driver, like Lee.'

'No, I work in a lab, I'm a pharmacist,' he claimed, stretching the truth.

She was impressed. 'You had a long training. Took a degree?'

'I have a degree, yes.'

The inquisition was ended by Lee's reappearance in fresh T-shirt and chinos. 'I think Tim had a couple of steaks planned for our meal tonight, but I don't mind a frozen pizza.'

They argued over who should miss out on the second steak and finally Lee overrode her objections.

'So what about veggies?' she asked. 'Shall I go and see what there is?' Tim started to follow her into the kitchen, but a fearsome waggling of Lee's eyebrows cautioned him to hold off.

'Jenny will give Mummy a hand, won't you, pet?'

The two men shut themselves into the sitting room for a parley. 'I'll leave in the morning,' Tim offered. 'It's been good of you to put me up like this, but I can't stay. It's better I contact Max Harris and go on as I originally intended. He'll find me somewhere to lie low.'

'You trust that man, don't you? I can't think why. He's a journalist. He'll take all he wants off you and hang you out to dry.'

'I always knew there was a risk in going public. Nothing's changed. But he sounds like a fair-minded man and I'm counting on him having enough powerful contacts to give me any protection I merit.'

'God! Just hear yourself. What happened to all that earlier virtuous conviction? You sound like a bloody lamb trotting to the slaughter, not a crusader.'

Egerton managed a weak laugh. He couldn't admit to Lee that since he'd been here he'd been totally put off his stroke. It wasn't only the terrible accident with the intruder, but the creeping suspicion that all his life he had been missing out on so much. He envied Lee's easy manner with his wife and children, accepting them as no more than he deserved. An ordinary man, big and rather clumsy; no Einstein, no hero, but he had acquired a secure base that Tim could never see himself coming close to. Nothing in his own life seemed other than hollow in comparison. What was the value of a fairly good degree, a prestigious job, the illusion he was doing something of value to his country, when it could be used with evil intent towards mankind? It was right that things should have gone wrong for him, so that he felt somehow apart from the rest of humanity.

He had a sudden recall of his mother, near to death, counselling him. 'My dear, you have too much conscience. Have a little fun now and again. Don't be old before your time.' And he'd never seen she was right.

From his armchair Lee was watching him. He wanted to help, but he wasn't going to beg the man to stay on. There was too much risk for his family. Wherever the intruder had come from, and whatever his real intentions, he'd been hostile. When it was known he'd gone missing, others could come looking for him. The only hope then was to deny all knowledge, demonstrate there was nobody here that they were looking for. Just a normal English family getting on with humdrum everyday life.

All the same, he couldn't help feeling some pity for the man in his dilemma. 'Tim, leave it for tonight. You can ring Harris in the morning, if that's what you're sure you want to do. And if you aren't, well, there's still time to contact someone at work and say you're unwell. Run out the mugging story again and I'll back you up.'

The door opened and Kathy looked in. 'I'm just starting on the meal. Lee, would you be a love and run Jenny's bath? She can manage on her own after that, then come down in her jimjams to say goodnight.'

Tim closed his eyes which suddenly brimmed. He wasn't sure what it was that he felt. Sentimentality, or self-pity?

Kathy was watching him, anxious that the injury to his head might be more serious than Lee had supposed. It didn't appear that any report of the mugging had been made to the police, and that was surely wrong. There wasn't a lot of violent crime locally. Any new outbreak should be looked into.

Tim opened his eyes again and smiled at her. She nodded to him and went back to the kitchen, still uneasy. It wasn't until she stood opposite Lee's duty chart on the wall beside the window that she realised what had sounded wrong in his story about the mugging: Lee was on Earlies this week, which meant Friday had actually started his long free weekend. Yet he'd mentioned the hospital's chaotic emergency department in the early hours of any Saturday morning. He shouldn't have been driving at all that night.

Later, she put this to Lee when they were settling for sleep and he explained about the party one of his shift had given up in London's West End. He was coming back from that, not driving at all.

She remembered then that he'd mentioned it earlier: Brenda's fortieth birthday bash. Batwing Brenda, as they cruelly called her because she'd had brawny arms before her crash diet and now loose skin flapped under them. A silly name; but then the shift called Lee 'Cut-throat' because of his surname, and Lee would never hurt a fly.

Next morning Lee stole out in his driver's uniform to go on Earlies. After that, for Tim, little went as expected. He stayed in his room waiting for all the family activity to settle. He heard scuttling footsteps across the landing and softly closed doors; Jenny's voiced raised in some plaintive protest quickly shushed by her mother. 'Jen, Stevie's still sleeping. Keep your voice down.'

When he thought they had gone downstairs he ventured out for a shower and shave. He was back in his room and almost dressed when there was a commotion outside. Kathy's voice, high-pitched in alarm, and then she was knocking frantically at his door. He opened to find her there, ashen and distressed.

'It's Stevie,' she cried. 'He's barely breathing and he's covered in bruises.'

Chapter Eleven

'What's the time?' Kathy snapped at Egerton.

'A quarter to eight.'

'She won't have left for the surgery yet. I'll take him to her home. She can't turn me away if we land on her doorstep.' She seemed to be talking to herself as she wrapped a blanket round the little figure in pyjamas.

'We'll need you to drive us, Tim. It's not far.'

'Of course: anything I can do.' He assumed she meant to the doctor's. They swept Jenny up on the way out. He held the car door as they all got in the back, Stevie in his mother's arms.

'Right and right again, then straight over the roundabout, two hundred yards and first left,' Kathy commanded as he fired the engine. They made it in less than ten minutes.

The watcher in the car parked almost opposite the Barbers' house was in two minds about giving chase. He assumed it was a family emergency; the scramble to get away had included a child in its night clothes and wrapped in a blanket. But it wasn't them he was interested in. Egerton would be alone in the house now and conditions were perfect for his purpose.

He left the car and walked the fifty yards to the driveway, scanning the windows for any sign of movement. Everything seemed undisturbed. He approached the porch and rang the doorbell. It sounded clearly through the house.

He waited for Egerton to reveal himself, ringing again after a short pause. Maybe the man wasn't up yet, or he was determined to lie low.

After the third ring he gave up and walked across the front of the house to the side gate. It appeared to be fastened from the inside but, as in so many suburban gardens, the bolt could be drawn if he stood on tiptoes and reached over. It slid back silently and he slipped through. Downstairs the curtains hadn't been opened, but the kitchen had vertical louvred blinds and the angle was sufficient to show a round table set ready for breakfast. Place mats and seating for four, plus a high chair for the toddler. Whatever had occurred to send the family rushing out must have been dire enough to make them miss out on eating. He doubted it was a sudden discovery that they'd run out of a favourite cereal.

He rapped smartly on the glass panels of the kitchen door.

Nobody came. The passage just visible through the inner door left ajar showed no movement. He stepped back on the stone-flagged terrace and scanned the windows on this side of the house. He rapped again. Finally he returned to the front door and shouted through the letterbox. 'Dr Egerton, it's Max Harris. I'm quite alone. Will you let me in?'

Still nothing. So the bird had flown. He'd wasted the early hours spent uncomfortably in the car. He should have come last night. Then he might have caught the man before he moved on.

It seemed he must wait for the missing scientist to get in touch again. If, of course, he was so minded.

Dr Sylvia Dunlop answered the door herself, a green plastic apron covering a floral summer frock. Startled at the sight of Kathy with the child in her arms, she realised at once that this was an emergency. The Barbers weren't a family to take liberties or enjoy imaginary illnesses.

'Mrs Barber, come in. Is it Stevie? What's wrong?'

She showed them straight into the living room. Through an open doorway the conservatory was bathed in morning sunlight. 'Sit down. I'm sorry, but I'll have to go and wash my hands. You caught me out there cleaning the shoes. Back in a minute.'

For the first time since she had started to remove Stevie's pyjama top and seen the purple-blotched little body Kathy had time now to draw breath properly. She moved the child from one knee to the other, cuddling him for comfort. He made no effort to talk, lying against her still sleepy, his eyelids drooping.

'Any temperature?' the doctor asked briskly, coming back

'I don't think so. I didn't try. I just took one look…'

'Let's see, then.' Carefully the woman lifted the child's cotton top and a long silence followed. 'Tell me what happened.'

'He was off-colour yesterday. We'd been staying at Granny's and I drove them home in the afternoon. On the way back he was sick. It was pink. And then, when he got up to go to bed, he fell. His face struck the door frame and he had an awful nosebleed. I stopped it with an ice bag, but he seemed so groggy I carried him straight upstairs and tucked him in bed. I thought that he just needed rest and he'd be all right in the morning. But I found him like this. These bruises are all over him, but it was only his face he struck.'

Dr Dunlop stared at her. 'No, I don't think so. He fell down the stairs, didn't he?'

'No. He went to sleep as soon as I put him down. He never stirred till I woke him this morning.'

Another silence. 'Is your husband with you?'

Kathy hesitated. Lee had gone off to work early. Should she tell her that they had someone else staying at the house? No, it was irrelevant. 'No,' she said shortly. 'What is it, doctor?'

'Well, as you see, it's bruising. And it's extensive.' She had never seen anything like this before. It was quite appalling.

'I was so taken up with the nosebleed,' Kathy admitted, 'that I never examined the rest of him. I even closed the curtains while I undressed him, in case it was something like measles starting, when it's best to avoid bright lights.'

Poor woman, Dr Dunlop thought: she's not to blame in all this. 'You did well,' she told Kathy. 'These bruises are fresh. Something happened to him late yesterday. I doubt they would have shown up before now. You were right to come straight to me. I have to ring the practice now and explain I'll be in late. Then I'll come back and examine him thoroughly; perhaps take some photographs for the hospital.'

'Hospital?' Now Kathy was doubly alarmed.

The doctor patted her on the shoulder. 'Best place, believe me.' She hurried to another room and Kathy heard her low voice explaining over the phone. There came a short silence and then she started speaking again, more briskly. It was impossible to pick up what she said.

The examination was, as she'd promised, thorough. At the end she listened to Stevie's heartbeat and checked the pulse at his ankles. 'M'm, you're lucky, Mrs Barber. It so happens that this afternoon there's a paediatric clinic at the hospital. You'll need to take Stevie there. The specialist in charge is a Dr Marius McCauley. You'll find he's very understanding. I'll ring him at his home and tell him you're coming. I'm sure he'll fit you in. Meanwhile keep Stevie warm and lying down. Plenty of water to drink. Above all, try not to worry.'

Which warning was, in itself, enough cause for alarm.

The doctor's manner in seeing them out was less businesslike than earlier. She lingered at the door, watching mother and child helped into the rear of the car beside Jenny. The man solicitously holding the door for her was a total stranger. Since Kathy had said her husband wasn't at home, how permanently would he be away? And to whom had she turned in his absence?

Dr Sylvia Dunlop sighed. They'd seemed such a close-knit little family, but maybe this was the early warning of yet another marriage break-up. There were too many sad cases like that nowadays. But in this instance there was a more sinister element. Little Stevie's bruising suggested more than a small child's natural clumsiness. Whoever was involved, there'd been considerable violence done to the boy. Someone was responsible. Barber was a big man and probably didn't know his own strength. Under emotional pressure he could have hit the child and sent him tumbling head over heels down the staircase. It was significant how Kathy had paused before denying he'd been in the house.

However, the matter was no longer in her hands. She had to get to surgery and catch up with her waiting patients. It was left now to Dr McCauley to notify Social Services, who would decide if the child was at risk in his parents' care.

Max Harris was no skilled detective. His watch on the Barber house had not gone unnoticed. Old Mr Godden, an inveterate curtain-twitcher, observed how the alien car reversed and took off some minutes after Kathy and the children had left. Painstakingly, with arthritic fingers, he wrote down the car's licence number. The least he could do was to warn Kathy when she returned. He hadn't liked the behaviour of the man she'd had staying at her home, and now it seemed there was a private detective keeping a note of her outings with him.

Poor Lee; he'd warned him there were dangers in changing to a job that involved night shifts, though he hadn't gone into detail. But it stood to reason that if a man wasn't there to keep a woman warm in bed, she was going to find someone else to take the job on.

Women weren't like that in his day. Well, not decent ones anyway. It was all this feminism and equal opportunities. The country was going to the dogs.

For Lee's sake alone, something had to be done before the damage was irreparable.

Freda called him from the kitchen. His egg, sausage, beans and bacon were getting cold. He tottered off to take them on board. As soon as breakfast was over and Freda busy with the dishes he'd give Sergeant Baldwin a ring. Just as well to get a bit of official notice taken. Nobody wanted a private investigator active in the neighbourhood.

He was not there to witness Kathy's car return, so – annoyingly – he couldn't enter the time in his exercise book labelled *N'hood Watch*. It was as he came back from making the phone call that he noticed her car was back in the driveway.

Nothing of any value had resulted yet from enquiries at all intervening stations and taxi ranks between Marylebone and the farthest reaches of the Misbourne Line. With so many of his team commandeered for the Egerton disappearance, Superintendent Yeadings was conscious of being left with too many plates spinning in his own act.

He was concerned that existing cases should not be left inadequately covered or abandoned in limbo.

Always happy to get back to some hands-on detective work, he was presently intent on doubling between his desk and following up a serious GBH of the previous week. It brought him to Wycombe General Hospital, where a security courier had just emerged from a five-day coma. He sat by the man's bed waiting for Cedric Albert Farrow to get his scattered wits together and give some account of what happened.

The man claimed to remember nothing, and so far forensic evidence had provided little to give a picture of the ambush the man had blundered into. Yeadings, familiar with the concept of memory shadow – that loss of time before the incident could equal the period of later oblivion – suspected that the man was less confused than he made out. He had been easily persuaded to accept a cup of tea in the nurses' office while Farrow had his dressings changed, and he had seized the opportunity to question the young student nurse who'd been left to watch over the patient while he was comatose.

'Did he have any difficulty remembering his own name when he awoke?' Yeadings asked.

'Not really. He said the usual things: "Where am I… what happened?"'

'What was his manner?'

'Well, confused, of course.'

'Anything else?'

The youngster screwed her mouth. 'I thought he was watching me under his eyelids. Usually people peer around a bit when they come to, sort of trying to focus.'

'Did you think he was more conscious than he was trying to appear?'

She grinned. 'I thought he wanted time to think before he had to answer any questions.'

'Well, he's had time,' Yeadings considered. 'I think I'll hang around until he's free to have a chat. I'm told he's lucky to be alive. Maybe he'll be grateful enough to make an effort at recall.'

'If Sister will let you. Actually, she'll be taking her lunch break in about twenty minutes. You could have another word with him then.'

Over in the Outpatients Department the clinic was scheduled to begin at two p.m. At a little before twelve the paediatric consultant's secretary had rung through to advise Kathy Barber that he could see little Stevie that afternoon. She gave no specific time for the appointment, so Kathy assumed it was a first-come-first-served system and made an early light lunch so they could get there as the clinic opened.

She had phoned through to Lee at work and his DSM arranged for an on-call driver to fill in for him. His car came racing into the driveway, pulling up with a scattering of gravel and he stormed into the house. 'What the hell's happened?' he demanded. 'What did the doctor say it was?'

Kathy tried to explain. There was no handy name to hang it on. Dr Dunlop had seemed quite puzzled. Stevie was so weak and covered in purple blotches like bruising.

With all interest turned on her little brother, Jenny

started playing up, insisting that she could now go to a birthday party which she'd had to refuse because of the intended stay at Granny's.

'Let her go,' Lee decided. 'That's better than having her wait about in the hospital while Stevie's being seen to. Ring through and see if she's still welcome. When Kathy explained the change of circumstances, she was assured that they'd be delighted to have Jenny after all. The children were to meet up at the swimming pool at three. The small Splash Pool had been hired for the afternoon and a special tea arranged in a room off the cafeteria.

While the others set off in Lee's car, Tim was to drive Jenny to her party in Kathy's Mini Cooper. She lent him her mobile so that Lee could ring him from Reception if there was any delay in meeting up afterwards.

Directed to the clinic, they saw about a dozen mothers with children already waiting for the doctor's arrival. They found a space on the triple rank of chairs, Kathy nursing Stevie on her knees and waiting her turn. About half an hour later a nurse approached to take her name. 'Ah, yes,' the woman said. 'You're Dr Dunlop's referral. I have you on our list. I'm afraid you've happened on a very busy day. It will mean quite a wait.'

The longer she sat there, the more Kathy fumed at the delay. Some of the other children brought in looked completely healthy; probably there for routine check-ups with nothing much amiss. Stevie, on the other hand seemed to be getting more lethargic and miserable by the minute. Kathy peeped under his pyjama top and found the bruising had spread and developed darker.

Lee, normally impatient at any delay, forced himself to stay calm, aware that Kathy was near to tears. He needed to be filled in on the details of the morning, so he took Stevie out of her arms and they withdrew to the corridor while she explained how she'd found the little boy like this and couldn't account for the state he was in.

'Dr Dunlop thought he must have fallen downstairs, but he couldn't have. We'd have heard him crying, and he'd never have gone right back to bed on his own without a cuddle.'

She was right about that, Lee thought. Stevie was no Trojan and normally enjoyed maximum sympathy paid over his little injuries. Perhaps they'd been making rather a noise downstairs, or the television was on too loud at the time. Or the little boy could have felt shy about making a fuss when there was a stranger in the house. Kids could be funny that way.

When they returned to the waiting room the crowd appeared even bigger. 'I think they're leaving us to the end,' Kathy warned him. Lee went to speak to the nurse acting as usher. She heard out his complaints and shook her head. 'The others have appointments. They could have been waiting weeks to see Dr McCauley, you see. The clinic's under a lot of pressure.'

As if we're not, Lee resented silently, returning to share the wait with Kathy.

She had been right. The crowd gradually thinned until they were the only little family left. There was still a pause before they were called, and then they found themselves facing a ring of nurses, with a small man in a black jacket seated in a swivel chair at a desk. He had his back to them and was writing up his notes.

'Undress him, please,' a nurse requested brusquely.

Kathy handed the blanket to Lee and with trembling hands removed Stevie's pyjamas. There was no need for everyone to be so starchy. A clinic for children should surely be more friendly and welcoming. This must put some mothers completely off coming a second time.

The paediatrician stopped writing, stood up and faced them. He was a hunchback, Kathy realised; then reminded herself there'd be some other less hurtful term required now. It made her face flush with embarrassment.

Dr McCauley bent and lifted Stevie from her. He dangled the poor little scrap by the armpits and moved closer under the lights.

'Oh, my goodness,' he exclaimed. 'I know what this is.'

He turned to Lee and Kathy, his face breaking into a smile. 'But it's many a year since I saw it.'

He laid Stevie gently on the examination couch. 'Come and look,' he told the nurses. 'This is a perfect example of infantile purpura.' They crowded around the couch.

He turned to the parents. 'What medication has the little lad got hold of? Was there something lying about at home? No? Well, tell me how this all started.'

'First of all he vomited,' Kathy said plaintively. 'That

was yesterday evening. Then he fell and had a nose
bleed. This morning I found him like this. It seems to be
getting worse. Is it serious, doctor?'

'It's spontaneous bleeding, a severe allergic reaction.
Serious, yes, because the minor blood vessels have
ruptured throughout his body. He will need to be kept
very quiet indeed to prevent more critical damage until
they've had time to repair themselves. It will be a matter
of several weeks. I'll get him a private room off the
children's ward, and you will need to come in with him.
They'll arrange for you to have a bed alongside for the
first week or two.'

'But I can't...' Kathy protested.

'Oh, I'm sure your husband will manage at home
without you for a while.'

'It's Jenny,' Kathy said. 'Our little girl. She's only been
at primary school for half a term. She's barely settled in
there yet. Lee can't give up his job to look after her.'

'Ah.' McCauley stood considering her. 'Yes, we have
to consider Jenny too. But I must stress how important
you will be to this little chap to help with his recovery.'

He returned to his desk and riffled through some
papers. 'I see your GP is Sylvia Dunlop. Well, let's find
out what she has to say about this.

'Get her on the phone, will you?' he asked the senior
nurse. He turned back to Lee and Kathy. 'Perhaps you
would wait outside for a moment. No, leave the little
lad. He's all right where he is. I shall need to examine
him all over.'

Kathy felt Lee's hand on her elbow, guiding her to the

door, which a nurse whipped open with a sympathetic smile.

'They're all sweetness and light suddenly,' Lee snarled as they found seats again in the empty waiting room. 'They'd thought he was a battered baby, for God's sake! Our Stevie! It would make a saint weep!'

Chapter Twelve

Arriving at the Leisure Centre, Egerton prepared to drop Jenny off. She had already undone her seatbelt and was waving excitedly at a group of five or six girls of her own age, who were going through the ticket barrier. Chatting together, they remained oblivious to her and continued inside.

'Your swimming things,' Egerton reminded her, standing beside the rear door as she climbed out.

He suddenly felt vulnerable, a half-familiar sensation of chill on the back of his neck despite the heat of the day. Someone, he was sure, was taking an unusual interest in him. He wanted to turn and see where the threat came from, but was afraid of a confrontation: better pretend he'd noticed nothing, get safely rid of the little girl and be on his way so the cars queuing behind him could find parking places.

'Buck up,' he told Jenny. 'You know what to do. Just tell them at the entrance who you are and you're one of Melanie's party, and they'll let you through.'

She stood looking bewildered as he slammed himself back in the driving seat and made for a break in the exit lane for the main road. He would take advantage of the lead, head for the motorway, leave it at the first opportunity and then double back. He needed to make a phone call, but wouldn't risk leaving any trace on Kathy's mobile. Once he felt safe from being followed he would find a phone box near the house and ring Max Harris, throwing himself on his mercy. Given this domestic crisis at the Barbers' over little Stevie, he would only be in everybody's way if he stayed on.

He double-checked that no one stayed in lane behind him, turning sharply into a pub yard and waiting for ten minutes under the inn sign. No other car pulled in or drove back after going past. When a stout man in rolled up shirtsleeves appeared in the doorway and stared pointedly at him, he felt obliged to go in and order a lager, persuading himself that time spent here wasn't wasted: just further insurance.

There were only five oldish country men lingering over their drinks, two occupied with a game of dominoes; and the others glumly watching. The barman was disinclined to talk. The dour silence, broken only by the slow click of dominoes on the beer-stained tabletop, played on his nerves, but he forced himself not to imagine the atmosphere hostile. He was in enough risk of paranoia without extending suspicion to a normal village coolness towards strangers.

After twenty minutes of contemplating his indifferent half-pint, he rose, grunted goodbye to the room in general and went back to the car.

He was almost back at Thame when the mobile lent him by Kathy sounded the first few bars of the Skye Boat

Song. He pulled in to the grass verge to answer.

'Tim,' she said breathlessly, 'we've seen the consultant, but it could take some considerable time yet. Let yourself in at home with the key you'll find on the ledge above the garden shed door.'

God, he'd totally forgotten the Barbers' troubles, but he recovered himself enough to ask after Stevie.

'It's pretty serious. They think he'll have to come into hospital for several weeks. And they want me to stay with him. I don't know how we'll manage…'

Because of Jenny, he realised. He guessed they wouldn't send her back to Granny's. There had been some kind of problem there. Was Kathy obliquely asking if he would help out while Lee was at work?

'Right,' he said, 'I'm heading back now.'

When he reached the old, twisted Wishing Tree at the corner of their road he glanced swiftly in the driving mirror. Still no other car behind, and nothing parked to wait for him. He turned into the driveway and drove straight into the single garage, although he knew that Kathy's car was the one normally left in the drive.

With the garage door dropped to conceal it, he went in by the side gate to the back garden and retrieved the spare key as directed. When Lee got back, he would have to play it by ear, see what was expected of him. It looked as though, once again, the appeal for Max Harris's help must be put on hold, in case he was needed here.

* * *

Superintendent Yeadings lingered over his salad lunch in the hospital cafeteria, not savouring it as a great culinary experience, but because it granted time for the afternoon shift to take over and the overprotective Sister to go off duty. He was quite a rarity in that he usually warmed to a hospital atmosphere. The mingling of medical and cleaning smells, the squeaky sound of soft shoes on vinyl flooring and the subdued bustle of activity never failed to bring back his early courting days at the old Westminster Hospital. He'd been an ambitious and newly promoted young detective sergeant in the Met, working out of Horseferry Road, and Nan an awesome theatre sister worshipped from afar. It had taken him almost a year of determined pursuit to get himself favourably noticed, but when eventually she had agreed to have dinner with him and discuss one of his cases, they found they shared more interests than that one.

Starting from such an unlikely subject – the victim of an IRA bomber, precariously clinging to life after serious invasive surgery – they had moved on to happier topics, finding they enjoyed each other's company. Mike's eager enthusiasms complemented Nan's steady caution; but both laughed at the same things, discovered they enjoyed the same music and films. They met often. She introduced him to wider horizons in reading; he taught her the rewards of weekend gardening at an allotment rented from the local council, raising roses, tomatoes, raspberries and fresh vegetables. When finally he proposed marriage she had been silent a moment, then threw back her head and laughed, 'Well, really. Why not?'

If ever Nan had regretted it, he knew he never had, never would, even though from the very beginning things started coming between them. The young man whose life she and her co-workers had slaved to save was proved to be the very bomber who had caused the devastating explosion. It was the specialist team Mike worked with that built the case that earned him a long sentence. Neither of them was young or naive enough by then to expect life always to turn out the way you expected.

Recovering from reverie, he returned to the surgical ward, politely introduced himself to the new senior nurse on duty and was taken to Farrow's bedside. The man's disgusted expression clearly said, 'Oh, not you again!' but by then the nurse had turned her back and was busy elsewhere.

Yeadings pulled up a chair. 'I've decided,' he began, 'that you need to get a lot off your chest. So I'm here ready to listen and see how I can help.' His manner was as expansive as his words, getting the message across that he would be perfectly comfortable to stay waiting until the injured man's resistance completely dissolved.

Farrow was disinclined to accept the invitation. His eyelids fluttered and he weakly turned away, feigning sleep. After a few minutes he opened an exploratory eye. The big policeman was still there, watching and waiting. He had a nasty feeling that a superintendent was too senior for him to have much chance of getting away with his planned story. Never before had anyone he knew been dealt with by a higher grade than detective sergeant. And this member of the Old Bill had a stolidity that warned he would be prepared to wait until something gave way.

It seemed that withdrawal wasn't going to work. Irritated, Farrow decided he must be given some guff and sent on his way, diverted into other channels of enquiry.

Yeadings continued vaguely smiling. His ally was silence. He let it build until the man was forced into speaking. 'God,' he said, 'I thought I was a bloody goner that time.'

Yeadings nodded encouragingly. 'Let it all out, lad. You'll find you feel better.'

It needled him. 'There's nothing to let out,' he almost shouted. He looked wildly around, but the arrival of a trolleyed patient from recovery meant that attention was directed elsewhere.

'Let me help you remember,' Yeadings tempted. 'How long have you known Percy Williams?'

'Percy who?'

'Ah, but then he'd have been "Wheeler" Williams to you. That's what he was called at school. Something about a box-cart his father knocked up for him. Of course, you had a real pedal car. No expense spared in your family, was there?'

Farrow looked sick. He hadn't expected there'd be any delving so far into his past. He wondered what had come up. Certainly the police would still have found some juvenile misdemeanours among their records.

'Let me help you. You became quite a skilled driver...' Yeadings complimented him '...for a ten-year-old. But it cost your old man a pretty penny to pay for the Mercedes you put in the river at Henley. You should have waited until you could see properly over the steering wheel.'

Farrow gulped. 'I was only a child then.'

'Yes, that was the point. Your father had the matter smoothed over. And from then on you were sent away to boarding school, out of local news-gathering. When you came home, it was to start working at Adison's Bank in the city, with flattering references from some of your father's business friends. How long did you last there? Two years, was it, or even thirty months? Some doubts were raised over your reasons for leaving the bank.'

'I left because Mother was ill. They needed me nearer home.'

'With some experience behind you, you took a security courier's job locally, and apparently turned over a new leaf. Until you met up again with your old school friend Wheeler Williams.'

'Old enemy, more like. He's set me up. He's lying.'

'He was always a better driver than you. You were the one with the brains. You're surely not suggesting it was he who planned the heist, it just happened on the day when the wages were being made up for the stationery warehouse, and the takings being counted from the Summer Fayre? And guess which of you could access the duplicate keys to the vaults.'

'They beat me up. I tried to get to the alarm bell. I didn't even know who the raiders were. They wore animal masks. You don't ask for their names when you're staring up the barrels of a sawn-off shotgun.'

'You're right there. It can be frightening. You must have thought he was getting quite a kick out of – well, giving you one or two himself. Only he was reminding you that brawn sometimes gets one over such brains as are available. Perhaps he was still envying the pedal car, Cedric. Professional criminals like Wheeler Williams can hold a grudge forever if you're fool enough to make him feel small.'

'It's only his word against mine,' Farrow protested. 'He's a known criminal.'

This time it was loud enough to bring a nurse across. 'I'm sorry, Superintendent, I can't have you upsetting him. I told you five minutes. You've had over twice that.'

'I'm ready to go, Nurse. Thank you.'

The smile Yeadings turned on the patient was false-friendly. 'Don't worry, Cedric. Your friend took good care of the detailed plans you drew up. He's passed them over to us for safe keeping. I look forward to a visit from you when you feel up to it. Meanwhile, get well soon.'

A bit naughty, that last, he told himself, walking out. He'd get one of his sergeants with a uniformed constable to come in and have another talk with Farrow. He was nicely on the boil now for a confession. And, knowing his partner in crime had been singing, he'd fall over himself to unload the blame.

Still finding the disinfectant and floor polish scents of the corridors agreeable, the superintendent reached the main exit, falling in behind a couple waiting for the automatic doors to open. The man, as well-built as Yeadings himself, was gently cradling a small child in a blanket. The woman had recently been crying. Little of the child's face was visible, but it seemed to have a bluish tinge.

An echo of earlier agony struck at Yeadings. Not all of his hospital memories were good ones. He relived the pang of heartache in bringing Nan home with their first child, and the unbelievable pain of having learnt that the tiny cherub would never be quite perfect.

He'd known little of Down's Syndrome then, but Nan hadn't escaped meeting it during training. She was like an automaton, unreachable, while he so badly needed explanations: why it had happened to them; whether it could have been avoided; what it would mean as the child developed, or failed to do so. There was no comfort to be had: doctors weren't so forthcoming in those days.

A corner of the blanket on this unknown child caught on the door as they went through. Yeadings reached forward to release it and the man nodded his thanks. No words. He looked stunned, and the father in Yeadings responded in equal silence. Then they were gone, turning towards the parking area.

Displaying his POLICE sticker on the windscreen, Yeadings had left his own car nearby, among the ambulance spaces. He felt as though part of him went along with the younger couple, but he didn't expect to encounter them again.

He sat for a few moments before driving off, thinking of little Sally. He would admit she was different from other children of her age, but for him she had *become* perfect, sweetly innocent and uncomplicated. The frustrations and sudden angers of her early years had been overcome because she was spontaneously affectionate and safe within a loving family.

She had her own kind of blunt-featured beauty, like a young puppy. She was fearful of large animals, but in her fondness for all plant life, by age thirteen she had struggled to find herself a future career, working for pocket money at a garden centre on Saturdays and mastering many of the easier names of the flowers and shrubs she potted up for sale. In all, a blessing; when at first he had believed her arrival a cruel stroke of fate.

They had put off having a second child for years, and then, almost by accident, young Luke had signalled he was on the way. And, miraculously, Luke *was* perfect, in the accepted sense; lusty and tough, and brimming with curiosity about the world around him. In later years, Sally would have a brother to protect her.

Yeadings got out of the car, relocked it and went back inside the hospital. The flowers on sale there weren't as good as many in his garden, but he needed to make a gesture. He spent some time making up a bouquet for Nan. So long, in fact, that when he went out again he found an ambulance driver fuming at the space he'd taken up. He apologised and made short shrift of easing the car out.

He headed for home, refusing the mental shift needed to face the criminal statistics piled on his desk.

Through the driving mirror Lee watched Kathy in the rear seat. 'Are you sure you'll manage on your own?'

'I don't see why not, if Dr Dunlop will visit every day, as she promised. I'll do everything Dr McCauley said, as long as I can keep Stevie at home. Maybe you'd bring down his old cot from the loft. Then I'll be sure he can't get out and move around.'

Not that the poor little scrap showed any signs of wanting to, Lee thought. He'd never seen Stevie so wan and lifeless. But *six weeks* Dr McCauley had insisted on: six weeks without putting a foot to the ground. It was unbelievable that so much damage could result from an allergy. Kathy would have to take enormous care what he ate and what was allowed to touch his bruised little body.

'What d'you suppose caused it?' he demanded.

Kathy's mouth tightened. 'Something he ate at Granny's, of course.'

'She's not all that bad a cook.'

'It's not that.'

'What is it, then?'

She was silent a moment, then, 'I asked her to lock her bedroom door, but she couldn't always be bothered. You know she keeps all her medication on the little table beside her bed: stuff for blood pressure and arthritis, and that dry cough she gets in the summer. A whole cocktail of pills and potions.'

She stopped there, then went on again; 'I caught Stevie in there on his own, looking around. He promised he hadn't taken any of Granny's sweeties, and I believed him. But just now, when Dr McCauley asked about dosing him, I remembered that. I think he did take something and was too scared to admit it. The problem is, just what?'

'By now, does it matter? He's been poisoned. Isn't that enough? The silly old bat, why couldn't she lock the stuff away, with children about? Anyway, I thought things like that were sold with childproof screw caps.'

'They are, but her hands are so rheumatic she can't open the bottles herself. So she gets her cleaning woman to transfer the drugs into old spice bottles. Stevie would be able to get in if he wanted. Manufacturers shouldn't make pills in bright colours that make them look like Smarties.'

Everyone's fault but Stevie's, Lee thought bitterly. He was too young to see it as stealing. He'd been warned never to accept sweeties from anyone without asking Mummy first; but he could have considered that helping himself was something different. There was no end to what precautions parents needed to take. From day one it seemed children were programmed to self-destruct.

Chapter Thirteen

There was so much to explain to Tim when they reached home that his own fears about being followed seemed irrelevant. This crisis with Stevie was so real; the other business possibly evidence of his rattled imagination. At the same time he kept in mind the saying – *Just because you're paranoid it doesn't mean they aren't out to get you.* He accepted he was paranoid; it was the rest he couldn't be sure of. So he said nothing.

Like Lee, he doubted Kathy was wise to take on full-time nursing of such a sick little boy, but she was adamant and it wasn't really his business to offer an opinion.

'What choice have we?' Kathy demanded of Lee. 'If I were to be away with Stevie in hospital, there's no one I could trust to look after Jenny except you, and we can't afford for you to give up working. Can you imagine the rail company granting sabbatical leave?

'It's not just seeing her off to school and picking her up. There's all the special time needed to reassure her and listen to her problems. This is the worst possible moment for her to feel I've abandoned her or value her less than her little brother. Children at her age don't understand illness or what it requires of you. No, keeping the family together comes first every time, Lee. Are you afraid I'll be less than meticulous in watching how Stevie gets along?'

'It's not that. But you haven't all the facilities of a hospital; the specialist treatments…'

'Total rest and quiet,' Kathy reminded him. 'That's what Dr McCauley insisted he needs. How much of that would he get in a children's ward, however much I tried to cushion him from all that goes on there? And anyway, since Dr McCauley agreed in the end, he must have had good reason to give in. Dr Dunlop has promised to look in every day, and she'll pick up on anything that could start to go wrong.'

Lee stopped his pacing and stared at her. She could be very persuasive, and McCauley was only a doctor after all, viewing cases from a distance. Day-and-night nursing was a hands-on job that specialist doctors were free of. And, of course, some of the time he could be here himself to relieve Kathy. And, for the rest, maybe if Tim stayed on…

His resolution faltered. He knew he was losing the argument. He should have stood his ground before driving her home.

Tim seemed to have picked up on his thoughts. 'If there's anything I can do to help…'

'Thanks, Tim.' Kathy darted him one of her sudden smiles and his heart leapt. 'You'll see, Lee; we'll manage, between the three of us. Have faith.'

So she'd got her own way. And made my decision for me, Tim realised. Contact with Max Harris was again postponed.

Dr Dunlop arrived after six, a doctor's unpaid overtime. She checked the little boy's bruises, seeming unusually subdued. As she should be, Lee considered. She'd have been the first one to believe this was a battered child case. It was she who'd passed on the suspicion, so that they got cold-shouldered at the clinic, left sitting there helpless when Stevie should have got priority treatment. And she offered no apology. Well, of course; because that would have been admitting a mistake.

She put her stethoscope back in her bag.

'Is there anything you can give him?' Kathy asked.

'No; he's taken more than enough. Is there no way of discovering what it was that upset him?'

'I think now he may have helped himself to some of my mother's pills, when we were staying with her.'

The doctor's voice sharpened, demanding what medication Granny was taking; when it could have happened; how much later the little boy had vomited. Kathy told her as much as she knew, but had no list of her mother's prescribed drugs.

'I know she was given something to control high blood pressure; then there's arthritis, and she had been taking something for a tickly throat.'

'Children go for coloured sweets,' Sylvia Dunlop said. 'I wonder about Felodipine: there's a version that's orange and shaped like a small Smartie. But I doubt it would have this effect. It would be helpful to know what she was using for her sore throat. Some adult preparations have warnings against children being given them. In any case it's extremely dangerous to leave any medication lying around.'

'I'd asked her to keep the door locked, and the children were told not to go into her bedroom,' Kathy said. 'But they'd been playing up a bit. Granny isn't good with children and she'd got rather snappy. That's really why I decided to bring them home early.'

'It's as well that you did. Anyway, the damage is done, and all we can do is give him the right conditions for his body to catch up again. Lots of water and soothing fruit juices, and anything he's particularly fond of to eat; though he'll probably not have an appetite for a few days.'

Before she left, she turned back and admitted, 'I'd not come across this before, so I've had to look it up. It's fortunately quite rare, but given the right conditions he'll pull through without any repetition of the blood vessel ruptures. He's a strong little boy. I'll drop in tomorrow about lunch time.'

DS Rosemary Zyczynski reached home before Max. She had the vegetables prepared and the table laid when she heard him coming up the stairs. There had been no sound of his car, which meant it was left at the front of the house because later he'd be going out again.

'Hello there,' he called from the landing, seeing her door ajar. 'Five minutes and I'm with you.'

It was more like fifteen. He came in breezily on a discreet waft of aftershave. 'Busy day?' he enquired after she was thoroughly kissed.

'Tedious. How about yours?'

'Energy expended to little avail. A sweaty day in all. When is this heat going to let up?'

He had brought in a bottle of claret, but she took it from his hand. I've put some Montrachet to chill in the fridge. We're having sole, if that suits you.'

'Perfect. Presented any way except *Véronique,* I hope.' He reached in the freezer cabinet for ice and filled the wine bucket.

'On the bone, lightly grilled with lemon. It's funny how tastes alter. As a teenager I thought *Sole Véronique* was the last word in sophistication. All those pretty white grapes for decoration.'

'And sloshy sauce.'

'Well, for sloshy you must wait for the dessert. I've made quite a mess of cutting up a pineapple.' She slid the grill pan under the flames and turned them low.

'So, who took you out dining in your teens?' he asked, his curiosity piqued.

'An old friend of my father's, Pavel Piotrowsky. He was a doctor,' she said shortly. If only 'Uncle' Pavel had been her real uncle instead of the disgusting old brute her Aunt Alice was married to.

Max nodded. She still preferred not to talk much of her early years after her parents' tragic death.

Now, as she waited for the vegetables to reach perfection, she was happy to change the subject. 'Did you hear any more of your elusive friend of Friday night?'

'Yes and no.'

He wasn't going to give on this, but she needed to know. There was still a chance they were both looking for the same man.

'How could it be both?'

'I traced him to his friend's house, but the bird had flown. Frankly, I'm getting a little tired of his quirkiness.'

She didn't believe him, knowing that complications served only to whet his curiosity further. Max had something of the natural hunter in him: not so different from her own CID team.

Max poured the wine. 'So what of your tedium? Is it worth itemising?' He knew she never discussed the cases she was working on, but it was worth a try to keep her off prying into his connection with Egerton. His Rosebud was sharp enough to scent when he could be on to something a tad dodgy.

'No?' he questioned as she shook her head, busy with serving the meal. 'No further adventures in court with our local Portia?'

'Nothing like that. The Boss slipped out of harness and did a bit of freelance investigating to some purpose. Just to show he hasn't had his edges dulled by deskwork.'

'Good for him.' He smiled to himself. 'The word tedium reminds me of a young parson I knew who deliberately pronounced the 'Te Deum' that way. He couldn't wait for matins to be replaced by a happy-clappy family service. Personally, I miss the old forms of the *Book of Common Prayer*.'

'As often as you ever cross the threshold of a church,' Z chided.

'Maybe we should do that more often. They do a nice line in a Marriage Service.'

She pulled a lump off her wholemeal roll and threw it at him. It struck him above the right eyebrow. He'd turned the conversation again. And back to the old irritant subject.

Several times during the meal she considered bringing the conversation round again to his missing informant, but she had to be wary, gleaning information without revealing any police interest. The search for Egerton was still under wraps, but with so many people already questioned it would hardly stay so for long. And Max was too wily a bird not to notice if all the information was flowing in a single direction. Then he would clam up on her.

Something had gone out of their usual free exchange of ideas. It wasn't so much a distance opening between them as a *paso doble* without flair. Unsurprisingly, Max stood up after his second cup, patted his pockets for his keys and announced, 'Wish I could stay on, but I have to see a man about a statement. I shouldn't be late back, but if I am I'll use my own flat. OK?'

'In which case, I will miss your snore.'

'I don't snore, minx. I sometimes breathe with passion.' He bent to kiss her.

As she left, for some reason she found herself saying, 'Take care.' It wasn't a warning either of them normally employed.

* * *

Paula Mott's mobile phone chirruped as she accepted the mineral water from her husband's hand. She scowled at the sender's name. 'Work,' she excused herself and listened to the message.

'Farrow?' she questioned. 'No, I've not come across him… I see. Not actually charged yet?'

She listened some more, flicking a quick glance at Angus who was studiously appearing not to overhear, while certainly alerted.

'This could be some time ahead,' she warned the caller. 'I could be otherwise occupied by then.'

With the new baby, Angus thought approvingly.

'Did he? That's very flattering. Of course, if I'm free I'll take it. Otherwise I know someone reliable who could probably step in. Shall we talk about this later? Yes, I understand. Quite; well, thank you. Goodbye.'

She looked slightly miffed. Was that because I was here to listen in? Angus asked himself. Or because – despite the obvious flattery of having been expressly asked for by the future defendant – she knew that choosing her as defence counsel could intentionally embarrass whoever prepared the police case?

Her mention of the name Farrow came close upon the Boss's description of his interview with the injured man in Wycombe hospital: Cedric Albert Farrow, courier for a security firm, a young man whose position there was possibly due to his father's financial pull locally. Paula, only recently making her home here, had evidently not heard of the influential family. And yet apparently Farrow had heard of her and was intent on booking the best possible defence in advance.

'A potential case some way ahead,' Paula announced shortly, dismissing the conversation. 'They'll probably want to call me out when I'm starting in labour.' She raised her glass. 'Cheers, love.'

Angus saluted her with his single malt, then turned the glass against the light to watch the prismatic effect. This set of crystal tumblers had been part of a wedding gift from Mike and Nan Yeadings, certainly not strings to make a puppet of him, but serving now as a reminder of loyalties. And Paula was set on walking all over them.

He had to be fair. She had her career, just as he had his. Neither had the right to insist on condemning, much less influencing, how the other operated. It was just unfortunate that Paula had made her name – and already a sizeable amount of money – defending accused put in the dock as a result of ball-crunching police investigation. It had struck him as ironic when she did it at some distance. Now that she had transferred from London to Thames Valley and was prepared to continue despite the imminent baby, it brought home the uncomfortable clash of interests. Right into their home, in fact.

It was left for him to grind his teeth, carry on notwithstanding, and bloody well see that all cases he was responsible for were made doubly Paula-proofed.

The Boss seemed to fancy his chances of building a case against Farrow, and the man's appeal through his solicitor for a standby barrister, instant upon the first hint of police interest in him, could imply guilt.

So, how deliberate was the choice of Paula for defence counsel when it must be common knowledge that her married name was the same as the DCI heading the investigation into the heist? He couldn't forget that the junior partner in the local solicitors had been a fellow student at King's with Paula and behaved possessively when Angus first met her. It could suggest a nose somewhat out of joint and a subsequent touch of quiet malice towards the lucky suitor.

Or was he underrating his wife's pulling power in court? Was she the indisputable dead cert locally for anyone hell-bent on proving his innocence?

The once-discarded cot had been brought down from the loft and reassembled in the Barbers' dining room; the table and chairs moved into the sitting room, as a temporary bedroom was set up for Stevie downstairs. Lee was drawing up a rota for the night shifts.

During the furniture moving, the sick child had been accommodated on the sofa, with Tim nervously in charge. He had no experience of children, and the added element of Stevie's precarious state increased his unease. He observed that the physical activity involved in setting up the new arrangements had restored some of Kathy's self-confidence. She appeared to have slipped into a new role of nurse-manager, while Lee, like himself, became an almost useless spectator.

Tim retired to the kitchen and started sorting vegetables for the evening meal. When he had the carrots grated and a mixed salad prepared, he laid the table for four.

Kathy put her head round the door and approved warmly. 'Jenny won't need anything else to eat tonight,' she said. 'Melanie's mum is a fantastic cook and never does anything by halves. There's a birthday tea at the Leisure Centre before a candlelit supper in the garden after the conjuror has finished.'

Unlike his own childhood, Tim reflected. He barely remembered their house in Wimbledon before his parents' marriage break-up. There had been a garden, but he doubted he ever played in it. Instead he was taken for walks in the park or along roads full of tedious shops. Other children weren't invited to the house, but entertained once a year, lavishly but uncongenially, at a nearby restaurant. Then, aged eight, he'd been sent away to boarding school, returning on holidays to Mother in her third-floor flat in Kilburn. Dad had meanwhile remarried and moved away.

The three adults had their meal in the kitchen, leaving the door ajar to hear if Stevie called out. He appeared to be asleep again, the purple bruising even more stark against pallid patches of skin between.

'Should I go and collect Jenny?' Tim asked as Kathy cleared their dishes.

'No need, thanks. Mrs Skinner offered to drive her back. We arranged it on the phone.' She glanced at the kitchen clock. 'But I thought she'd be home by now.'

Half an hour later, Lee went upstairs to bed, still being on Earlies at work. Tim and Kathy were to share the night watches. Jenny had still not returned.

Finally Kathy's patience snapped and she rang through to the Skinners' house from the hall telephone. Tim, reading the evening paper in the kitchen, heard her voice sharpen; the rushed questions.

She flung the receiver down and ran to confront him. 'Jenny's not there. She says Jenny never turned up. She thought we'd cancelled again.'

Frantic, she dragged a hand through her hair. 'You were supposed to deliver her. *What have you done with my daughter?*'

Chapter Fourteen

Her shouting must have disturbed Lee, already half-asleep. He came rushing downstairs to find Kathy beating at Tim with her fists and Tim, overcome, holding her against his chest.

Enraged, Lee towered over them, swung a right to Tim's exposed jaw, which sent them both crashing back against the kitchen table. 'What the hell's going on?' he roared.

'Jenny's missing,' Tim croaked. 'At least, we don't know where she's got to.'

Lee stood stunned. Kathy was past words. So much had happened – catastrophe on catastrophe with no pause for recovery between. Now she couldn't even weep, her whole body shuddering with shock.

'*Jenny…how?*' Lee demanded, stupefied.

Tim struggled to explain. 'She went to a friend's party…'

'Yes, I know. Melanie Skinner's.'

'I delivered her to the Leisure Centre. The other children were just going in. She waved to them and I thought she'd caught them up.'

'I rang Jean Skinner,' Kathy managed to get out.

'And?'

'She hadn't seen Jenny. She said she – never arrived.'

They both turned on Tim. 'I never saw any adults,' he protested. 'Just the little girls. Jenny knew them.'

'The *swimming pool*,' Lee shouted. 'My God, she could be…' His face was ashen. 'Phone book! Kathy, what's the number?'

She struggled to remember, though she'd used it often enough.

Lee tore directories from the hall cupboard and searched the pages. 'What the hell does it come under?'

'Try Bucks County Council.'

The number came up. When he dialled they heard the ringing go on and on.

'It could be a club evening. Reception closes once they're all in,' Kathy whispered.

Lee gave up on that call and stabbed out 999. 'Police,' he snarled, as it was answered. Then, sickly, 'And Ambulance. They're needed at Mardham swimming pool. A little girl's gone missing.'

He crashed the phone down. 'Get in the car,' he ordered Kathy. 'Tim, stay and keep an eye on Stevie.'

Kathy, almost out of the door, turned back, screamed, 'No! No, you can't. I'm not leaving that man here alone with my baby!'

'There's no choice,' Lee shouted. 'Get in the car.'

It fell to night shift at Mardham Police Station to take the call. A patrol car was at the Leisure Centre in less than five minutes. Banging at the entrance brought no response, but the brilliantly lit pool could be seen clearly through immense plate-glass windows at the side. Rapping brought a member of the water polo team, dripping water, to see what was wrong.

Once inside, the two uniformed officers made a rapid search of the building. There was no child in the women's changing rooms, the training pool, the showers, the cliff-face climbing area or refreshment kiosk. Everyone was out of all three pools by now. The water, glinting turquoise under the lights, lapped gently and innocently empty.

'No sign of any five-year-old little girl,' agreed the sergeant who had just arrived. 'Thank God for that much.'

A car delivered the shaken parents, but they were held back at Reception. Sergeant Bailey went through to get the story from them. There a pool attendant handed him a pink beach bag patterned with cartoon animals. 'There was this,' he said, 'tucked under the check-in counter. Someone handed it in for Lost Property.'

A sharp cry escaped Kathy standing just inside the doorway. 'That's Jenny's,' she said faintly. 'Her swimming things. She *was* here!'

The emergency operation involving a missing child had struck when uniform officers were thinly stretched. A report of a break-in at Chalfont St Peter Church Hall had come straight on a call for back-up at an affray outside the cinema at Gerrards Cross, where the casualties required two ambulances. The one meant for the pool was diverted there.

Sergeant Bailey wasted no time on calling in CID, and advising the Child Protection Officer at Maidenhead to stand by. Meanwhile he had to get the parents talking. The story was complicated. There had been a five-year-old's birthday party, meeting up first for a fun splash at the pool followed by tea, and going on to entertainment at the house. Jenny Barber, the missing child, had been one of the young guests.

He took down the Skinners' address and dispatched a constable to question them. 'And little Jenny was dropped off here with the others?'

'Dropped off separately by a friend,' the father told him. The sergeant was observing him. Barber was a big man, a head taller than Bailey himself, and he stood tense-shouldered, with his fists balled, ready for trouble.

'She joined a group of friends just going in.'

Bailey broke off to radio through to the constable he'd already dispatched. 'Get a list of all the children, with their addresses. They're vital witnesses. I want that asap.'

He didn't need prompting: such a young Misper wasn't all that common round here. Teenagers were different. If they didn't see themselves as indestructible, they were to some extent Tefal-coated and enjoyed taking risks. But a *five*-year-old… She wasn't going to run away from home when the alternative was a birthday party.

'Who was on Reception then?' he asked the group in general.

A name was offered. No phone number, but one of the water polo players thought he knew where the woman lived. Pulling on a tracksuit, he volunteered to drive and fetch her.

A disturbance at the entrance was caused by a grey-faced man shouldering his way through. 'I'm Malcolm Darby,' he said tersely. 'I manage the Leisure Centre. They called me from your station. Has the child turned up yet?'

He insisted on a fresh search, which he led himself, ending in the filtration and heating areas not already penetrated. Bailey steeled himself for the sight of a crumpled little body tucked away behind an oil tank in basement gloom. In the event he found the place well lit, tidy and, to his non-technical eye, impressively engineered. The enclosed space was stiflingly warm, redolent of oil and chlorine, but there was nothing more offensive there.

Superintendent Mike Yeadings had just reached the cheeseboard stage of the meal at home, at a later hour than usual after a long call to DCI Mott exchanging info on their recent interviews. When the call came there was no question but to take instant departure. For Serious Crimes Squad a missing child meant all leave cancelled and all hands to the pump. Angus rang back offering to pick him up on his way in to Area Station.

Yeadings spoke with the duty sergeant as they drove. An incident room was being prepared there with himself as SIO for the case. DI Salmon was on his way in from Bicester. Detective Sergeants Beaumont and Zyczynski had already arrived. The Chief Constable had been notified at home and demanded to be kept informed of progress overnight.

They found the station buzzing. In the pair of communicating offices set aside for the incident, fresh equipment was being hurriedly moved in. DC Silver was already there working at a computer keyboard. The nearby printer chattered and produced a list of known paedophiles in the area.

Mott snatched it up. He called over a civilian assistant and shoved it at her. 'Extend the list to cover the entire Thames Valley, and copies all round.

'DI Salmon, take Sergeant Beaumont and work through alphabetically. Sergeant Zyczynski, you'll work through in reverse order. I want you to report in immediately after each visit. If any listed paedophile is missing from home I want the family and neighbours questioned.'

Yeadings listened and watched, making himself as invisible as his bulk allowed. Mott was on the ball, closing the obviously dangerous gaps, but there could always be an unknown child-abuser slipping into the region unnotified, or one starting up without a record.

'What do we know of the child's family?' he asked Mott in a pause in activity.

'Not known to us locally. I've got someone chasing Barber up on HOLMES. The parents are on their way here with Sergeant Bailey on their tail. I thought maybe we should see them together, sir. They've found us an office on the first floor.'

'Agreed. I'll go and oversee the set-up. Ask Sergeant

Bailey to come up for a word on his own when they arrive.'

His allocated office already had the bare essentials plus a willing woman PC who sprang to her feet as he entered. 'Sarah Maple, sir,' she introduced herself.

Yeadings nodded a greeting and stared around at the monastic set-up.

'A bit of a cell, sir,' the girl apologised.

'I doubt the child's parents will be taking in the décor. How's your shorthand, Constable?'

'Passable, sir. Shall I get some coffee, sir? Or tea?'

'You can offer it when our visitors arrive.'

The desk phone buzzed. 'Internal,' PC Maple explained.

'Sergeant Bailey on his way up,' a voice announced when Yeadings lifted the receiver.

The uniformed sergeant's face was familiar to Yeadings, but the man had put on weight and his hair had greyed all over since they last met up. That would be not more than four years ago. 'The stud farm poisonings,' he recalled aloud.

'That's right, sir. Nasty business, but we got them banged to rights.'

'And now we have Jenny Barber, aged five, unaccountably missing. You've met the parents. What's your impression?'

'Genuinely distressed, sir. The father's a big chap, got a lot of anger in him. The mother's quite small, knocked all of a heap. No reason to think they're not fond of each other.'

'And fond of the child?'

'Gutted at what's happened. There's another younger child. He's sick at home. The woman's torn between being here and going back to see how he is. A live-in friend's looking after him: actually the one who dropped the little girl off at the Leisure Centre.'

'Name of?'

'Tim something.'

'Is he being checked on?'

'Not to my knowledge, sir.'

'Send someone out there to stay with him. He's a vital witness. And find out what the neighbours make of the family; discreetly, of course. The sooner we find out if either parent's abusive, the sooner we may be able to eliminate that aspect.'

'Yessir.'

'Then you can bring them up.'

The woman was nervous, the man almost aggressively protective of her. Yeadings was conscious of a warm relationship between the two. At the same time, he was reluctant to apply the 'gentle giant' label to Barber: it was too much of a cliché. He'd met so many vicious bullies displaying a tender manner when it suited their purpose.

They both refused the offer of refreshments. Lee Barber began to explain why they'd left it to the friend Tim to deliver Jenny to the swimming pool. Then the wife, Kathy, got a grip on herself, taking over the story, impatient at his slower manner. She was clearly the planner of the two, the one who would keep tags on family birthdays, keep lists of expenses, check on everyone's comings and goings. But right now she condemned herself for abandoning the older child, taken up entirely by appalling worry over the toddler's illness. 'Infantile purpura,' she explained. 'It's a really serious condition.'

Yeadings nodded to the WPC to take a note. She had already done so, writing the named disease out in full.

'This Tim,' he said. 'Would he be your lodger?'

The couple looked at each other. Awkwardly, Lee admitted he was a friend staying over as a temporary measure. Apparently he'd given up his flat in London and hadn't yet found another place to live.

The wife wasn't entirely at ease with this. Yeadings could see that this Tim had offended her. Was it only that she blamed him because he'd been slipshod in escorting Jenny to the pool? Or had she something further against him? She was so obviously eager to get home and take over care of her son for herself, despite the present need for her here.

'It's getting late,' Yeadings stated, looking out at the darkened summer sky. 'I know you would both feel better at home. I'll have someone run you back there now, and please be sure that everything that can be done will be put most urgently in hand. You can leave it with us. It's important you stay within reach of your phone, in case someone finds Jenny and tries to get in touch.'

Kathy stared back at him in sudden anger. 'You think she's run away? Jenny's not like that. Or has someone taken her? She's been kidnapped and they'll ring us demanding a ransom? Why would anyone do that to people like us?'

Her husband lumbered to his feet. 'Kathy, he's right. We'll do no good here. Best go home. And we don't need a lift. We drove here.' He was almost snarling.

Yeadings couldn't blame them for their anger. He knew how he would feel if either of his children had suddenly gone missing.

The couple had appeared vaguely familiar to him. He'd seen them somewhere, and recently, but the difference in context put him off full recall. They'd certainly given no sign of recognising him.

Sergeant Bailey had returned to the Leisure Centre on receiving a message that a Mrs Phyllis Forsythe, main receptionist there during the afternoon, had been brought in. She was a heavily built woman, earlier muscle turned to fat, her flushed face interpreted by Bailey as menopausal, his own wife being similarly afflicted. He knew better than to ruffle the woman further. He apologised for the inconvenience and stressed that the seriousness of present circumstances made her recall essential.

She faced him tight-lipped and self-important. Malcolm Darby, finding her equally formidable, stepped in to keep the peace.

'Phyllis has been with us for over eight years,' he explained. 'We rely on her for so much more than check-in and making up the daily accounts. She is responsible for keeping membership data updated. Perhaps more than anyone here, she is personally known to regular users of the facilities. You will understand that on occasion there can be a tendency towards – er, to rather lively behaviour among some of the more boisterous club members. We can rely on Phyllis to see that everything is kept under control.'

A fire-breathing dragon, Bailey registered. Right, so tread softly.

'I understand,' he began, 'that you were forewarned of the children's party arranged by Mrs Skinner.'

'Quite so.' Phyllis Forsythe's accent was superior, the tone clear as cut crystal. 'A private booking was made five weeks ago for the Fun Pool and Helter-Skelter Chute: from 3.15 p.m. to 4.45 p.m.'

She produced a computer-printed form from a drawer in the ticket office and waved it towards him. 'We were notified of the number of children – thirteen five-year-olds, as it happened, accompanied by seven adults. This is a perfectly adequate safety provision, Sergeant, as I'm sure you will agree. Two-to-one, and one spare. There should have been no difficulty at all in keeping a constant eye on the – er, little kiddies.'

Something in the tone informed Bailey that she had no children of her own. Would 'kiddies' be the normal way she referred to children? Was the lady too refined to employ the term 'little brats'?

'And you counted them through the turnstile.'

'Of course. And I reminded the adults that everyone was expected to put on plastic overshoes before entering the female changing rooms. This is a hygiene measure we insist on, Sergeant. There were, of course, no little boys among them.'

But a certain amount of milling around, Bailey envisaged: some children squatting on the tiles to pull on the bright blue overshoes, some wobbling on one leg and needing a hand to steady them: the inevitable squeaky excitement of small girls out on a birthday treat.

It would have been difficult to be certain of numbers, except that the turnstile would have recorded them. Was Mrs Phyllis Forsythe watching the figures clicking up on her screen, or eagle-eyeing them for possible misbehaviour?

She was still flipping the piece of paper under his nose. He took it and glanced at the booking. The number 14 had been crossed through in red biro and the number 13 substituted.

'There's an alteration,' he pointed out.

She took the form back and read it through. 'Yes, of course. One of the children withdrew for some reason. Thirteen were on the final booking and thirteen arrived. I remember the alteration now.'

She went suddenly tense, looking up, her flushed face now scarlet. 'Oh my God! There was another child tried to get in at the end, when the others had gone through.'

'You thought she was trying it on?'

'Well, you know what children are like.'

'So you sent her away. A five-year old. No parent with her?'

'I –I didn't see anyone.'

'But it seems her swimming things stayed behind.'

The woman looked appalled. 'Were they hers? There was no name on the bag. Someone leaving brought it in. That would have been later. It was found dropped in the car park. We thought someone would come back and claim it.'

Chapter Fifteen

He didn't know what to do. A radiator was ticking away, getting raging hot. It couldn't be good for them, these layers of bright woollies – cardigans, sweaters, even a knitted skirt – all carefully spread out to dry on top. Not far off dry: clammy-warm already.

He pushed his hands through their folds to the white flannelette sheet that covered the old-fashioned metal ribs. The *tick-tick* continued underneath as heat mounted.

She'd meant the sheet to protect her washing from any rust stains from the paint-chipped metal. But when had she done this – and how? So many multicoloured female garments; she couldn't have washed them all by hand; would never have trusted them to a machine.

And where was she? Gone to call on a neighbour – leaving these things spread out to dry on a radiator set to full power? Knowing they must all surely shrink?

She was a big woman. No, he'd got that wrong. Lately she'd shrivelled away, shrinking like the woollies certainly would. Maybe that was why she'd risked…

He became aware of other people circulating in the background, advancing on him but not coming close

– all women, middle-aged, slightly familiar and yet he didn't quite know any of them. He felt small and unprotected. Now they all seemed to be outdoors.

'Where is my mother?' he asked. One, in passing – tawny hair going grey, or white badly dyed – shook her head, closed her eyes and passed on. Somebody was distantly calling, 'Piers, Piers!'

And now again he was somewhere else, on a stony track between crumbling, once-white walls. Beyond them, to either side, large houses, vaguely Greek, lay back among untended gardens. He knew no one lived there. The place was deserted. A path wriggled ahead, taking him on minute detours round tall, prickly shrubs.

In the distance he could hear children's voices, shouting. They'd be down at the playing field. Maybe she was there with them. He rounded a corner and was faced by an immense thorny bush. The path had abruptly ended.

The voices were louder, becoming angry, demented. With a shudder he recognised them: Lee and Kathy arguing in the room beyond this shared wall. He came awake to worse chaos in his mind.

Last night, he had never thought he would sleep; but, after the police had come and gone, Dr Dunlop returned, handing out pills all round. She'd made him give up his vigil over Stevie and go to bed.

After Lee and Kathy left, the first to arrive had been a young constable, and on opening the door, Tim's heart had nearly leapt from his mouth. It must mean further disaster, little Jenny found drowned, something happened so that Lee and Kathy couldn't get back home.

But the policeman was only there to ask questions, wanting to know who else he'd seen, handing the little girl over at the Leisure Centre.

He couldn't answer, because that's what he *hadn't* done. Not properly, because he believed he was being followed. He had to drop her off and speed away before the other car could turn and catch him up. That Jenny could be the one in danger had never struck him. At the time, he hadn't really panicked. He'd had it all clear in his mind, how he'd throw off pursuit and get back to the house, garage the car, be sure that if anyone was still on his tail they'd assume he'd driven past.

He was ashamed. Scared for his own skin, he'd left Jenny to catch up with the other little girls. It had been no accident – no coincidence – that she had disappeared. Whoever was following him had seized the opportunity, dropping him for a more vulnerable victim.

It was all his fault. Ever since meeting up with Lee Barber he'd been a Jonah for him, bringing disaster upon disaster. But he couldn't explain any of this to the police. They'd want to know who he really was; who and what he was running from.

He'd sat stricken and dumb, shaking his head uselessly. All he'd managed was to give his name as Johnson, as he'd done earlier to the nosey neighbour.

This dilemma had swirled in his head as the tall blond detective, a Chief Inspector called Mott, followed on the constable with the same questions; creating deeper suspicion as he became tongue-tied. He'd broken off, rushed away, back to watch over the sick child. His head was in a turmoil; there had to be some way he could be useful, redeem himself.

Then Lee had returned, with Kathy, and the recriminations began in earnest. He would have run out of the house, got lost himself, but the doctor had driven up then, bringing a jarring hint of reason to the nightmare situation. And he'd actually slept. But now, with dawn's arrival, chaos had returned.

He knew he must get away before he brought even worse evil on this house.

Z, Beaumont and Salmon had worked into the night, following up the list of known paedophiles. All but two were accounted for and interviewed. Of those missing, Michael McKenny was believed to have returned to County Wexford. DI Salmon was involved in contacting the Irish Garda over the man's whereabouts. The other absentee had recently been badly beaten up in the street near his home and transferred from Wycombe Hospital to one in London, where anonymity would leave him less exposed to violence.

The two sergeants returned to base and learnt of DCI Mott's misgivings about Tim Johnson, Barber's friend who had been the last known to see the missing child. He explained the anomaly over the number of children at the Skinner child's party. Jenny's mother had accepted an invitation for Jenny before the trip to Granny was arranged; and afterwards had cancelled it.

A further change of plan had brought Kathy Barber

and the children home early. Partly to distance the little girl from anxiety over Stevie's sudden illness, she had been allowed to take up the invitation again. Kathy had rung Jean Skinner who okayed this; but, in the rush of last-minute party arrangements, no one had informed the Leisure Centre that the number of children was back to fourteen.

'Pretty hectic,' Z commented.

'Everything to do with a kids' party always is,' Beaumont assured her, having suffered them yearly until his son struck a superior attitude, opting for adult-free binges outside the home with unsuitable teenage friends.

At the pool entrance, Mrs Phyllis Forsythe's refusal to admit the little girl had a shred of sense to it, but this didn't excuse her lack of feeling. She could so easily have checked on the discrepancy and looked after the child until the position was clarified. Malcolm Darby, reviewing this, attempted to defend his receptionist to the police, and later, in private, tore several strips off her attempts at justification.

After a brief break, the Serious Crimes team met at 8.15 on Thursday morning to review what information had come in. Overnight searches had failed to find the missing child. Under portable floodlights police had conducted a fingertip search of the car park, extending it to the landscaped gardens beyond the Leisure Centre. The expected collection of unlovely litter from the area – cigarette stubs, paper drink cups, two used syringes, a single knotted condom and food wrappings – had been collected by Scene of Crime officers and bagged against the possibility of DNA sometime leading to witnesses, if not to actual perpetrators.

Frames on the current tape from the single swivelling CCTV cameras there were being enlarged and enhanced in the hope of identifying car licence plates, but its panning had missed the vital moment when the child was snatched.

'The beach bag was handed in, but the child wasn't,' Beaumont reminded the team. 'The tape shows it being picked up not far from the entrance, but not the act of it being dropped. For reasonable security there's a strong case for at least one more camera being installed.

'The dropped bag suggests that Jenny was suddenly alarmed after being turned away from the door; perhaps as she was being forced into a car.'

'Someone leaving could have offered to take her home. It could have been a person she knew slightly: a neighbour or someone familiar connected with the Leisure Centre,' Z suggested.

'But then wouldn't she have hung on to her bag? No, it's more likely she was taken unawares, panicked, and was struggling to get free.'

'Someone must have noticed all this. A number of cars were leaving at the end of the public session,' Salmon objected.

Beaumont shrugged it off. 'Who would interfere over a small child throwing a tantrum? God knows it happens all the time. Supermarkets are full of stroppy kids trying it on, yelling at gale force to make life difficult for the grown-ups. Other people feel embarrassed for the parents and look the other way.'

'But someone will remember the incident when reminded,' Yeadings assured them. 'I've prepared an incident report for local radio flash news. Exactly how much *did* the CCTV get?'

'We clearly have the Barber car arriving and Jenny getting out from the rear, with Johnson briefly helping with the door. She had two goes at slamming it and the car pulled rapidly away. She started up the wheelchair ramp to go in and then the camera swung past her.'

'That does seem a little indifferent,' Yeadings agreed, 'whatever the congestion in the car park. What do we know about this man?'

'Not enough,' Mott said shortly. 'DS Zyczynski and DC Silver, I want you to get out to the Barbers and their near neighbours. Get as much background as you can. Familiarise yourself with regular comings and goings. Then consider whether there's recently been any significant break in routine.'

'Such as the shortened week away at Granny's?' Z suggested.

'Yes, we need to know what went wrong there, to cause the change of plan. I'm not satisfied it was on account of the little boy's illness. It's likely that Kathy Barber had decided to come home early before she noticed he was sickening for something. Find out if she had any reason to check on her husband's behaviour in her absence. Look into her attitude to the man Johnson, who was staying at the house. Quite apart from blaming him for not seeing Jenny was safely handed over, she seems uneasy with him: discover why. Is there something funny going on between the two men? Johnson was too overcome about his carelessness over Jenny for anyone to tackle him properly last night.'

'Is there a chance he doubled back to pick her up?' DI Salmon asked grimly.

'The car doesn't appear again on the CCTV tape,' Mott told him. 'But it doesn't mean he's not involved. Get a photograph of him and show it around at the pool. Ask if anyone was hanging round suspiciously. Someone else could have been in it with him. In a case like this, everyone's a suspect. Hang on to that idea. Trust no one. Don't let the slightest hint go untested. If a marital break-up is on the cards, this disappearance could be a pre-empt by Barber to get custody of the daughter.'

The meeting dissolved, DC Silver following Z out to her car. He grinned across from the passenger seat as they pulled out of the station yard. 'Shall I be the nice cop? I guess you'd rather be the tough one.'

'We'll both be sympathetic ones, as far as the Barbers go. But I'd like you to concentrate on the man who's staying with them, follow him around with your notebook. He sounds in a very nervy state. Work on that. Maybe it is just a tender conscience over being a total prat, but there may be more to it. See what you can get out of him.'

Silver grinned wider. 'I told you: you're the tough one. Tigress on the hunt.'

Unsurprisingly, they found the Barbers subdued.

Kathy led them into the kitchen, since the dining room was given over to the sick child and the door between firmly shut. Lee Barber was seated at the cleared breakfast table, his head in his hands He had refused to go into work, but Kathy was finding him less of a comfort than an inescapable obstacle under her feet. There was no sign of the other man.

'How is Stevie today?' Z asked.

'The same,' Kathy said brusquely. 'He'll not show any improvement for some time. We just need to keep him quiet and away from all this.'

'Which can't be easy, with us coming back, I know. Does he seem aware of what's happened?'

'He's barely awake. Shows no interest. Doesn't even want his teddy. Just clutches his cuddly cloth, like a baby.' She was not far from tears but her voice had a sharp edge: more to keep her own feelings at bay than repel anyone.

Z turned to Silver. 'Why don't you take a walk in the garden with Mr Barber while Kathy and I talk?'

The two men looked at one another, Lee uncomfortable. He didn't need telling he was in the way. Kathy had already made that clear. 'Come on, then,' he granted, waving the DC out.

'I'll make some tea,' Kathy said wearily. 'Do sit down. I don't know what I can tell you. It's so incredible. I mean, why us? Why Jenny? It's not as though we're rich and could offer a big ransom.'

'We don't know why, because we don't know who,' Z said quietly. 'Not yet. It may be a random snatch, or it may even be personally aimed.'

She let the idea stay with the other woman until the tray of tea was there on the table between them. Kathy was struggling for control.

'Someone who might want to hurt you as a family, that's what we've got to consider first. Is there a spiteful neighbour, or someone at your husband's place of work? Is there some woman you know who has lost a little girl of Jenny's age?'

'Could it be that?' Kathy started up, a wild hope in her eyes. 'You do hear, don't you, of babies being snatched from their prams by mothers who've... Oh, that's awful! But it's not as bad as what might be happening to her if it's some filthy pervert... Oh God, aren't men bastards!'

'Not all of them, surely. You have a good husband.'

Kathy seemed hardly to have heard. She was fighting with some inner demon, her fists clenched on the table.

Then like a dam burst, it began pouring out: her dismay at coming back to find a stranger in her house, invited in while she was away. And Lee hadn't warned her, hadn't rung her at Granny's, not once. Usually he never let a day go by without keeping in touch.

Where had the man come from? What Lee had told her didn't make sense: about finding him in the early hours of Saturday, mugged near the station. Because Lee was off-duty then. He couldn't have been driving on that Friday night. Why would he be near the station?

He'd made up some story about going to another driver's fortieth birthday party in London, but it wasn't true. Brenda had rung to thank them for the gift, and said she was sorry Lee hadn't turned up. They'd all missed him. So where *had* he been?

And who *was* this Tim? All she knew about him was just that name. What kind of hold had he over Lee, to make him behave so strangely? It was true the man was injured, but she had this feeling it wasn't like they said. Lee was acting so weird, as if they'd been in a fight together somewhere, and since then he was running scared.

She stared at Z, wide-eyed. 'He had persuaded me to go to Mother's a couple of weeks back. It was his idea. Why would he want me out of the house?'

She was hysterical now. 'What is there between them?'

Her faith in her husband was badly shaken. And now this, Z thought: Tim had been the one trusted to deliver Jenny to the children's party. And he'd let her get lost. It was small wonder that Kathy was raging against him.

Chapter Sixteen

DC Silver wasn't getting much change out of Lee Barber. There was nothing much new he could tell him about Jenny's disappearance. It was all at second-hand, quoted from Tim Johnson. Lee had been too concerned about his son, accompanying Kathy when she took him to the paediatric specialist. He'd had no doubts about Tim: according to Kathy, the man was a competent driver. It had never occurred to him that anything untoward might happen to Jenny.

'No,' he said shortly, when asked if he knew of anyone who might wish to harm the family. He expanded to say his relations at work were reasonably good: you had to put up with the oddballs, like anywhere else. As for the travelling public, you sometimes got some ratty old person with a grievance come rapping at your cab window over something beyond your control. Then you told them where to direct their complaint or you acted deaf until you got your green light to proceed. It was amazing how someone supposedly pressed for time could waste so much on unloading their spleen. But no one ever took it further; not on this line.

'There are kids, of course,' he admitted, 'including the

nutters who would drop a concrete slab from a bridge as a train goes under, but none of them mean it personally. To their tiny, computer-blasted minds it's just scoring a hit on a moving target.'

They had reached the far end of the garden where a heap of ashes and charred branches indicated a recent bonfire. DC Silver turned as Lee kicked at the remnants with the toe of one shoe. In an upstairs window of the next-door house Silver caught a sudden glint of light. Behind it loomed a cruciform shape: someone was watching them through field glasses. That house should be the next on their list.

In gloomy silence the two men walked back towards the kitchen where Silver hoped Z had found time to unload Kathy Barber. She'd looked fraught enough to be on the edge of bursting into storm-force revelations.

Both women looked up as they reached the doorway momentarily blocking out the sunlight. Kathy dragged herself to her feet and started again towards the kettle. 'I'll make you some fresh tea. Lee, there should be some biscuits in the usual place.'

On automatic pilot, he opened a cupboard and stood staring sightlessly in. She pushed him to one side and reached up for the tin herself. Her face was flushed and Silver thought she had been crying.

'What sort of neighbours do you have out here?' he asked; then realised how patronising it sounded, implying this rural part of Thames Valley was the back of beyond.

'Just ordinary folk,' Kathy said. 'On that side' –

pointing towards the house where he had seen the watcher – 'they're an elderly couple. Mr Godden ran a sub-post office until it was closed down three years ago. His wife is some kind of office-holder in the local Women's Institute. On the other side they're much the same age as us, both out at work all day. We don't see a lot of them, except at weekends or out shopping.'

'You get along all right together? No disputes over Leylandii hedges or shared drainage outlets?' Silver probed.

'Good God, no!' This was an outburst from Lee Barber. 'It's live and let live.' He hovered by the door to the hall. 'Shall I call Tim down? I suppose you'll want to have a word with him?'

'If he feels up to it,' Z said cautiously.

'Don't call,' Kathy warned sharply. 'I don't want Stevie disturbed. Go up and fetch him.'

Lee glared at her. 'I intended to.' He left the room. Silver took a vacant place at the Formica-topped table. Kathy turned her back, emptying and refilling the teapot.

Drumming with his knuckles on Egerton's door, Lee heard a creak from the bed as Tim rose and then came reluctantly across to open up. He slid in and closed the door firmly behind him. 'What're you doing?' he demanded, viewing the two piles of borrowed clothing folded on the foot of the bed.

'Sorting out the clean ones. I'm sorry; I meant to put the others through the washing machine.'

'You're leaving?'

'I have to. You saw how Kathy is. And she's right. It is my fault. I should never have let Jenny out of my sight until she was inside.'

Lee didn't argue. 'You told me someone was following you. So what if that's the one who snatched her? It'll be you they're after. You could be our only chance of getting her back safely. You can't walk out on us.'

'Do you think I don't realise that? I'm prepared to have them pick me up. When they call you, say I'll be hanging around the Leisure Centre.'

'You can't go there. It's still swarming with police. It'd look as if you were setting up an ambush. That'll be the reason they haven't come here for you yet.'

'Well, somewhere else, then. Anywhere. Lee, does Kathy know the truth about me? About my job, and me running out on it?'

'No. I haven't told her, and that's killing me. We have to explain to her, at least enough to make her understand someone's out to get you. And that means telling the police too. It's the only way we stand a chance of getting any control over whoever it is. They have the facilities. They can give you protection. They're already on the job of looking for Jenny. The longer we hold back, the harder it'll be for them to follow the trail. They need to know everything.'

'Everything?'

'Well, starting with me finding you beaten up. The same thing we told Kathy.'

'It won't wash. Unless we tell them all about that Ince business and your attack on me, we'd have to invent a whole scenario to account for me being injured. I don't think I can do that; not to make it convincing. It wouldn't add up. They don't need to waste time looking for a non-existent mugger.

'No, it's better if I just disappear. Then, if you wish, you tell them everything. Otherwise we'd put the police on the wrong track from the word go. Ever since last afternoon I've been trying to think of a way out of this that's safest for Jenny. I agree the police must be brought in, but only after I've gone. Better if I leave it to you to tell them as much as you know, because they won't expect you to know the whole story about me. If need be, let them start hunting me too.'

His voice became bitter. 'Maybe they'll get to me before these other people do.'

Lee was a long time coming back and Silver decided to go up after him on the excuse of needing the bathroom. On the landing he heard voices beyond a closed door. It was not exactly an argument; more an urgent bit of strategy planning. The doorknob began to turn and the voices came louder. Silver darted through the door decorated with a ceramic seahorse and flushed the lavatory. He emerged as the other two did, Lee scowling with suspicion of him.

'We'll be off in a minute or two,' Silver assured him.

Downstairs, they passed the open dining-room where Stevie was being supported upright by Kathy in an old-fashioned cot while she gave him a fruity drink. Lee pushed into the doorway. 'Hello, soldier, howya feeling?'

The boy managed a wan smile, pushed away the beaker and slid down again on his mattress. His face was sheet-white between the purple blotches.

'Have they found out what he took?' Tim asked.

'His Granny's "sweeties",' Silver said dryly. 'We have confirmation from Mrs Whitaker that she found him in her unlocked bedroom. A box with her current medication was on the bedside cabinet and she thought a couple of orange cough pills could be missing.'

'Thank God he was sick on the way home,' Kathy whispered. 'Otherwise…' She shook her head.

'There's no treatment, just total bed rest. But he'll need weekly blood tests to check he's getting over it. It's awful seeing him so lifeless. He's normally such a tough little go-getter.'

They crowded into the kitchen.

'Have you made any progress?' Tim asked Silver. He left it to Z to give the stock answer: early stage of the enquiry as yet, but they were hopeful of something coming out of witness statements. 'Which is why we need to know if anything relevant comes to your mind to fill out the picture we're getting.'

Tim hesitated. 'On the way to the Leisure Centre…I just had this feeling…'

'Yes, Mr Johnson?' Z gave him a hard look. There was nothing familiar about the troubled face under the gauze dressing. Certainly she wouldn't have linked it with the much earlier graduation photograph of a confident, moustached young scientist the police were currently looking for.

'…that the car was being followed.'

'At what point was this?'

He seemed to be working something out in his head before he answered. 'Quite soon after leaving the house. Then, outside the Leisure Centre, it was rather congested, with cars leaving after the earlier session. I couldn't be certain then. I never got a proper look behind.'

'Can you describe the car at all? Size, shape, colour? Even make?'

'Oldish, I thought. And dark. That's all I can tell you.'

Silver was regarding him doubtfully. He hadn't offered this suspicion before. Maybe it was a by-product of nervy imagination after the event. If DS Beaumont were here he couldn't have resisted making some pun about *hind*sight via the driving mirror.

'If you should remember any further details, please contact us immediately,' Z said. 'You must realise how vital that sort of information could prove to be.'

She stood up, preparing to go.

'And you'll let us know…' Lee insisted.

'…as soon as anything positive comes to hand,' she promised. 'Meanwhile, a civilian technician is waiting outside to set up monitoring equipment for your landline phone. It's likely you'll be hearing soon from whoever is holding Jenny. You know to get as much information as you can and keep them talking while we get a trace.'

'Yes, if they'll fall for that.' Lee hadn't high hopes.

And there was still the hideous chance that maybe the kidnapper wasn't after money at all. It might be Jenny herself that was the prize.

'The Goddens,' Silver decided crisply, as they reached the road again. He described seeing the figure at an upstairs window watching through field glasses.

'Nosey neighbours,' Z agreed hopefully. 'That's worth a try.'

They rang at the next-door house and listened to the dulcet first bars of 'Greensleeves'. The woman who came to the door wore a densely flowered apron and had lightly floured hands wrapped in a tea towel.

'Police?' she demanded, seeming unsurprised. 'Come in. I'm in the kitchen, baking. You won't mind if I just carry on. Things are about ready to go in the oven.' She hustled them along a narrow passage towards a scent of cinnamon and lemon.

If she was so fully occupied, Silver deducted, it would be the old chap who'd been keeping an eye on their neighbour's doings. 'Is your husband at home?' he enquired.

'Around somewhere,' she answered impatiently. It seemed she was one of those ever-busy ladies who found men's retirement from work a further infliction on female life-management.

'Perhaps we could talk to you both together,' Z suggested, 'to save our going over everything twice.'

'Give him a shout from the bottom of the stairs,' Mrs Godden ordered Silver, already arranging her production line of patty pans ready for whipping open the Aga door to load them in.

Old Godden was already on his way downstairs, having spotted the police arrival and stopping off on his way only to ensure that his diuretic tablet shouldn't cause any interruption into what could be an enjoyable interview.

'Ah, I wondered when you'd get round to seeing us,' he announced enthusiastically, hanging on to the lower newel post. 'There's been some very strange things going on next-door.'

'Tea or coffee?' Freda Godden interrupted him. 'Fred, don't exaggerate so. They're a nice enough young couple.' She was rinsing her hands under the tap and paused to tuck back a loose strand of hair behind an oversized ear.

'Thank you. Whichever is less bother,' Z answered as Silver said, 'Tea'd be nice: strong, with a little milk and two sugars, please.' They'd no need to take further liquid aboard, but it could help the conversation along.

Godden plodded across and seated himself at the table. 'Sit yourselves down,' he invited. 'Smells as if she's got some buns just coming up.'

Silver sat and opened his notebook, ready to enter their names. These, he found, were Frederick and Freda Godden.

'Seemed sort of meant to be,' Godden offered. 'Fred and Freda, see? Couldn't do anything else but marry the lass, could I?'

The police couple smiled dutifully, overlooking Mrs

Godden's snort of contempt for an over-worn attempt at jocularity.

Godden pulled a folded school exercise book from his pocket and laid it on the table with some ceremony. He patted his pockets again, muttering under his breath.

'They're up on your head,' his wife said sharply.

He reached up and retrieved a pair of reading spectacles. 'Well, so they are. Look, I've been keeping an account of things since that Mr Johnson came to stay.'

'When would that have been?' Silver asked, with pen poised.

'It was on the Saturday morning I saw him first, in the garden. He must have arrived during the night, because the house was empty most of Friday, after young Kathy left with the children to go to her mother's. I heard Lee's car come back in the early hours. Two or three, I guess it was. Couldn't switch on the light to see my watch, for fear of waking the wife. That's later than the time young Barber usually gets back when he's been driving on Lates, but occasionally he'll do Nights and then he's not back until well into the morning. You know he's a driver on the railway, don't you?'

Silver grunted assent. 'We understand the visitor did arrive then, in Mr Barber's car.'

'So they'd met up somewhere during the evening?' Godden asked, fishing for information. Neither officer offered any, and he looked disappointed.

Godden consulted his notes. 'Well, as I said, that was Saturday. On the Sunday, young Lee went off in his car for most of the day, leaving the other one at home. He'd got one of those powered saw things that make a terrible racket. He'd obviously come to remove bits off their old apple tree and he didn't care a jot for upsetting the Sunday afternoon quiet. He didn't make too bad a job of it, considering he wasn't the build for toting a heavy thing like that. Anyway he got tired quite soon and went back into the house.' Mr Godden paused for dramatic effect.

'That's when this odd-looking man came and rang at the Barbers' front door.'

'*How* odd, Mr Godden? Could you describe him?'

'Swarthy, with a beard. Tall and heavily built.'

'Did he go in?'

'No. For some reason Mr Johnson chose not to open up then. Anyway, the man let himself through the side gate and went round to the back. That's when our phone rang. Freda answered it, but I had to go down and explain to the Secretary of the Indoor Bowls Club why there was a discrepancy in the previous week's takings for the Guest Tea. I'm Hon. Treasurer, you see.

'Well, it meant I never saw whether the man got in next-door or not. I never saw him again.' This he confessed with regret.

'Young Barber must have had next day off free. In the morning, the two of them were at it in the garage, sawing up the rotten branches from the apple tree. That was Monday. Then they went off together for the rest of the day, taking the sawn-up branches in black plastic sacks for the recycling plant.'

There was a sudden shrill beeping. 'Elbows off!'

shouted Mrs Godden, dealing out cork table mats with the speed of a cardsharper. She turned to open the oven door with hands encased in padded gloves and slapped out the trays of patty pans, now filled with golden muffins and tartlets. A gust of hot, fragrant air hit the three at the table.

Offended by the interruption, Godden continued with his tale. 'On Tuesday, Lee went off early to work, and Mr Johnson had a bonfire with the rest of the small branches and twigs. Inconsiderate again, but then he's like that. The wind blew smoke all over our garden. Lucky there wasn't washing on the line. I guess it would have made no difference to him if there was.'

'There wasn't any wind, actually,' Freda put in as correction. She started easing the edges of the buns with the tip of a knife. Then she carried each of the tins to the open window to cool, with everyone's eyes following her.

'He'd only just gone back into the house,' Godden resumed loudly to regain attention, 'when Kathy's car arrived. I know she'd meant to stay a whole week with her mother, and here she was back home with the children after only a few days. Lee was on Earlies, but still he wasn't home, so only this Johnson was there to receive her.

'I don't know what happened next, but yesterday morning, Wednesday, after Lee left for work, all the others bundled into Kathy's car with Johnson at the wheel, and they went off like the devil was after them. Then the same in the early afternoon, but I never saw when they returned. Since then, there's been a doctor and police coming and going like there was something really wrong.'

He looked slyly at Silver. 'I did happen to be close to the fence and overheard something about young Stevie covered in bruises. Well, who did that to him, I ask you?'

Nobody offered an answer.

'Anyway,' Godden continued, 'this should interest you.' He produced a digital camera from his pocket with the flourish of a conjuror.

He flipped it open and prodded a few buttons. 'See that? And that?' They were two shots of a dark car parked almost opposite his front gate. A dim figure could be made out sitting in the driving seat.

'He was waiting out there for over an hour,' Godden claimed, 'but as soon as they left the second time, after lunch, so did he, following them.'

The shots were taken from two different angles. It wasn't even clear that the cars were of the same make or who was in them.

In the morning photo it was just possible to make out the car's licence plate. Z leant closer to read it. With a quiver of shock, she recognised it instantly.

This was a car she saw every day. It was garaged at the house where she and Max owned neighbouring flats.

What connection could her lover have with the Barbers?

Chapter Seventeen

Zyczynski's reaction was an instant urge to warn Max. Which was impossible: she was on the job, and personal relationships were right off the map.

Silver was lifting a single eyebrow in her direction and she wondered how he could possibly have recognised the licence plate. But of course he hadn't. He was waiting for her nod before passing through the number for identification.

'No need,' she told him. 'It's known.'

Old Mr Godden's washed-out blue eyes were suddenly sharp as a squirrel's. 'A criminal?' he quavered.

They had to tell him then that Jenny had gone missing, otherwise his Neighbourhood Watch instincts would have supplied him with a dozen lurid reasons for a police presence at the Barbers'. He listened attentively, head tilted, and actually smiling. 'I guessed it was something quite serious,' he bragged. This latest development clearly justified his scrupulous chronicling of local movements.

'Jenny?' Freda Godden demanded shrilly. 'But she's such a good little girl. She wouldn't have run off and upset her mummy. How did it happen?'

Briefly Z explained about the children's party at the Leisure Centre and how Jenny had been refused admission.

'That's dreadful. Poor little soul. And you say this was yesterday? Where could she have been overnight?'

At least one of them was taking the crisis to heart. And by now the full significance was getting through to her husband. He sat with his jaw dropped, speechless.

'And you suspect that this man parked outside that morning could have something to do with Jenny's disappearance?' Freda demanded, horrified. 'He was up to no good? A paedophile, stalking her?'

'We can't jump to conclusions,' Z warned her hurriedly. 'There could be a valid reason for him being parked there. Any description you can give us will help to eliminate him, if he's perfectly innocent. After all, it's only the car that's been identified, not the driver.' She knew she sounded defensive and, conscious of flushing, turned away from the woman's stare.

'I never got a glimpse of him,' Freda said squarely. 'I don't have time for gawking out the windows. Fred, you'll have to do better than taking note of the car. What did the man inside look like? – if it was a man.'

'Well, I suppose it was. I never saw his face.'

'His clothing?' Z asked. 'Colour of hair?'

But Godden had no more to add. They had to be satisfied that at least he didn't have imagination enough to embroider his story. He was a simple note-taker, no more.

'We'll get your photographs printed and enlarged for

you,' Silver said comfortably. 'Just let's have the camera and we'll see to it.'

Godden protested. The camera was new, a digital one, and he was waiting for a compatible printer to come by post. Couldn't they wait and let him do it himself?

Z pictured him slowly wading through pages of almost incomprehensible instructions on the complementary functions of camera and printer. She doubted he would manage it, and busy Freda could certainly not spare the time. Not a technically sophisticated pair; it was likely they didn't even possess a computer.

'Write Mr Godden a receipt and we'll take it now,' Z told Silver firmly. 'I promise it will be perfectly safe with our specialists.'

The old man was still torn between its loss and the celebrity status implied in helping the police in a serious investigation but, with a hastily written receipt in his hands, he gave way.

'Blueberry muffin or cinnamon custard tart?' Freda asked, asserting practicalities. 'And did you say tea or coffee?'

On the return journey, if Silver wondered why Z hadn't immediately opened up on the subject of the suspect stalker he kept it to himself. She had elected to drive and appeared to be concentrating on the traffic in a grim manner that didn't invite interruption. Arriving at the nick, she asked for a minute with DCI Mott before he joined them. His not to question why, he thought. She was the Sarge, after all.

Angus wasn't in his own office, nor in the CID room. A uniformed constable, passing in the corridor, said he'd been called up to see the Boss.

That meant leaping in at the deep end, Z thought, apprehensive of the coming interview. She knocked on Yeadings' door and was invited to enter.

'Ah, Z,' he greeted her over a steaming mug of coffee. He waved towards the machine on the windowsill. 'Help yourself.'

'Thanks, sir, but I'm awash already. Hospitable witnesses.'

'So what progress?'

She described the situation at the Barbers' house and the tensions between the adults there. 'Johnson spoke of being followed on his way to the swimming pool, but didn't take note of the car's make or colour. Just oldish and dark, he said: no more than an impression. He gave it as an excuse for pulling away before he'd made sure that Jenny was safe inside.'

'This wasn't in his earlier statement,' Mott noted, 'which was sparse, anyway. So was he being creative, trying to justify his actions?'

Z paused. 'He seemed convinced. But I wouldn't like to say how easily he can fool himself. He's – well, rather an oddball: not like the Barbers at all. Maybe a more complicated person. I tried to get some background out of him, but he was wary. He claimed he was a civil servant and currently on leave. He gave a London address in Kilburn, which was a flat left to him by his late mother.'

'Anything more on his mugging on the night of Friday-Saturday?'

'No; he repeated that it was very dark and he was approached from behind and robbed. All the same stuff. I felt he was keeping something back. The only obvious injury was to his temple, but he was certainly attacked. Taken with his story of being followed to the Leisure Centre, it could be that someone is out to get him a second time.'

'Or they found something of interest from his rifled pockets which seemed worth following up on?'

They all considered this. 'Do we have a list of property taken?' Yeadings queried.

Mott nodded. 'The sort of things you'd expect: keys, diary, cheque book.'

'Credit cards?'

'Apparently not.'

'It would be interesting to know if he's used one since the attack.'

'See to that, Z,' Mott ordered.

'Yes, Guv. We visited the elderly neighbours on one side. The others were out, at work. Mr Godden gave us a fairly detailed rundown on the Barbers' recent comings and goings. Johnson had been acting like a friend of the family, doing jobs in the garden in Barber's absence.'

'...and while the wife was away at her mother's,' Mott remembered. 'Coming back early, she wasn't at all pleased to find him installed in her home. Some strong resentment there, wouldn't you say, Z?'

'Yes. Even suspicion of Johnson. Of course she blames

him for not taking good care of Jenny. He's conscious of this, but he's still staying on there – which I don't see as being for our convenience. We left him free to leave.'

'We'll slap a restriction on him now, I think,' Yeadings decided. 'He could have more to tell us if you push harder.'

There came a knock at the door and Silver was invited in.

'I'll expect your written reports in by 3 p.m.,' Mott told him and Z. He rose, ready to leave.

'There's something else.' Z said hurriedly. 'Mr Godden, living next-door to the Barbers, photographed a car parked for a considerable period near his house the morning before the disappearance. He thought the male driver was watching the neighbourhood.'

'…which could give us a possible stalker,' Silver assumed with satisfaction.

'Actually,' Z said, 'that doesn't seem likely. I recognised the car in his photograph. It belongs to Max Harris.

'There was a later occasion the same day. There's a rather smudgy shot taken that afternoon after the Barbers had rushed the little boy off to the paediatric clinic. It might or might not be the same dark car. It followed when Johnson drove off with the little girl. We have the digital camera used.'

In the CID room Silver and Zyczynski sat at neighbouring keyboards, filling in their reports. She was aware of his occasional glances across at her and recognised his suppressed thirst for more on Max Harris.

Yeadings and Mott had refrained from comment on her news, the Boss merely, after a slight pause to meet his DCI's eyes, asking, 'Is that the lot, then?'

But the inquisition had to come. It must have struck both of them that, if Max Harris showed an active interest in one of their cases, it could be because Z had talked out of turn. She was taking the last page of her report from the printer when DI Salmon put his head round the door and nodded peremptorily to her. 'The DCI's office, now,' he barked.

Oh God, she thought, why does Salmon have to be dragged in? As if he hasn't enough against me already. Angus wasn't always such a stickler for protocol. If now he found it necessary to involve the middleman, it was to distance himself from her personally. She could expect no easy ride.

Mott was standing at the window, looking out on the visitors' car park, hands in pockets and shoulders rigid. He barely turned as the other two came in. 'You know what this is about, Sergeant Zyczynski. Have you anything to tell me?'

'Not really, Guv, because I don't know much about it myself.'

'Perhaps you can share what little you do know.'

It was chillingly formal. She wasn't even being offered a seat. If it hadn't been so serious she would have found the unreality laughable.

'I have no idea why Max should be keeping a watch on that neighbourhood. Nor why he should have lent his car to anyone else who would do so.'

That was strictly true, so far. If she went further – and Mott's silence was certainly meant to induce her to do so – then she could risk putting her lover on the spot. Surely Mott – in his more usual, human mode – could understand her position of divided loyalties?

'No idea at all?' He had picked up on her equivocation.

'I try not to get involved in his work, as he does with mine: it's a matter of mutual respect. Why he should be interested in that neighbourhood I've no idea. It doesn't need to have any connection with the Barbers.'

'That is not for you to judge. Great care has been taken not to reveal the address from which the child is missing. Yet a newspaperman and close friend of yours has latched on. Your link with a possible suspect we shall need to question forces me to take you off the Jenny Barber case; which is particularly inconvenient with present work pressures. You are instructed not to mention our suspicions to your friend, and to distance yourself completely from any work he may be following. Is that understood?'

'Yessir.'

'I have discussed this with DI Salmon, and he will allocate an alternative enquiry for you. Unless you have more to tell us on this matter, that is all.'

'Sir.' Her face flaming, she let herself out, closing the door firmly, but quietly, behind her.

Hot tears forced themselves into her eyes, but she blinked them back as she almost ran down the corridor. Damn Angus and his suddenly upright, regulatory stance! He could have made some effort to understand her position, especially since he was in much the same situation himself with Paula, on the opposite sides of law enforcement and forced into extra discretion. But then, perhaps it was *because* of that, and feeling equally vulnerable, that he'd run short of sympathy. It looked as though, whatever assurances she could give, he would assume she passed on restricted information as casual pillow talk.

All the same, Angus needn't have taken it out on her, especially in a set piece with the unpalatable DI Salmon as audience.

Beaumont had joined Silver in the CID office. As she entered, their conversation broke off and both turned to look at her. 'I'll put you out of your misery,' she said angrily. 'I'm off the missing child case.'

'Hard cheese,' Beaumont commiserated.

'And since you might as well know all the facts, I don't discuss anything about work with Max Harris. Blame his crystal ball, or whatever he uses. *If* he has strayed on to the same track we're on – and I'm not entirely convinced that's so – then it's entirely off his own bat, not mine.'

Frustration was making her talk nonsense, ridiculously mixing her metaphors, and the realisation only increased her anger. She picked up her written report, which, in her absence, Beaumont had been reading, and fiercely stapled the pages together. She swept the contents of her desktop into a drawer, slammed it shut and announced, 'I'm off home.'

Beaumont grunted. "Bye, then.'

She knew that he must be privately rejoicing at her temporary removal from the team. It permitted him more scope for making a good impression, if not some spectacular breakthrough. Their rivalry was something that warred constantly with an established sense of team partnership.

She fled to the incident room, in which opposite walls were now devoted to the two Misper cases. The Office Manager took his copy of her new report, rapidly read it through and passed it to a woman PC at a computer terminal. 'Any sightings yet?' he asked. Everyone, Z thought, was specially affected by a lost child incident. Everyone except her now.

Sitting later in the car, she puzzled over where to go. Away from here, certainly; but she couldn't go home. Max might be there and she'd given her word not to discuss the situation with him. She had to let enough time pass to allow Yeadings to call him in for questioning.

Or would Mott be going out, accompanied by Salmon, to interview him at home? And would they find him in her apartment, or his? She wrinkled her nose at the thought of the disagreeable DI staring at her personal things, pricing them, picking up on her private habits, assessing her lover on some male scale of his own.

Maybe, after all, she should get there ahead of them and ensure Max was found in his own quarters. But she wasn't poker-faced enough. If she encountered him he would see at once that something was upsetting her personally. Best leave well alone for the present.

And I shouldn't be anxious for him, she warned herself. I know Max. He takes risks, but he wouldn't be involved in anything he couldn't easily explain if he came under suspicion. That is, if he *chose* to explain himself. He could be stubborn as a mule if he saw himself under unwonted pressure.

She wasn't hungry enough to go out for a lonely meal, and she wasn't the sort to be driven to drink. Most of her friends were in the job, so she couldn't safely drop in on any of them.

Which left the cinema. Doubting she'd be in the right mood for sloppy romance or male action drama, she could nevertheless curl up in the shared dark and lose herself among anonymous strangers.

Chapter Eighteen

Jenny stirred, reached for the edge of her pillow, and found instead the broken corner of a cardboard box. A vague sense of something wrong hung on from her dreams but she couldn't remember where she'd been or who with. Confusion grew as a square of dim light showed that the window had moved to the opposite side of her bedroom.

Then came instant recall of what had happened at the Leisure Centre. She sat up, rough fabric slipping from her bare shoulders. This wasn't her bed at all, but something harder, which crackled under her as she moved. And the room was a strange one; small, with dingy, yellowish-grey paper hanging off the wall in one corner.

She was still with those strange people who had offered to help when she'd been turned away from going swimming. Melanie's mother was supposed to have sent her a ticket that she could hand over. The woman at the desk had been horrible, thinking she was trying to sneak in free. The image of her came back vividly: the frizzy, reddish dyed hair, the dark-rimmed glasses with their glittery gold chain dangling from her scraggy neck. She was like an angry chicken, darting her head in and out as she scolded. Only much, much bigger. And frightening, because it was so unexpected. Parties weren't meant to start like this.

It was more awful because the girls who'd just gone through, laughing together, were all ones she knew from school. Only one of them had looked back and seen her, but that was Jody Watson, and right from the start something wrong had started up between the two of them. Jody had a way of staring at you, and you didn't know why, or what she was thinking. But it wasn't friendly, that was certain. Jody had seen her, but she hadn't told anyone to let her through the barrier. So, instead, that pecking chicken-woman had turned her away.

By then it had been too late to tell Mr Johnson, because, once she'd got clear of the car, he'd roared the engine and gone off in a flash. So these other people had offered to give her a lift home.

There was nobody else, and Mummy had warned her about strangers; not to go anywhere with them or accept anything they wanted to give you. It had never happened before, but she knew what to do. She'd said, 'No, thank you,' quite politely, but they wouldn't take that. The woman had tried to take her swimming bag off her, pulled at it quite roughly and she'd had to let it go. She saw it flung behind her, on the gritty ground. And then the woman had grabbed her wrist, so tightly that she squirmed in pain. And before she knew what was happening she was pushed into the back of a car and the woman nearly fell in on top of her. And so, they'd roared off with her trapped inside.

She'd managed to twist round and look out of the rear window, but there was no going back. A whole stream of cars was following them out of the parking lot, and none of them was a car she recognised.

She could see nothing of the driver except the back of a long neck with things Daddy had once called 'jug ears'. The man didn't say anything, but he must have known she didn't want to come with him and the rough woman.

'Excuse me,' she started to say to him, but the woman snarled 'Shut up!' so fiercely that it dried the breath inside her throat. She wanted to cry. Or, rather, her eyes wanted to, while she screwed up her mouth to stop it trembling.

Then she'd been stopped from looking out at the traffic and the passing buildings, pushed to the floor and a blanket thrown over her, which was prickly and hot and smelt of sweat; but she didn't dare stir. That was a very fierce lady up there, and her shoes were nudging sharply into Jenny's side.

She didn't understand why they were doing this to her. She hadn't done anything naughty that she knew of.

And now it was next day. She sat up in the half-dark and wondered where she was; what Mummy and Daddy were doing; whether poor Stevie was still sick.

If she crept across to that lighter patch, maybe she could open the curtains and see out. Then if she opened the window she could call to someone. Except that it was some place she didn't know at all. The people out there would be strangers too and could be dangerous. She wasn't allowed to talk to them.

She found there weren't any curtains. At some time the glass had been painted over. She chipped at a corner with one fingernail and a small piece of grey flaked away. The hole was just low enough for her to get an eye close, but all she saw was a jumble of roofs and chimneys. Then suddenly a swoop of gulls wheeled up behind them, soaring to float, wings wide-stretched, effortless as the gliders she'd watched with Daddy at Booker Airfield.

There were other birds scattered among them, black ones which flew more clumsily, but mixing merrily, black and white together, as though they were all friends. One of the gulls darted down out of sight and came back with a lump of something in its beak. Then the others turned on it, shrieking and stabbing at it savagely with their beaks. They weren't nice at all. The lump of bread fell away and another gull swooped on it as it dropped, to be attacked in its turn.

Jenny closed her eyes, and just then she picked up another sound, distant but familiar. It was the *hoo-ha* double note of a turbo train before it entered a station. Somewhere out there a driver like Daddy was at work. It could be Daddy, and he didn't know she was shut away here, listening out for him. The sound didn't come again. The train was gone and she knew she could never catch up with it.

She shivered, having no clothes on. At home she had silky pyjamas, pink, with comic little animals all over them, but when the woman had taken her clothes away she'd just been given a scratchy blanket to cover the makeshift bed. Which wasn't a real bed; just two wooden boxes with two cushions covered with a sort of crackly groundsheet like Daddy put down in the tent when they'd all gone camping. There she'd had her own little puffed-up sleeping bag and it had been better than this, although here she was under a roof. In somebody's house.

She couldn't remember what its outside looked like. They had hustled her in between them. She remembered stumbling over the doorstep and falling on her face. Then the man had picked her up and she saw his face for the first time. It was long and thin, a bit browny-yellow, but what she couldn't miss was the purple stain down one side of his forehead and cheek. She'd been reminded of Stevie, how he'd looked bruised all over. And that made her feel sorry for the man.

He wasn't as rough as the woman, and he didn't want to talk. Once he'd put her down on a chair in the kitchen, he turned away and went outside again to get rid of the car. The front door was left open and she heard the engine sounds fade and disappear. She was left with the woman.

She hadn't eaten much at lunchtime, to leave room for the party food. There would have been baby sausages on sticks, tasty little pastry things and trifle with red jelly and a big sponge cake – probably pink – with lit candles on the top. Melanie would have blown them all out while they sang 'Happy Birthday'.

But she'd missed out on all that. She was hungry and the woman hadn't said anything yet about feeding her. She heard her tummy give a little, round gurgle and thought something moved slightly inside. 'Can I have my tea now?' she'd asked.

That set the woman off again, using some bad words, but she had clattered a plate off a high shelf in the cramped little kitchen and slammed it on the rickety table. Then she had worked on a red-labelled tin with a wicked-looking sort of curved-beak knife, not like Mummy's whirring little electric tin-opener. But it got the lid off. Before the woman slung the empty tin into an open cardboard box, Jenny worked out the word on its side: To-ma-to. So she expected soup. But it wasn't. Instead, there were little chunks of tomato along with all their skins and pips, which she was used to having removed.

She thought it wouldn't have been so bad warmed up, but the woman slopped it out cold onto a slice of greyish bread. Everything was grey in this house. The kitchen was lit with a lamp standing on the draining board because the only window had wooden boards covering the outside. She supposed that was because the glass was broken and the edges would be all jaggy. Nobody had bothered to clear the bits away.

'You can cut it up yourself,' the witch-woman said. 'And count yourself lucky.'

The knife and fork were enormous, but she managed with them, cleared the plate and said, 'Thank you,' at the end.

That was when the man came back. The woman hustled him into another room and Jenny heard her voice going on and on at him through the wall. It was funny they hadn't introduced themselves. When the woman came back Jenny asked her, 'What are you called?'

The woman stared as if she couldn't believe her ears.

'What do I call you, please?'

'You don't need to call me anything. Now just you sit quiet here while I get upstairs and make up a bed for you. Not a squeak now, mind.'

Jenny had relented, but as soon as she was alone in the kitchen she fixed her eyes on the outer door. She didn't have to stay, but she didn't know what was outside. It could be even worse, and there'd be more strangers. All the same, she had to try.

The door was locked and bolted. There was no key, but she lifted a corner of the dingy net curtain that hung over the upper glass panels and peered out. A narrow yard of cracked concrete and two metal dustbins gave on to a dirt path between twiggy green bushes and ended in a high wall with a brown-painted gate. Beyond that was nothing.

Jenny went back and sat on the chair by the table. Melanie and her friends would have finished at the pool now and would be playing party games in her garden, a real garden, not like this one. She thought of her own garden at home and how they'd be able to put the swing back now because Mr Johnson had made the apple tree safe. She decided that when the woman came downstairs she would tell her she didn't want to stay here. She'd ask her to ring Mummy and someone could come out and collect her.

The woman laughed at her. More of a *cackle,* and her eyes went all small and black like currants – which was when Jenny knew for sure: she *was* a witch. A real one. Then she began to be really scared.

As Max Harris drove back towards the house, he saw DS Beaumont's car on the circular sweep of gravel before the front door. He thought nothing of it. Rosemary often had CID colleagues visit her. But it did merit a raised eyebrow when DI Salmon climbed out of the passenger side and stood leaning with one hand on the roof, obviously expecting his return. Beaumont slid out from the driving seat and nodded. It was himself they were here for, then; not his Rosebud.

In his mind he ran over his recent activities. There seemed nothing that might have incurred what already looked like an official police visit. For a shocking second he thought they might be bringing bad news: his Rosebud injured on duty? Oh God, not that!

But no. Yeadings would have come himself, knowing how things were between the two of them. By now the Superintendent and his wife ranked almost as friends.

'Hello there,' he greeted the two CID men, getting out of his own car. 'Something up?'

Salmon was doing it formally, holding up his warrant card and loudly announcing who and what he was. Beaumont was at his most po-faced, spoiling the effect by suddenly and wildly rolling his eyes behind the other's back.

That was reassuring. Max grinned at them both. 'Yes,

we have met, Inspector. Do come in. No doubt you could do with a cup of tea.' He preceded them inside, across the impressive galleried hall and up the grand staircase he shared with DS Zyczynski. The pores at the back of his neck absorbed Salmon's sour reflections on the suspicious splendour in which one of his subordinates, a mere woman, chose to live.

And his disapproval would automatically extend to her lover, Max acknowledged. Well, hard cheese: DI Salmon was not a person whose admiration he secretly coveted. He let them into his flat.

'We'll dispense with the hospitality,' Salmon said brusquely. 'This is an official visit.'

Max waved them both to chairs but the DI preferred to stand. Max wasn't particularly tall but he could give him four or five inches and Salmon preferred to have the advantage. Beaumont took up a position behind his superior officer, but he'd given up pulling faces. So, something quite serious, Max warned himself.

'How can I help you, officers?'

'Where were you between twelve and three yesterday afternoon?' Salmon began, diving in without any preamble.

'I was having an early lunch, I believe. I could recite the menu, if necessary. But I hardly think it would interest you, Inspector.'

'Where would that have been, Mr Harris?' Salmon was breathing heavily down his nose.

'In Old Amersham, at Gilbey's. They're good. Do you know the place?'

Salmon's lips tightened. It wasn't likely he'd throw money away on fancy restaurants which overpaid newspaper men frequented. 'Was anyone with you?'

'Most of the tables were taken, yes.'

'Would anyone be likely to remember you?'

'That rather depends on how observant everyone was. I didn't actually start a fight or dance on the table. I'm sure that as a detective you must often find how unreliable witnesses can be.'

'Are you known there? As an *habitué*?' Salmon struggled with the term.

A swift smile crossed Max's face. He was sure if he looked across at Beaumont the eyes would be rolling again.

'I have been there before, if that's what you mean. The staff would recognise me.'

'Then they will have no difficulty in telling us whether you were actually present at that time? Or not.'

'Again it depends. They are very discreet. If they thought it was to my disadvantage they might well find it hard to remember. On the other hand, if it was to provide an alibi, I should like to believe that they will assure you that I was there. In any case, you could rely on their absolute honesty.'

Beaumont sensed fireworks about to go off and intervened. 'How did you pay for the meal, sir?'

'With cash, almost certainly. My guest could probably back me on that.'

'And this guest, Mr Harris: who would that be?' Salmon was back, snapping at the bait.

'The clerk to the local magistrates, a young woman called Peabody, Inspector. I regret that the subject of our discussion is strictly confidential.'

It was time to change tack. Salmon struggled to appear unruffled. 'And when were you last in Thame, Mr Harris?'

Max hesitated a fraction and Salmon darted in. 'In Rigsby Road, to be precise. I would warn you to be very careful of your answer, Mr Harris, as we have reliable witnesses as well as photographs.'

'I had no idea I was such a celebrity. Let me see, it would be yesterday. Yes; Wednesday morning. And before you ask, the subject of my interest is again restricted information.'

'Not in this case, I can assure you,' Salmon decreed, 'since it impinges on the investigation of a serious crime; the abduction of a minor. Any withholding of information germane to the case will be regarded as obstructing the police in the performance of their duty.'

'Is that so?' Max said quietly. He was utterly serious now. 'And what child is this? Not a small boy, by any chance, covered in bruises and wrapped in a blanket?'

Chapter Nineteen

Jana Simekova caught the sound of light footfalls crossing the upstairs room. Her brother had once said she had the ears of a bat. She thought that, maliciously, he'd meant their size too. They served a good purpose anyway: enough to tell her the child was awake and would soon have to be dealt with.

She rummaged in her travel bag and found the tailor's scissors she used for cutting up felt for the puppets' clothes. They would probably be sharp enough for the purpose. It had been difficult to pack in everything they would need at this makeshift lodging: just a few basic foodstuffs, a blanket or two and some bedding. The beasts of the field and the fowls of the air had less with which to nest and take refuge.

She was used enough to finding asylum in hard times, barely seven years old when she had fled from Prague with her mother, leaving behind her older brother. It seemed that, ever since, she had been searching for somewhere to lay her head in safety.

When Pavel returned with the morning paper, they would put their things in the car and be away again, stopping only at the post office to drop off the little package.

She heated water over the portable oil stove and made thick cocoa for their hostage. It must be strong and sweet to hide the taste of the addition. There was enough bread left to allow the child some to dip in the drink.

She filled the enamel mug and added the two little white pills, stirring it all briskly. A loud thump on the wall and a surge of rough laughter told her that the gang of young people next-door were recovering from their raunchy night. They too were squatters, but long-stay. It was surprising they had not spread into this boarded-up end house of the condemned Victorian terrace. Perhaps they had had enough time to make their own quarters fairly comfortable. Anything can be thought of as home once you've marked your boundaries and left your scent.

She heard Pavel at the front door and went through with the steaming drink in one hand, the chunk of bread in the other. 'Well?' she asked him, eyeing the newspaper under his arm.

'Nothing yet. It's too soon.'

She didn't believe him 'But the police must know.'

He shrugged, defiant. Not a man for many words. She sometimes wanted to scream out loud and pummel him until he made some response. But she knew better than that. There was no knowing where it might end. He was not like her gentle husband.

And where was Karel? If only they knew what had happened: whether, failing to find the research papers, he had run out on them for good, or by now would be waiting at home for their return. He had used this squat himself and Pavel had instructed him to bring the file back here, where they would pick him up. Since his phone call from the house, there was only silence. One way or another he had let them down. So they'd had to take this extra risk, burdening themselves with this child, as a longer way round to getting the information they needed.

Karel had always been weak. But it was better not to have been Pavel breaking in at the house. He might have done something rash there. Even now she wasn't sure they had done right to risk taking the little girl, but it had been so opportune, following the car and then seeing her get out and be left alone. He was a strange one, that Egerton, to abandon his small daughter where anything might happen to her.

Pavel had made up his mind on the spur of the moment, shoving Jana out to snatch the child before she'd even had time to think. She was too used to doing whatever he said, to keep him from being violent. Anything for a quiet life. But now – this! It was complicated.

She continued up the uncarpeted stairs, the heavy scissors in her skirt pocket knocking against one knee as she climbed. On the landing she had to put down the mug on the floor, to have a spare hand to turn the key in the lock. It made her nervous, because the child might try to rush out and push her down the stairs while she bent to pick the drink up again.

She needn't have worried. The girl had climbed back into bed and covered herself with the blanket. Only the round blue eyes stared over the top, with half of her blond hair wild over her forehead. One of the pink ribbons had come off and the second still bunched the other half: the half she must cut off, ribbon and all.

But not until the child was asleep again, because surely she'd scream. Jana couldn't stand that.

She thrust the drink towards her. '*Snidane*,' she said. 'Breakfast.'

The little girl continued staring, wide-eyed, so that the whites showed all round the blue. She said nothing.

Jana bent and put the mug on the gritty floor, the hunk of crust alongside. 'Eat up. That's all you get till tonight. I come back later to make sure it's all gone.'

In the depot the news had been received in stunned silence. Then uproar broke out among the drivers due to go on duty. Lee was popular enough, even if a bit la-di-da for a relative newcomer, with his ideas of being only temporarily here on the way up to something better. But he enjoyed a good laugh and he was learning to take a joke against himself: under the skin just an ordinary bloke like the rest.

So how could it happen that his little girl got snatched? It couldn't be for ransom, and the little mite was only five, not a flirty thirteen. So that meant a nonce had got hold of her; a ruddy paedophile.

Brenda decided they had to do something to prove solidarity. She'd been the nearest when Bascombe had taken the phone call from Lee: that he couldn't get in for duty. Even before calling for a stand-in driver, the

DSM had blurted out the reason. It was incredible. Bad things happened in families, but not on this scale.

'Well, that's a first as an excuse for skiving,' said Norman Harker as the others stared astounded. They rounded on him. But Norman hadn't kids of his own, so who could expect the stupid sod to understand?

'I'll go round to see Kathy,' Brenda volunteered, 'soon as I've done me shift. There must be something we can do to help.'

'Like a whip-around?' Bob Kettle offered.

'What use'd that be?' someone asked. 'By the time we got a decent sum together it could be only good for a wreath for the poor kid.'

He was shushed roughly. That seemed like calling down worse luck. There was still a chance that Jenny had run off on her own, got lost and taken shelter overnight. Thank God it wasn't winter so they'd find her shrivelled and frozen under some leafless hedge.

'Search party,' Malc Dobbin said suddenly. 'That's what they do when a kid goes missing. The police'll want volunteers. We should let them have a list of when we're free. Boss, can you do that? I'm sure we'll all want to join in. And Kathy'll need back-up if she's staying home to be near the phone. I'll give the wife a bell and tell her to go along for company.'

Bascombe, who'd stood apart, coughed loudly to get their attention. 'I'm as sorry as anyone, but before the Aylesbury Posse saddles up to ride into the sunset, let's not forget we're trying to run a railway here. You guys have to stay focused on the track. I don't want someone dropping a bollock because they weren't concentrating on the job. Right?'

But, sensing he'd spoilt their moment with his well-worn dogma, he added, 'Leave it to me. I'll get some flowers sent.'

'Right,' Brenda approved. 'But, for God's sake, no white lilies!'

Lee Barber swore at the one called Salmon. It was a thing he tried to avoid, especially in front of Kathy. 'Why the hell aren't you out there looking for her? Why can't I go?'

'We have officers enough covering the Leisure Centre and surrounds. It's better you try and tell us where your daughter would be likely to go once she'd been refused admission.'

'There was to be a party afterwards,' Kathy put in. 'Maybe she would try to get to Melanie's house and wait there until the girls came back from their swim. Only, it's quite a way for her to walk. And she's only been there once, in the car.'

'That's Ivy Lodge, 14 Meldrum Way?' Beaumont prompted. 'Yes? Well, we've sent officers there to check. The house was empty at the time, but someone may remember seeing her hanging around. So they'll be questioning neighbours door-to-door and reporting back any moment now.'

'Other friends she might drop in on? Relatives? People she knows you know?' DI Salmon thrust out an aggressive chin.

Lee turned to Kathy. She shook her head. 'This is her first year at school. She doesn't have any other friends outside the ones she was going to spend the afternoon with. We never sent her to nursery school because I taught her to read and write a bit at home. She met a few children at Sunday Club at St Mary's Church, but she wouldn't have any idea where they lived. I suppose I could get their names from the Club Leader.'

'Yes, do that. But I think it really boils down to who was around and saw her leave the Leisure Centre,' Salmon decided.

'There's a CCTV camera in the car park,' Lee reminded him. 'Have you got the film?'

Salmon ignored him. Beaumont grunted. 'It's useless: shows her walking up the ramp to the door. Then it pans away. When it turns back, she's gone.'

'What about the other cars there? Tim said it was crowded with them, leaving in a stream. Haven't you…?'

'All licence plates are being followed up,' Salmon said grimly. 'All drivers will be questioned. We do have methods of procedure, sir. Everything possible is being done.'

'Except us being out there, looking for Jenny.' Lee's voice was almost breaking. Kathy moved closer and put a hand on his elbow.

'God, I am so sorry,' Tim muttered from his chair in the corner. He had collapsed into it, burying his ashen face in his hands. 'I've brought nothing but disaster to you all.'

Lee swung round on him, torn between denial and an

outburst of spleen. He beat one fist into the other, trying to keep control.

'I don't think there's anything more we can tell you,' Kathy pleaded. 'Please, I'd like you to go now.'

Beaumont eased towards the door, but Salmon stood there looking bullish. 'We have arranged for interception of any phone messages, and an unmarked car with two plain-clothes officers will be in the street keeping watch at all times. If any message gets through, it is essential you get in touch immediately. Is that understood?'

He didn't wait for an answer, following the DS out.

'Does he take us for fools?' Lee shouted at Kathy.

She moved away, shuddering. 'Well, maybe we are.' Her voice was barely audible. Lee stared at her, saw the look of detestation she turned on Egerton.

There was so much she didn't understand. But he couldn't spill it all out. Not now. He needed her to believe in him. And the whole present chaos resulted from that one crazed attack on the man he had thought was Ince. Everything that had followed was nobody's fault but his.

He could see she wanted Tim gone, but Tim had to stay, because it was Tim these people were trying to get at. It was only through him that there was any chance of bargaining to get Jenny back.

Standing at his open door, Max heard Rosemary let herself in downstairs. There had been no sound of her car. She must have coasted down the last hundred yards of the lane. She was keeping suspiciously quiet.

Avoiding me, he thought. How badly have I dropped her in it?

It had been clear from DI Salmon's attitude that he'd suspected her of leaking information about police matters so that he could turn a few quid on it in Grub Street. The man had tunnel vision: no idea how press intelligence worked, nor how delicately approaches from the public could be dealt with by journalists.

Over Egerton he was confident he'd been discretion itself; the only gaffe being to let Z take that call from his PI. That was what had led him to the address in Thame. And, by sheer bad luck, something had happened there that day which aroused police interest. A child gone missing. He knew nothing about it. The only child he remembered from that morning was the little boy wrapped in a blanket driven away in a huddle with his family. Some domestic accident, he guessed. They'd most likely headed for Casualty at the hospital.

He'd managed not to reveal what had taken him there, persuading them he had no interest in any police investigation, and eventually they'd had to accept his word. He'd no interest in a family called Barber, let alone their little girl who'd disappeared. He'd passed over that news item in the media without it having any special significance: not his kind of professional interest. And how could he have had foreknowledge of any snatch later that day unless he was part of the plot? Did his track record suggest he would indulge in criminal conspiracy?

It seemed a suspicious neighbour had observed him

sitting in the car that morning waiting for a sight of Egerton and photographed him there. Quite properly under the circumstances, the man had reported it in. And the police inference had been that he was a stalker, waiting for his moment to snatch a five-year-old female child from some house in the road.

It was a real stinker, the way the two cases overlapped. He hadn't let on to Salmon and Beaumont that he had ever heard of Egerton. And it seemed that they had no interest in Rigsby Road other than as the place where their missing child lived. For them there was no connection yet with the missing scientist. There were simply two parallel inquiries in a busy caseload, occurring within days of each other.

He had been able to persuade them that he had never heard of Jenny Barber at the time he was seen parked in that road. How could they believe he'd had foreknowledge of any snatch? But, then again, given his presence there, what else were they to think?

Yet by now Rosemary could have guessed why he'd been there, because previously she'd taken the PI's call for him. So was she seeing some kind of connection between the two cases? If so, how much of her suspicions had she passed on to Mott or Yeadings?

She came almost silently up their shared staircase as he stood in the shadows. 'Don't jump,' he warned her. 'I'm here.'

She looked up at him. It wasn't his imagination that she seemed pale and anxious.

'It's all right,' he said. 'They've already been to see

me, Salmon and Beaumont. I swore that you hadn't talked about any of your cases.'

'Did they believe you?'

'Not at first, but I can be very convincing when I try. I think, though, it's time we did talk. There's a child's safety to consider.'

'I still think we can't.' She looked utterly miserable. 'But we should both go and explain, separately, to the Boss...tell him everything. Because I believe you already had some connection with that address, and now pressure's being put on the family there through their little girl.'

'Let's not waste time then. Come inside while I ring him. We'll go together.'

She walked past him into the room. No kiss, no touch: like a stranger.

Chapter Twenty

Nan Yeadings picked up his call in the kitchen between serving courses. 'He's having his dinner,' she said, ever protective. 'He'll not be best pleased. He's only been home five minutes.'

'Nan, I'm really sorry, but this is urgent, concerning the current case. Max and I need to tell him something, separately.'

She hesitated. 'I'll put him on.'

When Z asked for a meeting, Yeadings sounded cautious, as though expecting bad news.

'Not here,' he stipulated. 'Be at the station in half an hour.' His tone was sombre.

They made it in twenty minutes and sat in the reception area, waiting at either end of the visitors' bench, not talking. Occasionally the desk sergeant gave them a sideways glance, puzzled why DS Zyczynski hadn't taken her witness into an interview room. When Superintendent Yeadings arrived, with DI Salmon in tow, within an hour of quitting the station, he was frankly intrigued.

'Evening, sir,' he opened, hoping for enlightenment.

'Sergeant Hopkins, good evening. Are both interview

rooms free?' Assured that they were, Yeadings motioned Max and Z to precede him. Z opened one door, switched on the light and went in, DI Salmon following. Yeadings nodded at Max to enter the other.

Hopkins lifted the flap, came out from behind his desk and hovered. 'Anything I can get you, sir?'

Yeadings stared at him and he got the message, bobbing back into position like a weather-house doll.

Max seated himself. 'We wouldn't have disturbed you…'

'…but it's a matter of urgency. I understand that. What have you to tell me?'

'That some ten days ago I was contacted by Piers Egerton, a scientist who had read some of my articles. He wished to inform me about secret researches he was carrying out for a government authority. He suggested we should meet.'

Yeadings considered this. It wasn't what he'd been expecting. Max Harris had been mentioned in an entirely different context. How did the missing scientist come to be linked with the investigation of a possibly abducted child?

'You realised this could have run you into trouble with the security services?'

'Possible embarrassment, yes. But at that point I had no idea what he was likely to tell me. I don't turn down material out of hand before I've taken a look at it. So I tried making some enquiries of my own, on the quiet.'

'Using what resources?'

'Personal contacts, perfectly legitimate, typical press intelligence.'

'And a police informant?'

'Only indirectly, and without success. When a leaked rumour was running round Dockland that Special Branch was hunting for an important civil servant who'd gone missing, name unknown, I assumed this could be Egerton. Earlier, he'd made a call to a number I had given him, requesting an urgent meeting at Beaconsfield railway station in the early hours of last Saturday. I agreed to be there, alone.'

'And you met?'

'He never turned up. I had to assume that he had missed the last train, which would have been on the down-line leaving Marylebone about midnight. But since he might have found some other means of travel, I waited a further two hours. Nobody came.'

'There was a follow-up?'

'I heard nothing until the next afternoon, Sunday, when he contacted me again, using a landline. He was having second thoughts about meeting me. He sounded upset and undecided, but he gave no explanation for not having turned up. He apologised for any inconvenience I'd suffered, then rang off.'

Max paused, shrugged and waved a hand vaguely. 'I remembered the local code number that came up on my phone. I used a contact to trace the call to Thame. That is why, a couple of days later, I started hanging around on the off-chance of spotting him.'

'You could have explained this to my DI when he visited you. Instead, you left him thinking you had some connection with a totally different case in the same area, which made you a serious suspect, Mr Harris. Especially since you were seen to follow when a family living near where you parked left in a great hurry.'

Max said nothing, simply waited for more.

'So, I must ask myself,' Yeadings said, eyeing him evenly, 'whether there is some link between an apparently abducted child and a missing scientist.'

Max was in a quandary. If there was a connection, how could he break confidence with Egerton? Surely the man had enough to worry him without suddenly getting involved in kidnapping a child?

'Perhaps Egerton isn't missing at all,' he offered. 'Simply staying somewhere, incognito, while he sorts himself out.'

Yeadings remained silent, waiting for the other to fill the gap, but Max, although uncomfortable, wasn't intimidated.

'So what do you know of a Timothy Johnson?'

'Nothing,' said Max. 'Who's he?'

'And little Jenny Barber? Where does she come into this?'

'You said it's a case you're working on. Like everybody else, I first read about her in today's newspapers. But the address wasn't given, and I made no connection until DI Salmon questioned me.'

Yeadings considered this. 'Have you ever seen Piers Egerton or a photograph of him? Would you know him if you saw him?'

'No. There's been no publicity at all. As far as the press is concerned, he doesn't exist.'

The superintendent nodded. 'An anonymous cog in the nation's secret research machine. Which is how he should remain, according to Special Branch.' He sighed. 'They will wish to interview you, of course. I have only one more question. Can you give me your assurance that there has been no leak of information between you and DS Zyczynski?'

'None, in either direction. I protected my information, and she didn't mention any case she was interested in. We recognised we could be on the same track less than an hour ago.'

'Thank you for coming in, Mr Harris. You are free to go.'

Max left Interview Room 2, observing the red light still glowing above the door across the corridor. He went back to reception and sat again on the visitors' bench to wait for Z to emerge. Yeadings had disappeared towards the stairs and his own office.

'Can I get tea or something sent up, sir?' Sergeant Hopkins enquired, hovering helpfully.

'Nothing, thank you.' Max assumed that in the interval someone had informed the sergeant of his relationship with Z. Ironically, for Hopkins he was now almost *one of us*.

The door to Interview Room 1 opened abruptly and DI Salmon came through, darting a sharp glance in his direction: there was to be no similar acceptance from him. Max Harris was definitely, even more now, one of *them*.

Rosemary returned apparently unruffled but with

a marked flush to her cheeks. She grinned at him. 'It's been a long day,' she said; nodded at Hopkins and made for the exit. Max caught up with her in the car park and opened the passenger door for her. 'Settled the problem?'

'I'd like to think so. How did the Boss take it?'

'It seems we've given him food for thought.'

'About us?'

'No. I meant about a possible link between you-know-who and the little girl. It could be our missing man is staying at that house under the name of Johnson; if so, Egerton was the one who delivered Jenny to the Leisure Centre, and the last person known to see her before she disappeared.'

Z stopped, halfway into the seat. 'That's not good. What did he think he was doing? Max, did he ever strike you as mentally unstable?'

Jenny came slowly awake. Her head felt heavy and muzzy. Her tongue seemed to have swollen; the inside of her mouth was rough and dry. There came a sound of soft whirring. A thin slice of light showed from the doorway and in the half-dark she could make out the shape of the man hunched over, doing something with his hands against the opposite wall.

He grunted. The whirring stopped. 'That'll do,' he muttered, standing upright and swinging some tool in one hand. He moved towards the open doorway, stood there a moment, black against the yellow light, and then the door slid shut. There came the sound of a key turning.

She was locked in again, left alone in a more solid dark. She wasn't sure if she was very hungry or about to be sick. It felt wrong anyway. She wanted to be at home, with Mummy who would cuddle her and make her feel better.

She remembered the witch feeding her that awful tomato slop and dry bread. And later a mug of hot chocolate that tasted bitter. If she called out now, would she bring her some water to drink? No, she dared not risk it. The witch would be angry, for sure. She'd told her she had to be quiet or there'd be trouble.

Jenny sat up and this time she seemed to be on a real sort of bed, with springs which creaked as she moved. The room spun a little before it settled again. Cautiously she pushed back the sheet and felt for the floor with her feet. It wasn't bare boards, but the shiny stuff some people put in their kitchens or bathrooms. She was in a different place. She felt sticky. One of her ribbons had got lost and her hair felt funny where a chunk was missing.

As her eyes grew used to the dark, it didn't seem as solid as before. At one point, just opposite, a single spot of light shone out clearly. It was just how a cat's eyes showed up at night. But this cat had only one. She thought it might be the sort that was always spitting and fighting. Perhaps that was how it had lost its second eye, scratched out by some other cat it had been in a battle with.

It would be black – which was why she couldn't see its outline. All witches' cats were black. Mummy had

read her a book with a witch's cat in it, called Grimaldy-
something. It had played spiteful tricks. They had giggled
together over the story, frightened in a nicely excited
sort of way. She didn't feel like giggling now, although
little noises started struggling up her throat and trying
to come out. She clamped her hands over her mouth to
make herself stay quiet. She drew her feet in and covered
herself again with the sheet.

She wished the cat would go away and stop staring.
But the door was locked and there didn't seem to be a
window. Maybe she should try to be nice to it.

'Puss,' she said in a quavery voice, 'what a beautiful
pussy you are.'

It took no notice. Not a blink. Jenny lay back down,
pulled the pillow from behind her head and covered
her face with it. She still felt muzzy. In a little while the
trembling stopped and she slid again into asleep.

'I've boarded it over.' Pavel said.

'Good. That'll protect the glass and keep her from
looking out. Is she still asleep?'

'I didn't look.'

Jana sighed. 'Well, didn't she wake with your
hammering?'

'Didn't hammer. I used screws.' He grinned to himself,
because she didn't know what else he'd done. With Jana
you had always to be a step ahead. Sometimes you'd
think he wasn't her older brother but a little kid.

'Have you taken your medicine?'

He glared at her. 'What d'you think?'

The trouble was that she didn't know what to think. That was no sort of answer to reassure anybody. But then that was probably what he meant by it: keep her guessing, make her worry.

He went out by the kitchen door into the neglected little garden. She heard him laughing all the way down to his shed. Jana moved through to the front window and stared out at the road. She'd really expected Karel to be here before them, with the papers he'd gone to the house for. Well, perhaps not *expected* exactly. More *hoped*. Anxiously hoped.

So had he stayed on in Thame, still trying to get to the man? They shouldn't have left him there alone and driven straight off, but there was no other car parked in that street, and Pavel hadn't wanted to draw attention by staying on. When he'd phoned them here before breaking in, Karel had said he'd be all right, because he'd rung the doorbell and the house was empty. He'd just have done what he had to do, was taking his time getting back, but would catch up with them later.

She acknowledged he was always the one made to do the difficult bits, because it was his nature to give in. And he was always careful not to get on the wrong side of Pavel. He said he'd seen what could happen if you did. But even Karel couldn't imagine…

She shook her head. It didn't do to dwell on such things. Her brother had shown fewer signs of violence since he'd joined them this summer. Whatever the stuff was that he got from the clinic, it helped to keep his anger in check. The terrible scenes she remembered from her younger years were best not dwelt on. She had to accept that Pavel had his problems, and what he'd suffered as a boy had turned his head for a while.

She still wasn't sure he was reconciled to finding her married when he'd come to England. He had no right to mind. Where had he been when she and Mother were left all alone to fend for themselves, fleeing from their home?

After Mama had died Karel had turned up here, in much the same sorry circumstances as herself, and they had thrown in their lot together. Better with him, she thought, than living with one of the sort of men her brother associated with.

She dropped the edge of the curtain and sighed. There was no sign of anyone approaching the house. Waiting for Karel to come home was like watching a pot that never boiled. She went back to the kitchen. She must stretch their food to cover the girl's needs now. Perhaps it was just as well that Karel was away for a few days. But he mustn't be too long gone. They needed him to bring in money with his puppet shows. She didn't want to cancel the children's party they were booked for next week.

In his shed Pavel Hlavacek slotted the screwdriver into its sheath on the wall and returned the drill to its box, with the bit removed. He looked around, approving of the neatness he'd imposed on what was chaos when he'd arrived. The shed had been wasted on Karel, who was just as happy whittling his puppet figures indoors. The kitchen was always sticky with his glue, and the floor littered with wood shavings and the cut-offs from fabrics Jana made the little garments from. Children's toys! And they had the brains of children themselves.

He uncovered his carbon wheel and laid out the row of knives to be sharpened. This was man's work, he told himself, gently easing a block of wood alongside a honed blade and watching the silken cut lengthen like a throat slit cleanly open. One day Karel should see what real entertainment these instruments could produce.

Jenny awoke again, sat up and cleared the bedding from her face and shoulders. The room seemed slightly less dark than it had been. Less dark than in her dream. But the cat was still staring.

Perhaps it wasn't real. It could be one of those china ones some people liked to have as ornaments. Bolder now, she whispered, 'Shoo!'

It didn't move. She shooed it again, a little louder; finally clapped her hands. The thing wasn't scared away.

She reached out her feet to the linoleum and waited. Still no movement. Groping at the darkness ahead, in case she might bump into things, she crept towards the spot of light. A wall confronted her. She dared to touch it where the top of the cat's head would be. There was just plaster, which came away gritty on her fingers. She traced her way down to the eye and felt a hole there. One finger went in. The light slid over it and then was cut off.

There was no cat.

She bent and looked through the hole. Where her finger had been was now a picture, showing part of another room properly lit. No, she thought, it was a real room, and she could make out a small corner of a window. In there it was daylight. Not night, like in here.

Why wasn't it light in here? Shouldn't there be a window here too? There ought to be a switch somewhere near the door, so you could reach it as you came in. She patted her way along the wall to where she thought the door must be. Her outstretched fingers found wood panels, moved back a little, and then explored higher. Stretching on tiptoes she discovered the switch, pressed it and a light came on.

Now she could see the room. It was small and square, not quite as awful as the other one she'd been in. And it had a big, shiny wooden wardrobe, with travel bags balanced on top. There was a tiny table and a straight chair. But no window. Instead, there was a flat board of speckly wood with brass screws in it on all four sides.

And that, she guessed, was to stop her getting out.

Chapter Twenty-One

Lee Barber looked out from the front landing window. The street was empty except for old Godden shambling by with an empty shopping bag on his arm. Freda was sending him off to the fish van with strict instructions while stocks were plenty; because, of course, it was market day.

Their own fishmonger, who also did poultry and was pricy, had closed down a fortnight back, despite an imploring *Use Us or Lose Us* sign displayed for three months above the marble slabs.

Maybe he should offer to go and do likewise, same as old Godden – try to be of some use. He doubted Kathy knew what day it was. Gradually she was falling apart, the reliable, ever-steady, coolly efficient Kathy. Now, with her family under threat, she was miles from him when both most needed each other's close comfort.

He knew well enough what the reason was. He was responsible for Tim being here. And what Tim had done was unforgivable, although it was no more nor less than he might have done himself, driving off before he was one hundred percent sure that Jenny was looked after. With the pressure of traffic building up behind, you did the reasonable thing – cleared off and made way. Because it was a safe place. Everything was supposedly under control; Jenny was expected there.

Except that Mrs Skinner hadn't passed on Kathy's message, advising the Leisure Centre that the children's numbers were back to fourteen. Not Tim's fault, not his own fault either, certainly not Kathy's fault. But the awful outcome, on top of Stevie's sudden illness, had been too much for her. It was as though her faith in all of life was totally eroded.

His mother-in-law had been careless, leaving her medication where a small child could find it, but he knew Kathy. She would be sharing the guilt, because she'd been there and hadn't prevented it. That was behind the crumbling of her confidence. She was mad at herself, and the anger had to be poured out on everyone around her. Nothing he could say would alter that. Only Jenny's safe return and Stevie's recovery could help.

The only hope was that Tim could somehow contact whoever was holding Jenny. In any case, he must tell the police who he was and that he'd made enemies because of his work. It was up to them to follow it up. And then the terrible truth would come out about the dead intruder and his, Lee's, part in disposing of the body. It made him an accomplice to murder, which would inevitably mean prison, and plunge Kathy in further distress.

Lee crossed the landing and banged on Egerton's door. Without waiting for an answer he walked in. The bedclothes were flung back. The borrowed pyjamas lay folded on a chair. There was nobody there.

There was no note, but he knew at once. Tim had gone. Either he intended some move to save Jenny or he meant to disappear entirely. Lee remembered the moment in the boat when Tim had stood grasping the gunwale, ready to jump in the sea. He could have reached the same point of desperation again and gone off to kill himself.

Lee felt a new fury surging inside. How could the man have run out on them? Did he think it simplified anything? Jenny was still gone, and now any hope of contacting her captors had gone too. He, Lee Barber, had been left to make all the explanations, confess his part in an appalling crime.

He sank on the bed, beating his fists against his thighs, fighting nausea. Briefly, he hoped he could escape police harassment, plead ignorance of everything except the man's identity, and leave it to them to unravel the whole business.

But that was as cowardly as Tim's running away. Better the shame of exposure than the shame of opting right out. That was something they shared; he couldn't live with himself if he simply did nothing. But he wasn't ready to end everything. There was one chance for him, he realised. Tim had spoken of Max Harris, a newspaperman. Through the Internet he could find what papers he wrote for and, through them, get an urgent message to him. It might even be that that was where Tim was heading even now, and between them they could... Could what? Somehow find Jenny?

He was fooling himself if he expected that. But what other option remained? Stiffly, he stood up and made for the staircase. He'd have to tell Kathy that Tim was gone. It was ironic that she'd probably be relieved.

Then he had to make up some reason to log on to her computer and make a search for Max Harris.

There had been no chance of obtaining a search warrant overnight, but at 8.30 a.m. Yeadings had rung Henry Ludgate JP at home and made the request. The magistrate was reluctant, pressing him for proof of the family being suspected of child abuse. The alleged bruising of the younger child, reported by Max Harris, was insufficient to imply that one, or both, of the parents was involved in the older child's disappearance.

Yeadings agreed, but he was almost sure that theirs was the house the missing scientist had drawn Max Harris's attention to. If Egerton, possibly unstable and on the run, had taken refuge there and been the last known person to see little Jenny, that added the necessary weight. DS Beaumont was despatched to get the warrant signed, and a police raid at the Barbers' address was set up for 9.30 a.m.

Beaumont and DC Silver arrived with two squad cars of uniformed police to find only Kathy Barber and her sick son at home. The husband had been sent shopping, and their guest, Tim Johnson, had left overnight without so much as a note to say goodbye or thanks for their hospitality. This seemed not to worry Mrs Barber, who had more grim matters on her mind.

A motherly WPC was left with her in the kitchen while the police spread through the house on a detailed search, causing as little disturbance as possible. Just the same, Kathy marked her protest by removing Stevie from the cot in the sitting room and nursing him on her knee as the policewoman prepared to make tea for them both.

Lee had left his mobile phone behind on the kitchen table, or she would have tried to call him back from the market. As the minutes passed, sounds of heavy boots and furniture being moved about overhead made her more and more incensed against the invasion. In particular she detested the plain-clothes sergeant, whose wooden features and sharp nose made her think of Pinocchio in the children's book. He had declined to say what reason they had for the search, and his prolonged stare at the bruises on the uncovered parts of Stevie's body recalled the original suspicions levelled against her and Lee at the hospital.

She felt hot blood rising in her own face but refused to make excuses. If he could hold back on explanations, so could she. Let him think what he chose. His opinion was nothing to her.

An hour passed. They had finished downstairs. Kathy put Stevie back in the cot and sat close to him, reading until his eyelids drooped and he fell asleep. He had shown no interest in the unusual activity in the house. Normally he would have been excited to see so many policemen and been bouncing around, chattering to them.

Lee hadn't returned. She couldn't understand what

was keeping him. The shopping list had contained only three items, all easily obtained in the weekly market.

There had been two phone calls; one from the wife of one of Lee's fellow drivers offering help, and the other was from Dr Dunlop asking after Stevie and promising to drop in during her lunch hour. Which it nearly was, Kathy saw. She supposed she'd better start putting a meal together, but just then Detective Sergeant Beaumont opted to come in and question her about Tim Johnson.

'I know nothing at all about him,' she said flatly.

Beaumont stared at her with his round, puppet eyes and she felt compelled to add, 'He was here when I got back with the children from Mother's.'

'A friend of your husband's then?'

'I wouldn't say that. He was just someone Lee came across Friday night. Well, in the early hours of Saturday, actually. He said he'd been mugged.'

'Johnson was mugged, or your husband?

'Johnson. It was true he had a plaster on his head, and next day I noticed marks on his throat. He did appear rather confused.'

Beaumont took time to consider this and make her feel more awkward. 'Do you mean to say that your husband brought home a complete stranger? Sort of Good Samaritan thing? Offered him a bed, all out of the blue? Had he ever done anything like that before?'

'No.' Her voice was low. She was acknowledging the story was thin. It still worried her that Lee hadn't simply given the man a lift to A&E at the hospital.

'Would it surprise you if I said there was some doubt about his name being Johnson?'

'Nothing would surprise me about him!' Now she sounded waspish.

She hadn't cared for the man at all, Beaumont noted. Now why was that? Was it only that she blamed him for losing Jenny, or did she suspect some questionable connection with her husband?

She was frowning. 'If you think he wasn't called Johnson, who was he?'

Beaumont hesitated. 'He could be someone the police are interested in speaking to.'

'A criminal?'

'Not necessarily.'

She recognised his caution and shuddered. 'But he came back here. Straight after taking Jenny to the Leisure Centre,' she protested. 'If he'd been a – a paedophile or something…'

'We don't think that,' Beaumont hurried to reassure her. He knew the man hadn't had time to dispose of the child outside the area already tooth-combed for traces of her. And, if he was Egerton, as suspected, he'd have had enough on his mind already without launching into a new bit of quirky behaviour.

He allowed a little sympathy to show. 'I'm a father myself,' he said. 'I can't imagine how I'd feel in your place. We are hoping to pick up some proof of who exactly he is, but he seems to have left nothing behind.'

'Except fingerprints, surely.'

'Yes, plenty of those, since he's been here almost a

week; which is why we shall need to bother you for your own, for elimination. And your husband's too.'

'I see. Does that mean you already hold his prints, for matching?'

'Not in police records, if that's any consolation, Mrs Barber. But we're expecting them, from another source.'

There was the sound of a key in the front door lock and voices as Lee came in with Dr Dunlop on his heels.

'What the hell's going on?' he demanded. 'The street's full of police cars.'

Max Harris had taken two calls in rapid succession. One was from *The Independent* and the other the *Spectator.* The messages were similar. He wrote down the number both gave. It looked to be for a public phone box, and the local code was the same as the one Egerton had used to ring him days ago. So, the scientist was trying to get in touch again, but why hadn't he called directly to his mobile, as before?

Max punched the figures in and heard the receiver lifted almost instantly.

'Max Harris here,' he said levelly. 'I've been hoping to hear from you again.'

There was a short silence, and then an unknown voice said breathlessly, 'My name is Lee Barber. I need to talk with you. Urgently. It's about Tim Egerton. He was staying with me, but now he's gone off God-knows-where.'

* * *

Jana was cleaning in Pavel's room and had just turned down the sheet on his made-up bed when she heard a little scratching sound. It seemed to come from the wall. A small framed picture of a coastline with seabirds, hanging low over the side of his bed, swung slightly as if in an earth tremor.

It usually hung on the landing. Pavel must have just brought it in. She'd never known him take an interest in pictures before. As she reached out to straighten it the frame started easing out from the wall. Something alive was moving behind it.

With distaste she lifted it off its hook and stared at the wall's surface. A thick length of wire wriggled out at her and then was withdrawn, leaving a round hole.

Her heart pounded in her chest. Pavel had made that hole, to spy on the room next to his own. She bent across the bed, leaning close to look in.

A round, blue eye stared back at her.

There was a startled gasp and a scrambling sound as the child withdrew. With a metallic clatter, a wire coat-hanger fell to the floor in the next-door room.

Jana was trembling all over. She sank on the bed, her face contorted in horror.

Not this again? Her evil brother! Had he kept this up all along? Was this why he'd fled here to England six years back? – maybe running from a criminal charge? That could be why he had risked entering the country illegally, taking refuge with Karel and her.

She'd thought he was cured; that the medication had stabilised him. But then, just lately she'd had doubts.

She saw now – he didn't want to be normal. This suited him better, to be getting all sorts of wicked satisfaction from preying on defenceless children. She should have known he couldn't change.

She shuddered, remembering how as a little girl, younger even than this one, she'd frozen in her bed as the door opened and torchlight searched her out, dancing across the room, then shining back into his devilish face. Her older brother! And how he'd hurt her, threatening to kill her if ever she told what he did.

Now she knew why he'd made her grab the child. It was nothing to do with the cruel work Egerton was involved in, which so revolted Karel and herself. No, Pavel had wanted Jenny for himself. What a silly, limp fool she'd been, to do as he'd ordered.

If only Karel had been there, he would have stopped her. But he'd been gone for days now, and she was worried out of her mind, thinking he'd left her because of Pavel always being there. The two men had disliked each other on sight, and God knows what had gone on between them in private.

And now, this child. What was she to do?

She stood, catching sight of herself in the old-fashioned oval mirror set in the wardrobe door. For a brief second she thought it was her mother come back to haunt her. There were the same sallow, sunken cheeks under high, slanting bones; the same small, black eyes, and the dark hair, going grey, dragged back behind large, ugly ears.

And the same fear in her eyes. Her mother, who had

hustled her out of the only home she knew, to flee across Europe for a new life. Protecting her daughter and leaving her son behind.

Had she guessed? Guessed and never spoken of it, all these years? Not even on her deathbed? Because she thought Jana was safe now. It had never struck her that eventually Pavel would try to follow them here.

Shakily, Jana went out on to the landing. The key was in the child's door. She unlocked it and went in. The little quivering thing was wound in a tight ball, eyes screwed shut, waiting for her anger. A small, defenceless, pink-fleshed mammal, like some scared puppy so young that it barely had hair yet upon it. All the pity Jana had poured out on abused animals welled up in her again. She wanted to pick it up, cradle it; take it away to a place of safety.

She remembered then how they'd caught one of the staff fleeing from the research lab they'd burnt down. The girl had turned on them and shouted. 'Leave us alone! We're animals too!'

And she hadn't understood until now.

'I'll get you a nightdress,' she said, and went out, leaving the door ajar. There was a clean one of her own in a drawer. She brought it to the child and made her slip it over her shoulders. 'Stand up.'

The child crept out of bed, still cowering. The coarse white cotton pooled around her feet.

'Come into my room.' Jana held out her hand. A moment of hesitation, then fearfully the child took it.

Jana reached into her sewing basket for the shears.

'It's all right. I won't hurt you. I just want to shorten the hem.'

She snipped around the child's trembling legs, taking off about eighteen inches in length. 'There, that's better.'

But the neck opening was so wide that the nightdress was slipping off the tiny shoulders. She could sew it up and make it fit better; but covering the child's nakedness wasn't going to save her from Pavel. Somehow she would have to get her away from him.

Downstairs the front door slammed. She heard him go through to the kitchen. Then he was shouting up to her, 'Jana, where the devil are you?' His heavy footsteps followed on the stairs.

'Quick,' she said, 'under here,' lifting the valance and pushing her under the bed. Jenny fell on her knees and crawled into the darkness.

'I'm coming,' Jana called back. Even to herself, her voice sounded unconvincing.

Under the bed it was fluffy with dust. Jenny could feel it tickling at the back of her nose. She put both hands over her face and tried not to breathe in too hard, but she had to: her heart was pumping away, as though she was running in a race.

The man with the stain on his face was just outside the door now, talking to the witch. She listened but the words made no sense. It was some other language she hadn't heard before. He didn't sound pleased.

And then she sneezed.

From under the valance she saw the heavy boots come in and circle the room, the woman's slippers pattering after them. And then, as she sneezed again, more light flooded in on her and a hairy arm reached in.

'What have we here?' he demanded. His voice was all funny, as if he was angry and sort of pleased all at once. He pulled her out to stand on her feet, and the overlarge nightdress started sliding off her shoulders, leaving almost all her chest exposed. He was staring at her and smiling. The old witch wasn't. Her face had gone twisted and dark. Jenny crept close to the man.

'Go back to bed,' the witch snarled.

The man's closeness gave Jenny courage. 'I'm tired of bed. I want to go home.' She didn't like the old woman's nightdress harsh on her skin. She tore at it and it slid right down, so that she had to step out of it, holding on to the man's trouser leg. He gave a great laugh and she knew he was pleased with her.

If she could stay with him, the old woman couldn't harm her. Maybe she wouldn't lock her in again. Although the man didn't say much, she could see that the witch was afraid of him.

'What is she doing out here?' he demanded.

'I found her something to wear. The nightdress, but I need to alter it to fit,' she said, stumbling over the words.

The man rested an arm on the child's bare shoulder. Jenny stared out from behind his bulk. 'I want my own clothes back,' she said, suddenly bolder. Why shouldn't she have them, even if she needed clean knickers and socks?

'Come with me. I'll get them for you.' But Jenny didn't

trust her. She pushed out her bottom lip and scowled back.

'Such pretty, pretty hair,' the man said in a sing-song voice. He ran his fingers over her head and stopped at the lopped-off bunch. She remembered Daddy, how she'd sat on his lap for him to read a book to her. She wanted so much to be home again. There was a story about a gingerbread house and two children who'd been kept prisoner. The witch had meant to shut them in the oven and cook them, but they'd managed to escape. She wasn't sure quite how. Maybe a woodman came in with an axe. Or that might have been Goldilocks he was saving, in another book. Perhaps that would happen for her.

But it wasn't to be yet. The witch suddenly made up her mind, stepped forward and seized her roughly by one hand. The man didn't stop her; just stood smiling in that funny sort of way he had while she was pulled out on to the landing and hustled back into her room.

But he was still there. Sometime he would come and rescue her. Hadn't she seen him make that little peephole in the wall so she could look out?

When the witch had left and locked the door again, Jenny went across and put her eye to the hole. But it had gone black. Someone had covered the other side so she couldn't see the light any more. And she knew who that was. She closed her eyes and saw again the witch's fierce black eyeball boring into her.

Chapter Twenty-Two

We should meet up, Max thought, but Barber can't leave the house at present, and the area is seething with police. After Yeadings' caution, I have to stay away. But there is a lot more that I need to know.

Short of Egerton getting in touch again directly, there seemed no way now that he could get a fix on the man. Frustrated, he made himself some strong coffee and settled to write out everything he remembered from Lee Barber's conversation. The man claimed to have acted Good Samaritan to Egerton on the night he should have met Max at Beaconsfield.

Barber was a train driver. Sometime after midnight, driving home from Aylesbury station, he had come across Egerton lying in the gutter, unconscious. And, instead of calling for an ambulance, he had taken the man to his own home.

The details weren't clear. Why was Egerton found at Aylesbury, when he should have got off the train at Beaconsfield, several stations earlier? It seemed unlikely that, with such a momentous decision on his mind, he should simply have fallen asleep and gone past his stop. So something had prevented him. Was it because of something that happened on the train, or someone glimpsed on the platform at Beaconsfield who had to be avoided? Max had taken a good look around there and had seen nothing untoward.

The timing needed clarifying. Barber had been vague over that, sounding almost nervous. Max suspected he wasn't getting the whole truth from him; or, at best, a sanitised version of the truth. If so, why? Was his intention to make Max believe Egerton had gone missing again, when he actually was still lying low? To discourage Max from following him further? Surely not, since he'd bothered to make the phone call. Tomorrow could produce some clarification, either through further police actions, or by their issuing a press statement. However, time was something he didn't have, especially in view of a child going missing, and Max was sure Egerton's actions had had a direct bearing on her disappearance.

From the man's first approach, all Max had picked up was the dangerous nature of his scientific work, but with nothing specific on the research itself. He might have doubted the story was genuine, because the man's subsequent behaviour was eccentric, but the immediate interest sparked at Special Branch tended to back him up.

His continued delay in contacting Max could be because he was in danger for his life. The attack on him at Aylesbury bore this out, but why had the assault been broken off? Barber had said nothing of seeing any muggers fleeing. The two men had had enough time together by now for the scientist to have confided in his rescuer. Certainly he'd admitted to his true name, although Barber had referred to him as 'Johnson' when questioned by the police. So, if the train driver knew so much, perhaps he knew a helluva lot more than he was prepared to admit to anyone. And was it more than coincidence that he worked on the very Misbourne Line that Egerton had travelled when he'd been attacked?

Suppose the assault had actually taken place on the train and Barber, feeling some responsibility, had agreed with him to hush that fact up?

The more Max considered this, the more he liked the fit of it; and the more urgent it became that he should get Barber somewhere on his own and make him talk freely.

He could even guess where Egerton would head for if he was left out on a limb.

So where had he come *from*? Porton Down research labs, or somewhere more secret? Barber had mentioned his mother's flat in Kilburn, but that Egerton was from Essex. He'd made it sound as though the man had been brought up there – the music hall joke of Essex Man. But with a more possible London background, it could be that he simply worked in Essex. In which case, one of the local press stringers there might have picked up on recent police interest in some medical research centre. It was certainly worth looking into.

From her window Zyczynski watched Max leave the house. Since she'd been suspected of leaking police information to him, he had kept scrupulously to his own apartment. She knew it was out of discretion for her professional reputation, but it hurt, and she missed him. It seemed out of character that he'd buckled under without firing off a salvo in return, but then there was more to Max than met the eye on first sight.

His car roared off with a spurting of gravel. She might be off the case of the missing scientist, but it didn't look as if he was.

Thoughtfully she picked up her present brief: Yeadings' neat, handwritten notes on his interview with one Cedric Albert Farrow, security courier, recovering from GBH in an armed raid. The haul was a little over a quarter of a million pounds in used notes due for delivery to Grimsdale's factory. The notes ended with the single word, *Why?*

Did the Boss query why that particular raid, why so large a sum of money, or why so violent an attack? It was an open question. Z doubted a second visit so soon to the recovering man would give greater focus. Perhaps at the security firm's office someone handling the delivery order could supply the necessary background.

She phoned ahead for an interview, was informed that the chief executive had been called to headquarters; but his assistant, a Miss Marilee Hobbs, was instructed to grant the police full cooperation.

Zyczynski checked in her mirror, retouched her lipstick and went down to get on the trail.

Jana Simekova turned down the flame under the simmering dumplings. The aroma of slow-cooked beef, carrots, peppers and onions, flavoured with basil and grated orange zest, filled the kitchen. It brought her brother to the door. 'Is it ready?' he demanded, almost salivating.

'Five minutes. Cut some bread, will you?' She watched while he brought the saw-edged knife from the locked drawer and hacked off two thick doorsteps of bread.

'Three,' she stipulated. 'We have to give the girl some.'

His shrug was surly but he cut another slice. She noted where he laid down the knife at the edge of the wooden board.

'Do you remember,' she said hurriedly, to divert his mind, 'how Mama used to make this for us on our birthdays?'

'For yours, maybe. Never mine.'

'Oh, but she did. You never noticed.' That was true. He would have been in too great a hurry to be off out with his horrible friends.

She took two clean, blue-and-white checked napkins from the dresser and laid one at his place. The other she dropped, as if by accident, over the edge of the breadboard. Later she would wonder just what she had intended, how much she was planning ahead, and quite how far she would have dared to go. But just then her head was in a whirl. She tried to hide the trembling of her hands. He mustn't suspect anything.

Pavel reached in the lower cupboard for the bottle of Slivovic and slammed it on the table. Jana nodded: that was good. She would have suggested it herself but was afraid he might think she was overdoing the occasion. It must seem just an ordinary meal on an ordinary day. Only she knew that it wasn't: that she had put up with enough.

It was clear by now that Karel was not coming back. He had turned his back on them because of Pavel, sickened by his coarse ways, no longer able to excuse him because he was of Jana's blood.

And she was revolted too, mindful of so much that was vile from their childhood, kept secret but never forgotten – not only herself abused, but also what happened to the pathetic little kitten, gone floppy, its fur streaked and clotted with blood, hanging on a cord from Mama's washing line.

She had thought they'd left all that behind when Mama and she escaped across Europe, but even here she'd found there was cruelty enough. Meeting up with Karel, and learning to love him, she had shared his detestation of animal abuse: the fur farms, the illegal cock-fighting, the baiting of badgers and now the diabolical use of innocent animals in scientific experiments. He had inspired her with his thirst for justice. Karel had been an Angel of Nemesis. Release of the innocent tortured creatures had become the core of their lives together, filling the empty space owed to children who by then she was too old to give him.

And then, after Mama died, suddenly her brother Pavel had reappeared from the past, expecting to share their little home. He had pretended to take on their crusade, but there'd been no tenderness in him, only a passion for destruction and fire-raising. And now, while supposedly helping to seek out this evil man who killed in the name of medical science, Pavel had sought only his own ends, taking this child to satisfy his depraved appetites.

And the girl was not even that man Egerton's daughter. In the papers her name had been given as Barber. It was all a mistake, they had snatched the child of an innocent man. And she, Jana, distressed over Karel's absence, had allowed herself to be dragged into it.

This had to be put right, but she didn't know anyone who could help. From childhood she had never trusted the police. There were only other members of *Release*, all dedicated to ending the misery inflicted by humans upon God's frailer creatures. She dared not admit to them what she had done, endangering the child.

And the people employing Karel were the ones who organised and paid for the secret work done at the hospital. Karel had been only a cleaner there and not allowed to talk to anyone who mattered. Nobody he worked with had felt the way he did, so he'd had to hold his tongue and bide his time, until he had overheard the man talking on the phone and knew he was leaving, taking all his secret work-notes from the safe.

So, Karel had left London to follow him to some place called Beaconsfield, as overheard, phoning back once, but she had been out shopping. Pavel had taken the call; which was how he knew of the house in Thames Valley that Karel was keeping a watch on. Karel's old Triumph was left parked beside their cottage. Pavel had insisted they take it and follow Karel to Thame.

There they had found not only the house he spoke of, but also the squat where he'd stayed over. By then Karel had left, never to come back. Maybe he obtained the papers he was looking for, or maybe not. Once away, he must have decided that life under the same roof with Pavel was impossible. That had mattered more than any affection he still felt for her, Jana. So he had set his back to them both and gone his way.

It was all Pavel's fault. Once again he had ruined her life, and there was nothing left to her but bitter emptiness. At Thame, he had followed Egerton's car and made her pick up the child left outside the swimming pool. They had held her a prisoner overnight in the derelict house Karel had spoken of, before coming back here. And this was no longer the home she had made with Karel.

She tried to eat, but the bread stuck in her throat. She made retching noises, louder than her brother scooping up the last of the gravy from the casserole dish, and he scowled at her.

'You will need to find yourself a proper job,' he said, 'now that that waster has abandoned you. Someone will have to bring in the money, and you know I can't. I'm not supposed to be here.'

She looked across at him. No, you shouldn't be, she thought. With all my heart, I wish you weren't. I'd rather have you dead.

Eventually he swilled his mouth out with the Slivovic,

gave a final belch and rose to go. There was fruit for dessert but he didn't bother with it. Jana listened as he went upstairs, not to the child's room, but his own. She supposed he would sink on his bed, remove the picture from his wall and apply his eye to the peephole. At least the child had some decent covering now, and in the almost complete dark of the boarded-up room he'd not make out her curled-up form in the bed.

She waited for half an hour before taking the small bowl of goulash from the cooling oven, slid the bread and a spoon into her apron pocket and retrieved the bundle of the child's clothes from the cupboard in the hall.

In her soft slippers she crept upstairs, listened at her brother's closed door and was satisfied to hear heavy breathing. She unlocked the child's door and slid into the darkened room. Enough light slanted through from the landing for her to make out where the child lay. 'Hush,' she warned. 'We mustn't let him hear us.'

Jenny sat up, wide-eyed. She was ravenous, but it was her clothes she reached out for. It didn't matter now that they were the same knickers and socks she had worn before. Anything was better than this harsh cotton gown.

'Have something to eat first,' Jana whispered. 'We are going out for a walk. You need something inside you.'

The child looked startled, as though she had been shut up here so long that the idea of something different appeared a new danger. She cowered away as Jana held out the bowl of goulash. She saw little chunks of meat and pale dumpling floating in it but the spicy aroma repelled her. 'It smells stingly,' she whimpered.

'Here, I'll soak some bread in it. Try that. It's lovely.'

Too scared to disobey, Jenny took the bowl, holding it while Jana dropped a lump of bread in and offered it covered in rich red-brown liquor. When the child opened her mouth and swallowed it, Jana grunted, pulled off another lump of the bread and went across to plug up the peephole.

Jenny continued spooning up the goulash, and Jana watched her until it was all gone. There had been no more protests. Then she exchanged the empty bowl with the bundle of clothes and watched the little girl dress.

'Not your shoes,' she cautioned in a whisper. 'Here, I'll carry them.'

'Where are we going?' She didn't want to go anywhere with the witch. She'd rather the man with the poor bruised-looking face was coming along too, but the witch was trying to stop him hearing them leave. At least the man had smiled at her, and he'd given her the little peephole so she could see out a little way, into the light. The witch never smiled. It was a terrible yellowy-brown face, covered in ditches and little ruts like a country lane.

'Where?' she insisted. The witch seemed not to have heard her the first time, listening with her head against the wall.

'To your home, of course. Don't you want to see your mama?'

Jenny supposed she meant Mummy. 'And Daddy?' she begged.

The witch nodded, putting a finger to her screwed-up lips to caution silence. She would have to explain later that they must leave it to someone else to complete the journey. All she could manage was to get the child away from here, far enough not to be able to lead anyone back That meant a long walk, and perhaps a bus or two, even a train ride so that the child, when found, would be absolutely lost.

'Come on,' she whispered impatiently. 'We haven't got all night.'

'Halstead,' Max repeated into the phone. 'That's on the way to Colchester, isn't it?' He had a vague memory of driving out there. It would not be far from West Bergholt, which had been where Randolph Churchill once lived. There was a wooden spire built for the church tower there, but because of high winds it had stood for decades on the grass of the churchyard. Or was he thinking of *East* Bergholt?

'That's right,' the stringer assured him. 'You must head for the A604. Tell you what, Mr Harris, I'll get over there and wait for you in the main street. Look for a metallic green Toyota. Only too glad to help you out.'

Jamie Carr had once had aspirations to make Fleet Street, but over the years they'd been honed away by a series of misjudgements, the first of which had been to make an honest woman of Sue Waring with her bun in the oven. It had anchored him, soured him and led to an inconvenient habit of backing nags that were fitter for the knacker's yard than the racecourse. Meanwhile, instead of his transfer to the Metropolis, Fleet Street itself had moved out, to Dockside. He'd remained the empty-pocketed provincial hack, covering the proceedings of the local Chamber of Commerce, police court summonses and occasional amateur dramatic performances. The very name of Max Harris, when he phoned, had been a sort of glorious Epiphany. And now he was to meet him in the flesh!

Lee Barber stole a look at his wristwatch. How much longer were they going to stay on? Right, so they were his mates from work, but anyone could see Kathy was finding it tough going. Stevie's bruises were gradually fading but he still wasn't up to noisy company, and the cheerful delegation from his shift filled the dining room, Norman Harker sprawled on the floor at the feet of the cot. He would keep moaning on about his bloody bike, how it was stolen from the station and amazingly turned up near this road in someone's hedge. Anyone would think he, Lee, had taken it, though everyone knew he always drove to work and back. With Kathy's little car as spare, he'd no need ever to nick a bike.

'You should have locked it,' Brenda said wearily.

'Hell, I did! The bike stalls were full when I came on duty, so I padlocked it to the guard rail. The chain wasn't damaged. The effing rail tore away, didden it?'

'Damage to Railway Property,' jeered Dusty Miller. 'They'll have you on that.'

'When exactly was this?' Lee asked, suspicion forming in the back of his mind.

'Near a week back. Friday night, Sat'day morning.'

Yes, thought Lee. He had reason enough to remember that night. While he was in the sidings loading Egerton's lifeless body into his car, somebody could have been nicking Norman's mountain bike hard by the station – someone else who'd come off the same train? And watched what he was up to in the sidings?

He couldn't believe any of his near neighbours would have stolen a bicycle to get home: hereabouts everyone was in bed with the lights out by half past ten.

So could it have been the intruder who broke into the house two days later?

Godden claimed to have seen him around earlier. Had he been trailing Egerton, stealing the bike and keeping a watch on the house where the scientist had taken refuge? He could have left the bike hidden in the hedge until the police notified Norman where to pick it up. Certainly their intruder had been incapable of riding it away.

His head pounding, Lee pictured the man following his car back to the house. He'd have been pedalling like a madman to keep up, although Lee, after all that unaccustomed drink, was keeping his speed well down. He seemed to remember there'd been no headlights coming up in his driving mirror. But the wavering lamp of a distant bicycle – that he might not have noticed.

That must have been what happened. How else could

the man have discovered where Egerton was taken? It was lucky the police regarded bicycle theft as too trivial to pursue, otherwise they might have picked up a connection with this house earlier. And if they'd come snooping at that point, God only knew what they might have walked in on!

He sweated at the thought. He had to shut Norman up before Kathy started wondering if the bike had belonged to 'Johnson' and imagined Lee had knocked him off it, accounting for the man's injuries. It was bad enough to have so much truth to keep hidden from her, without other fantasies heaped on top.

Finally he managed to herd them, sated with coffee and sandwiches, to the door. Even there, Harker lingered, shamefaced. He punched Lee's arm in a matey way. 'No grudge over ribbing you about the overrun, eh? You know we've all done it sometime. In the end, marking your record won't make a shit's difference to any plans you've got for the future.'

Now he tells me, Lee thought; but it was too late to feel anger over it. More shattering things had happened since then.

The shift had meant well by rallying here, but sympathy got you nowhere. Jenny was still missing and there'd been no reliable sightings of her. Stevie was still condemned to a further five weeks of not stirring from his cot. Now Egerton had scarpered, so he'd no bargaining power left if the kidnappers got in touch. And there'd been nothing since that awful little bundle of blond hair that came for Tim through the post, without any demand for ransom. He'd grabbed it before Kathy could see it; still dared not let her know.

It was locked away in his toolbox in the garage: all he had left of his lovely little girl.

He must let the police see it, *some* of it. He could never let her go entirely.

Chapter Twenty-Three

Detective Superintendent Mike Yeadings was getting more than a little tired of Special Branch. Though remaining perfectly willing for his team to liaise with them, he found their officious manner irritating. While divulging no useful information, they seemed to be waiting for pearls to drop in their laps.

He was glad he hadn't disclosed to them his brief uneasiness about Z's relationship with Max Harris. Since Salmon's suspicion of her leaking information had proved groundless, he found he missed her input for the major case. He rang the CID room and called her up to his office. She brought with her a page of notes on the security courier they had both interviewed in hospital, with the added news that, since twice being questioned, he had consulted a firm of solicitors. And they were the ones who had recently instructed Paula Mott to conduct the defence of their clients in court.

'Ah well,' Yeadings commented mildly. 'Possible storm clouds on the horizon, in that case. Actually it was something else I wanted to see you about. I appear to have mislaid young Max's mobile number.' He moved the papers on his desk in a vaguely helpless manner which didn't fool Z for a moment. The Boss was never genuinely helpless, and she guessed Max had never given him the number in the first place.

However, it seemed any breach between the two was mended, so there'd be little harm done if she complied. Max could choose whether he accepted the call or not when it came up on his screen.

She reeled off the required number and watched as the Superintendent wrote it in his daybook. 'Is that all, sir?'

'For the moment, Z, thank you. But don't leave the building. I may need you shortly. The others could be off chasing rainbows.'

So did that mean she was to be taken back on the Egerton case? – one which now appeared to involve the missing child as well.

Having dismissed Z, Yeadings pressed out Max's mobile number. There was no answer, but the ringing continued. He left a text message: *pls contact yeadings asap*. A few minutes later his direct line rang.

'Harris here,' Max told him. 'You rang, sir?' He sounded the perfect butler, and it wasn't lost on Yeadings.

'Never mind the silver salver for the moment, Max. Where are you, and what mischief are you getting up to now?'

'Touring Essex with a local stringer. Sniffing the air for something slightly off, such as a microbiologist might take an interest in,' he admitted frankly.

'Ah.'

'And wishing I had a photograph of Piers Timothy Egerton to show to the locals to confirm he used to work near here.'

He heard a faint rasping as Yeadings ran a hand over his chin. The photograph – an old one from student days, because it seemed he had avoided cameras ever after – was to be on the press release next day.

'H'm. Have you discreet access if I fax you one?'

'Why not the local nick at Halstead?'

'I'll tell them to authorise you access.'

'Perfect.' That offer invited cooperation, Max decided, and plunged in. 'I've come across an Animal Rights group here who might have been bothering him. They've been making threats against a hush-hush medical institute a few miles away.'

'That sounds possible. Who put you on to Essex in the first place?'

'Sorry, sir: privileged information. I have to protect my sources.'

Yeadings grunted; he'd expected nothing else. 'You'll be there overnight?'

Max hesitated. Yeadings had made the question sound innocent, but it was a *non sequitur*, therefore suspect. 'Can't avoid it,' he admitted.

'Right. Well, keep me updated.'

'So have you any information to trade with mine?' Max enquired. Yeadings stayed silent, grimly smiling unseen.

Max sighed. 'I know the answer: you're the one who asks the questions. Thanks, anyway.' And he rang off.

'You'll be lucky to find anyone awake at the station,' Jamie Carr warned him when Max returned and explained where he was bound for. But he put the little green Toyota in gear and headed for the police building.

Inside, an initial blocking at Reception by the constable on duty cleared when a uniform sergeant burst from the back room with fresh instructions. Max was ushered into a nearby deserted office and accorded the freedom of the fax machine. The copy came through, he signed for it, thanked the sergeant and rejoined Carr in the Toyota.

There was no need to request a list of possible *Release* members from the station, because Jamie's notebooks held the names of all those charged with offences throughout the area. 'Crowd of turnips and muttonheads,' was his opinion. 'They'd sacrifice the animals fast enough if they had a terminal disease that research might cure.'

'More likely sacrifice their grannies. Humans count for less to them.' It was better he leave Carr ignorant of the nature of Egerton's research. If whispers were true, then the implications were massive.

The gospel of inevitable climate change was spreading, with acceptance that by 2050 Britain would be suffering coastal erosion, increased flooding inland, disastrous storms and long summers above 30 degrees. But still it would be comparatively temperate, and further mass immigration could be expected from areas worse affected, swamping the existing population: extra mouths to feed at a time when food, mainly imported, was no longer available from earlier sources already scorched or inundated.

Even now, Max knew, secret training was under way

to deal with outbreaks of civil unrest in a climate of cut-throat survivorship. In the worst possible scenario, a silent weapon for use on crowd control would be welcomed. Could this be the motivation behind microbiological research such as Egerton claimed he was engaged on? The Russian Polonium 210 deaths had been horrific enough, and apparently the work of a state agency, but it was surely unthinkable that anything on a similar level could be considered in a democracy like Britain.

Jamie Carr was still grumbling about his present minor issue: the letter bombs mailed to vivisectionist workers, and the lasting effect on local wildlife of earlier raids to release mink from fur farms. 'Vicious little buggers, if you ask me. As if we haven't enough native vermin.'

'A pie and a pint?' Max suggested lightly, to change the subject. 'Then I'm turning in. It's been a long day.'

He managed eventually to lose Carr at the Talbot Arms, borrowing the list of known *Release* members which the stringer wrote out in longhand in the bar while sipping his real ale.

'Bedtime reading,' Max promised, waving the paper at him before disappearing into the residential part of the hotel.

It was barely ten o'clock by then, but even Carr had a home to go to and a wife who'd demand a dozen reasons for him staying out late. Also, it was the night for putting out the recycling bins, so his early return was vital.

Max removed his shoes and stretched out on the bed, his mind returning to the disturbing thoughts of global warming. It was one that often exercised him, the threat to all forms of animal and plant life on Earth. People were waking up to the dangers too late, preoccupied by vigorous consumerism and warring tribal factions. There were times when he saw worldwide disaffections, whether political or nominally religious, as symptomatic of a repressed fear that the planet was already doomed.

It must briefly have been like this in 1962, when the Cuban missile crisis had the world holding its breath, waiting for nuclear war. That was before he was born, and nobody seemed to take account of it any more. But by now one thing had become plain: there was no need for artificial means of wholesale destruction when the environment alone could eventually achieve that.

He sighed, sat upright and gave himself a mental shake, pushing his specs up to the bridge of his nose with his right-hand forefinger. Dwelling on such apocalyptic visions was futile when he had closer problems to deal with. Hadn't Voltaire suggested the right conclusion to a succession of dilemmas? – *Il faut cultiver nos jardins.* His present plot to dig over was the list Jamie Carr had written out. Several of the addresses lay within a thirty -mile radius. Since he was disinclined to sleep, he would scout them out under cover of darkness. And next day go visiting known members of *Release*. It was only a dim hope, but perhaps one of these people might know something about a little girl held prisoner as a move against her supposed father.

* * *

Jenny knelt on the ground outside the kitchen door and fumbled to tie the laces of her trainers in a bow. The wicked witch stood beside her, ready to snatch her hand again and drag her away from the house. Although it was a prison, Jenny didn't want to leave. It had felt safer while she kept close to the man, because the witch was scared of him. Now, there was no one to come between, and although she hadn't pushed her into the oven like the gingerbread witch did, there was no way of knowing what this witch would do. She'd muttered something about a long walk, and soon it would be getting really dark. Already, after sundown, it was cooler. Jenny shivered in her T-shirt and shorts.

'Hurry,' the woman hissed. She drew the child past Karel's old car parked beside the cottage. The overgrown thorn hedge tore against her dress.

She should have learnt to drive when Karel offered, but it had been so cosy always sitting there beside him, being looked after: a welcome break from all the housework and sewing for his puppets. If she could handle the car now, it would have been so much easier to get the child away and lose her on the other side of the county.

To be quiet they kept to the grass verge until they were well away from the cottage. There were no made-up paths here and no street lighting like Jenny was used to at home. She stumbled on in the dark, jerked along by the witch's harsh hand. She recalled the row of little wooden figures hanging on strings along one wall of the witch's bedroom, and wondered fearfully if they had ever been children like her. Maybe that's what she'd be turned into in the end. Just her wooden bones left, and strings for the witch to pull her along by.

One following the other, two huge birds swooped suddenly down from a tree to rush heavily over their heads. Owls, she guessed: like Wol in the Pooh books. But these were real birds, quite enormous, and they were hunters. It was scary being out in the wilds at night.

'I want to go back,' she pleaded, trying to pull her hand loose.

'You're going home,' the witch argued, gripping her more tightly, but Jenny didn't believe her. It was all a trick, and Jenny knew that sooner or later the witch meant to eat the flesh off her.

Pavel Hlavacek grunted, half asleep, turned over and squinted into the light. He must have left it on when he came to bed. His head felt muzzy, as if a heavy cold were coming on. He tried to sit up and the room tilted round him. He looked down and the grubby cuff of a shirt sleeve came feebly into focus. He was still dressed, sprawled on the bed covers. It was years since Slivovic had affected him like this.

That fool woman! She'd let something noxious get in the goulash; gone gathering fungi in the woods and mistaken a poisonous toadstool for a mushroom.

But it wasn't his stomach cramping. There was no nausea: just his head, this swollen, drugged feeling, making his limbs lifeless and feeble.

Drugged feeling, he thought again, and remembered the sleeping pills Jana sometimes took at night. Each day they'd fed one or two, crushed up in milk, to the child to keep her quiet.

But use them on him? She wouldn't dare! And why would she want to? Now that Karel had abandoned her, he was all she had: her own blood brother. Had the cretinous woman actually meant to disable him?

Slowly he moved his legs to the floor, stumbled a few steps and steadied himself against the far wall. He made it to the bathroom and swilled his face and arms under the cold tap. He dried off, threw the towel on the floor and swayed towards the stairs. Leaning on the banister rail, he went down step by step. The cottage was in darkness, but pale moonlight lit the kitchen. The table had never been cleared of their supper things. Jana always washed up and made everything tidy before she went to bed. So she was ill too.

He went into the passage and shouted for her to come down. There was no answer. He couldn't face pulling himself up all those stairs to go and find her. Back in the kitchen he slumped on a chair, and then suddenly knew what she had done.

Lined up, beside the door into the yard, there should have been her outdoor shoes and the child's small white trainers. Jana never missed out on changing into slippers when she came indoors. And all the little girl's things had been taken away from her.

He couldn't believe they would dare to do this – go out at night and leave him alone. Not unless they meant to run away!

He thought of the child, a little pink and blond

creature, so tender to the touch, so unspoilt and sweet, like a fragile porcelain doll. She was for him to make his own. Losing her would be unbearable.

How could Jana do this? In time she would have come round to understanding he had needs as a man. Soon she would have passed the child over to him. It had not been so difficult to persuade her to snatch little Jenny. So already she was halfway to giving in.

Couldn't Jana remember when they were both children? Those magical, exciting nights when he had possessed his sister, almost as young then as this little angel, but never, never, half so pretty.

They couldn't get away. He wouldn't let them.

He had a sudden wild fear that maybe Karel had come back and they'd all gone off together, to be a family, leaving him behind. But then surely they would have taken the car, and it still stood there, a dark shape feebly outlined by moonlight, close to the hedge.

He stood by the window, staring out into the night. Of course, the car! He could follow, catch them up and take the child away by force. He knew she wanted him. She had those flirty eyes. No peeping then through a wretched hole in the wall, but holding her, touching, enjoying, breathing on her and feeling the tiny heart beating under his hands.

He wrenched open the unlocked back door and staggered out into the dark, feeling in his pocket for the car keys. His mind seemed to be clearing a little. He felt ready now. He would hunt them down and show them just who he was.

Chapter Twenty-Four

Superintendent Yeadings swallowed the last of his cold coffee and stared at the small area of wood grain showing between files stacked on his desk He wasn't happy about Max Harris ploughing his lone furrow out in rural Essex. Having been warned off interfering in the Thames Valley search for Egerton, it seemed he was continuing to show interest in the missing scientist. It was too risky; he hadn't the necessary training. There were enough complications in pursuing this case without having to explain away an injured civilian crowding in. And just what leads had drawn him to the area where Egerton had worked? That was an aspect the Security Services claimed to have covered and they wouldn't take kindly to press intervention.

Max had been surprisingly open about his whereabouts. There could be a good reason for it. Yeadings had a feeling in his bones that Max could have stolen a march on the official search.

One hand hovered above the internal phone while the other rubbed uneasily over his chin. A moment's hesitation, and then he lifted the receiver and pressed in the number for the CID office. 'Z there?' he demanded as the receiver was lifted. She came on the line and answered instantly. 'Boss?'

'Um. Message for you. Max'll likely not be home tonight.'

There was no response.

'So he said,' Yeadings added.

Zyczynski frowned. When had the Boss started acting go-between for Max and herself? There was some ulterior message here. Yeadings was up to something. Best go along with it. 'Did he say where he would be?' she asked cautiously.

Yeadings' voice came over lighter. 'Out in rural Essex, Halstead area. Snooping, as I understand. Well, that's all, Z. You can knock off for the night now. Nothing seems to be coming up here.'

A slight emphasis on the word 'here'; or did she imagine it? 'Thanks, sir. Goodnight.'

Halstead was not an area she knew; except once or twice driving through on her way to the east coast. And Max had never referred to it in any context. She searched in Google and brought up a map of Essex.

Special Branch had mentioned the county in connection with the missing scientist, Piers Egerton. He'd worked at some kind of medical research station out there, hadn't he? Oh, Max, Max! What are you sniffing after? The Boss isn't happy about you being out on a limb.

So was the limb strong enough to bear the weight of two? She'd be a fool not to take the hint and chase after Max, at least to see he didn't get into trouble with the local constabulary. He was a big boy now and he'd survived enough rough and tumble on his travels, so she wouldn't insult him by acting the nanny. All the same, her warrant card might come in handy if tangling with Security earned him gutter-press treatment. And the Boss had told her to sign off for tonight.

She went out to check the fuel level in her car, set the Satnav system and headed off east.

Jenny stumbled in the tussocky grass and the witch yanked her up roughly. The suppressed sobs rose into a wail. 'I want my mummy and daddy!'

'That's where we're going, child.'

'I can't walk any more. I think I've got a blister.'

Jana tried to see the time, but her watch dial was dark. Even the thin crescent moon was hidden now behind cloud. There was nothing for it but she must carry the child or they'd miss the last bus at the crossroads.

Jenny screamed as she lifted her under the armpits. She beat at her chest. Distressed, Jana shook her hard and it shocked her into silence.

What would Karel have done? He was good with the children he'd met through members of the group. He used to tell them fairy stories and pull faces like the ones on his puppets. This big man with the soft voice and the broken accent could hold them spellbound. Perhaps she should try that.

'Be quiet,' she cautioned, 'or the Big Bad Wolf will come and get you.' She felt the child shudder in her arms. Her knees came up and desperately gripped the woman's gaunt waist. Jenny hid her face in the coarse cotton of the witch's dress. A smell of the kitchen came off her, like the lumpy stew she'd been made to eat.

The child was small, but a surprising weight. She seemed to get heavier with every step Jana took. She couldn't keep this up for long. If they didn't reach the crossroads bus stop in time they'd have to find somewhere to shelter overnight and start off again in the morning. If only there was a farm cart or van still on the lane. When you didn't need a lift they were forever trundling along here with their loads of fruit or hay, so that you had to draw back against the hedge to let them pass.

Just as she felt she could go no farther there came a low sound behind, the drone of a car's engine steadily growing closer. She turned and saw headlight beams bouncing towards her as the vehicle took the potholed macadam: some late-working labourer heading at last for home.

She stepped out into the centre of the lane, holding the child to her with one arm, and raised the other to wave the car down.

Max wasn't having much success with locating some of the addresses. Satellite navigation was fine with officially named streets on the edge of town, but not with these isolated cottages at the back of beyond. He'd imagined the zealots of Animal Rights would mostly be townies, the sort who'd pressured the government into a ban on hunting. Apparently the movement had different adherents hereabouts, and that could imply strong opposition to the local siting of the secure medical research centre. *Not in my back yard.*

This meant its existence wasn't as secret as intended. Egerton couldn't have been ignorant of the propaganda being circulated against the establishment and scientists such as him. It wouldn't have been easy, working there by day while living in a hostile social environment. Little wonder he'd appeared so uncertain of his own intentions.

Max peered into the darkness. He'd arrived at another dead end. Ahead of him lay long, low buildings centred on a concrete yard stacked with wooden crates. There were no lights on. The gate to the complex was padlocked. From the smell he guessed it was another fruit-packing centre: nothing for it but to turn around and find an alternative minor road.

His mobile started vibrating in his jacket pocket. He opened it and read Z's number. 'Hello love,' he said. 'What's up?'

'I've arrived at the Talbot in Halstead and I've taken a double room, in case you're interested. Or is this an all-night jag you're on?'

He didn't answer at once. His Rosebud stalking him? This was something new.

'I get it,' he said slowly. 'Yeadings has put you on to me.'

'In a manner of speaking, yes. Actually I'm my own woman at the moment. If you prefer to be your own man and stay aloof…'

'On my way back,' he offered promptly. 'Give me fifteen minutes.' He switched the mobile off.

He had sounded eager. When over an hour went by she began to wonder. Another twenty minutes and she made up her mind. Something bad could have happened to Max. She'd need to get out there and see what it was.

Dazzled by the headlights, Jana stepped towards the car, set the child down and took her hand again, but Jenny pulled free. The driver was getting out and the child ran towards him.

With horror, Jana recognised the burly shape of her brother. All motors sounded much the same to her, and in the dark she hadn't seen it was Karel's car until too late.

'No!' she cried, but her tired legs refused to take her forward. Rooted to the spot, she watched horrified as Pavel swung the little girl up high over his head, roaring with rage or laughter. She couldn't tell which, but it was terrible.

He shouldn't be here. There'd been enough pills in his supper to keep him asleep until dawn. They had always worked for her. Now she saw he'd be different. Bigger, healthier, he needed drugging more deeply.

He was shouting at her, calling her names she hadn't heard since she was a child running from the military. And now he was bundling the little girl into the back of the car, covering her with the rug they'd used when she was snatched from the Leisure Centre.

And still she couldn't move, wanting so badly to stop

him taking the child, and yet terrified of his anger.

He slammed the door shut and reached inside the front for an object on the floor. Then he was coming at her, brandishing some kind of heavy stick. In her imagination she could hear it cracking against her skull, feel her brain shudder from the impact.

She spun on her heel and blundered towards the thin copse behind. In between was a hidden ditch, and she went down, landing on elbows and face among brambles. As she scrabbled to sit up she glimpsed him towering over her, waving an axe handle, and she was reminded of farmers, back home when she was a child, flailing the harvested wheat.

She covered her face and bent her legs up close, rolled in a ball. The stick came thudding down but it missed her, landing in the thick tangle of undergrowth. She sobbed aloud and heard his caught breath as he drew back to aim again.

This time she was ready, and when the blow exploded on the brambles she reached out and tugged at the axe handle, making him lose balance. His arms made windmills as he tried to regain a foothold, and then one boot slid in and the heavy body followed it, crunching down only inches from her.

But at last she could move. While he floundered she clawed her way up and was away, the brambles tearing at her skin through the cotton dress, but she made it up the bank and headed towards the darker mass of trees away from the road. She fled through them, lurching against low boughs and tripping on exposed roots invisible in the dark. The only sound was her own soughing breath and then, as she tired, the crashing of a heavy body forcing its way through brushwood behind her.

She must go on running and running until she was done. If she drew him far enough away it could give the child time to escape.

Back in the car, Jenny started screaming, in short, staccato pulses like jetting blood.

Heading posthaste for Halstead and his lover, Max managed to lose himself again, not aided by the yokel humour of reversed signposts. He reset the Satnav for the Talbot hotel, and calm-voiced 'Doris' took over again.

Remote cottages he passed showed little light. You couldn't blame hardworking labourers for shutting down early. For the second time he approached the high walls and electronically guarded gates of the place Egerton must have worked at.

As he slowed he observed the tall pole where a mounted camera pivotted and focused on his car. Under present circumstances Special Branch would doubtless be visiting him tomorrow to question his intentions. He drove on.

At last came some sign of human life: a car, its headlights set on beam, was pulled up at the side of the lane. Curious, he slowed in passing and peered inside; saw a small white face pressed against the window; heard screams, regular as a high-pitched pager.

There seemed to be only the one child, alone in the car.

He braked and clambered out, heart pounding. He couldn't reach her because the rear doors were locked. But the key was still in the ignition, with the engine left running. Who the hell would abandon a child like this in the dark? He reached in and reversed the rear locking.

The child was rigid, arms tight against her chest, fists balled. His sudden appearance had shocked her into silence.

'Jenny?' he whispered. 'Jenny Barber?'

She stared at him with wide, scared eyes.

'Jenny, I know your daddy who drives trains. And your little brother, Stevie. He's not been well, but he's getting better now. You want to go home and see him, don't you?'

It took minutes to get her to speak. 'Who left you here?' he kept asking. 'Where are they?' At any moment the people who had left her might come back and catch them.

'Mummy,' she whimpered at last. 'I want my mummy.'

'Of course you do. Would you be happier in my car? You don't want to stay here, do you?'

She let him lift her out and carry her across. As he laid her on the rear seat he heard shouting from the darkness beyond a nearby spinney: a man's voice, furious, and a woman's fearfully pleading, ending in a strangled scream. 'Who the…?'

'The Wicked…Witch,' Jenny whispered, covering her mouth with both hands. She was crouched up small, as if waiting to be beaten.

He could drive away, keep the child safe, or – but

then there were the other two. It had gone suddenly quiet. Anything could have happened. He had to go and see.

'Don't make a sound,' he warned as he eased the door shut and turned towards where the voices had been.

The man was coming at him. He looked enormous and he carried some kind of cudgel. Not funny, Max told himself. His only weapon was a heavy flashlight.

This was no time for introductions. 'I heard voices,' Max challenged. 'A woman. Is she in trouble?'

The man halted, then came rushing at him, the stick raised. He roared and Max flinched. The man was out of his mind, almost upon him, and then he pulled up short. Max could just make out the way ahead. Between them was a ditch, too wide to leap over, but at least it gave temporary protection.

Discretion, the better part of valour, he reminded himself. 'I'm ringing the police,' he shouted, retreating to the road and scrabbling for his mobile phone. He had turned it off after speaking to Z, and now he found that at a mile or so from that point the signal was weak. He was wasting valuable time repeating his threat while the big man was clambering down, struggling through the ditch, was almost out and raising the stick which Max now saw was an axe handle. He backed away; lifted the heavy torch in self-defence.

He heard the first blow whistle past, wildly aimed at knee level. Then the man had found a purchase on the bank with one leg braced, and lunged out again. The axe handle caught Max across his middle, flooring him and knocking all his breath out. His glasses slid from his nose and fell to the ground. He was helpless without them. The torch had disappeared.

He was crouched, feebly searching about him, as the man suddenly bellowed beside him. The cudgel fell from his hands and he swayed on his feet.

Over him stood a tall, gaunt woman. As Max watched she crumpled to her knees. Blood was pouring down her face from a great gash in her left temple. Her tangled hair was slick with it. Both hands were still clasped together but the knife stayed plunged in the man's back. His body jerked spasmodically and he gasped for air. Then, a fine trickle of blood ran from his mouth and his head fell sideways. At the same moment the woman collapsed too.

Sitting in his own car, cuddling the child on his knees and with the radio playing soft music, Max was prepared to wait as long as need be until they were found. He had left the man's body where it fell, and he'd had the devil's own job to get the woman across the ditch and stretched out inside the other car, warmed by his jacket. He'd bandaged her head temporarily with cotton pads from his first aid kit. She was still unconscious, probably badly concussed, but hadn't vomited. There were countless other scratches to her face, arms and shoulders caused by running through the wood. Her dark cotton dress was shredded, one sleeve torn almost off. But she was breathing and he had found a pulse.

He hadn't dared care for her alongside the child, who

was petrified at the sight of her injuries. This, it seemed, was the one she'd called the Wicked Witch. But, if so, what did that make the man?

There'd be plenty that needed explaining, and he was glad that wasn't up to him. Let the police do their thing. He'd had more than enough of it tonight. Some hero he'd proved himself to be! – couldn't even drive the bloody car back, because without his specs he was blind as a bat in a spotlight.

It was his Rosebud who arrived first, guided in by his directions of half a mile short of the medical research station. She came over as a real hard nut, snapping questions. 'Max, you took an awful risk.'.

'Got results all the same,' he bragged mildly, and she burnt him up with her glare.

Following on the police came two ambulances. Max found himself bundled into the same one as little Jenny, which seemed to reassure her.

The injured woman was driven off for emergency hospital care. One paramedic stayed with the body until a doctor could arrive to declare life extinct. From a white van, equipment was being unloaded to set up a tent and secure the area as a crime scene.

'Don't imagine,' Zyczynski warned severely, before the ambulance doors were slammed on him, 'that you'll get off lightly over this. You could have been killed.'

Chapter Twenty-Five

Two days later, over a late breakfast, Max opened a bulky package postmarked Thame. He unpacked it and sat a long time pondering, with the weathered black briefcase across his knees. The morning light picked out worn silver lettering on the leather flap: INCE. He wasn't sure what he would do with its contents. Or if he ever would be ready to decide.

What he had started to read appalled him, although he had been prepared.

It's not for me, he thought. There's nothing in my remit that compels me to do anything about this. What had Lee Barber expected, sending this to him? It was because he'd felt powerless. As he, Max, now did.

This was the business of VIPs. His concern was with little people, their ordinary, mundane lives. Not that their ups and downs weren't mountainous to them. But those he could cope with, write about, raise a wry smile here, a fresh hope there. Light stuff; nothing global.

He thought about Lee Barber, train driver, in the grand scheme of things a nobody. But the salt of the earth, loyal to family and job, a good citizen; at the same time a stranger he'd met only once, when Jenny was returned. Apart from that, there'd been just that earlier hoarse message from a public payphone, and now this thing of Egerton's which he wanted nothing of.

And Egerton was dead: that clever, feckless man choosing his own way out. It was Yeadings who, after the suicide, had passed on the letter marked 'Strictly Private' and addressed to him. Police had found it in the hired car beside the cold body. Egerton had gassed himself with carbon monoxide, parked among trees half a mile from the entrance to his workplace, registering a protest against what he had been drawn into doing. *And leaving decisions for others to deal with.*

Max stood, letting the papers slide to the floor. He went across to the window and looked down. Outside, Zyczynski was washing her car, vigorously sponging the roof with hot soapy water.

A sixth sense warned her he was watching. She stared back coolly before lifting a rubber-gloved hand in acknowledgement. It was she who'd brought up the special delivery package, and she'd asked no questions about it.

There had been so much to clear up before Essex police let him go, holding him as a possible suspect for child abduction and murder by stabbing with a bread knife. He'd taken just so much questioning and then he'd walked out of the interrogation. Superintendent Yeadings had sent DS Beaumont to bring him in, Z having already gone back to give her own account of what happened.

When he reached home, a line of light had still

shown under her apartment door. He had let himself in and found her in the bathroom, wrapped in a towel and patting cream on her face. He touched her lightly on the shoulder and asked, 'Rosebud, how are we?'

'I'm fine,' she said. 'Congratulations, *sleuth.*' There was a brittle edge to her voice.

Later, in bed, physically close but still with a coolness between, she had taunted him. 'Maybe I should try writing a piece for the dailies.'

For a second he froze, then, 'Why not? Let's set no limits to what we do.'

And then the distance had disappeared. They were both laughing in each other's arms, together again, complete; back to their accepted position of separate professional lives and a shared private one. That much had come out all right.

At the window, Max grinned down at her and went back to his dilemma over Egerton's confession. Its most disturbing fact was that he had killed a man, albeit accidentally and in self-defence. It even seemed possible that Barber had been party to his disposal of the body at sea, and reasonable to suppose that the dead man was the husband poor Jana Semikova believed had abandoned her.

Was it wrong for him to believe she'd known enough grief without being told that her Karel was dead? The manslaughter charge against her would not be heard until late in the autumn, but when all the details were revealed there was every chance her plea of self-defence would be accepted.

And what of Barber's complicity in Egerton's crime? Nothing could be proved, once the damning suicide letter was destroyed. For everyone's sake Max should make sure it would never be seen once he'd read it.

And now these papers covering Egerton's research had turned up. In his mind's eye Max pictured Lee Barber picking up the briefcase from Railway Lost Property, mailing the package on and feeling an enormous burden slide off his back. Not entirely gone, but passed on elsewhere: to Max.

He didn't want Egerton's problem dropped on him: he was equally unwilling to do anything about it.

And yet shouldn't he? What about the press being a public safeguard for all those ordinary, unsuspecting people out there? Shouldn't they know what was secretly being done in their name?

'Conscience doth make cowards of us all', he recalled. Hamlet had it right. But what a bloody end he contrived for everyone when he finally opted for action.

Perhaps the wisest move would be to consign the evil thing to the flames. There must be copies of it elsewhere, but it lay in other hands to use or refuse what it contained. Leave it to government conscience, Fate, or God, or whatever you called the guiding hand behind the cosmos, to make the final decision.

It's not for me, Max finally convinced himself. Like Lee Barber, I'm made for smaller acts. I too shall merely pass it on. Into a locked vault with a lost key, for history to ponder…if ever it comes to light again.

He had a sudden feeling of *déja vu, déja fait*. It was like picking up chess pieces spilt over the floor and setting them all back in their right places. As though no real damage had been done.

Or had it? Only next day the question stared up at him from the front page of the *Guardian*. Professor Clara Foulkes wasn't quite a household name, but in the last New Year's Honours list she'd achieved a DBE, presumably for her services to Science. There were two photographs; one showed a covered stretcher being lifted into an ambulance, at the rear entrance of a West End hotel. The other was a studio portrait of a handsome, grey-haired woman with a determined face.

Yes, that is how he remembered her at their only meeting. It had been two years ago at a reception given by the Royal Society at Carlton House Terrace.

Dame Clara was accustomed to mixing with important people, and now she had elected to join the distinguished dead.

In the blurb below the portrait Max recognised a journalistic nudge. Without declaring a connection, the writer commented on the coincidence of two well-known scientists' presumed suicides taking place within three days. Piers Timothy Egerton, found dead from carbon monoxide poisoning in a hired car in Essex, had once been a student of Dame Clara at Cambridge. Both had followed distinguished careers in microbiology and deserted academia for private research.

It was the word 'private' that intrigued Max. Egerton had given Barber to suppose he worked for the government. Had he lied about that, or had he been hoodwinked himself? At some point the earlier department had been closed down and Egerton's project relocated to Essex. Had Dame Clara taken over control at this point? And had she intended the research results to be auctioned on a global market for weapons of mass destruction?

The possible inference was overwhelming. It could mean that, once aware of Egerton's absconding with his research papers, and every day expecting revelations in the press, Dame Clara had committed suicide, assuming she would be named and the game finally up?

So it appeared that the government had had wiser counsels about such monstrous research and Egerton been hoodwinked, unaware he had then become part of a private money-making initiative.

This brought another dimension to Max's present dilemma regarding the briefcase's contents. They could never be made common knowledge, but sent in confidence to the Head of Security Services.

Chapter Twenty-Six

Lee Barber's step was lighter. He felt like a condemned man who'd been granted a last-minute reprieve and saw all the old familiar things as vibrantly new and vital. Kathy, Jenny and Stevie were a fresh joy to him each time he returned to his secure and glowing home. Back at work, he had never enjoyed driving as much as he did in the next few weeks, until gradually it became commonplace. But through it there remained a shadow of the passing stranger who for a time had come closer than any other living creature, through shared guilt and mortal fear.

Then, without warning, disaster struck. On Early Turn, he was driving the first semi-fast of the day to Birmingham Snow Hill, its carriages sparsely filled until West Ruislip. At dawn, the sky had been pearly, and by 6.20 a golden light slanted through trees thinned along the track in readiness for winter snows. A beautiful day, the sort when it was good to be alive.

Pulling out of Gerrards Cross, Lee settled for the straight run to Seer Green, only one corner for slowing before the open track crossing to the lower woods. He came on it steadily, conscious of a figure waiting among the trees for him to pass.

Then horror, as the man walked out, faced the oncoming train and started forward in a robotic, plodding walk. Lee frantically toggled the two-tone horn. Was the man deaf as well as blind?

Neither, he saw, appalled. Already he'd slapped the emergency brake plunger. The juddering was hideous, but ineffectual as the man still advanced slowly towards him. An agonising, impotent wait, and then it all happened so fast that he heard only the sickening crunch as the windscreen cracked, cutting out the view ahead, but he thought the man had stumbled, falling sideways before he was hit.

The train ran on for some five hundred yards.

As it was slowing to a stand, Lee called the signaller, briefly to report a collision. 'Possible fatality,' he ground out.

'Well, it's your call. Are you prepared to go back and see what you hit?'

'I guess so.'

'OK, Driver. I'll get Emergency Services on their way.'

Lee picked up the public address handset, steadied his voice and warned his passengers there would be an unavoidable delay. Then he picked up his hi-viz jacket and Bardic lamp. Once the signaller confirmed that the line had been protected, he left the cab, swinging down to the ballast and running, heart beating wildly in his throat, the full length of the train and beyond.

'Never run on the lineside: always walk steadily and stay calm,' he reminded himself of the mantra from his training days. But he couldn't be calm, adrenalin surging through to his legs.

The body had disappeared. He had to thrash around in the undergrowth before he came on it at the foot of a birch tree, yards from the track.

It wasn't how it should have happened. He knew from grisly stories told back at the depot. Normally you never saw much; little more than a sudden blur coming at you from the platform's edge. And the force of the collision like an explosion. Usually there was little to be collected afterwards.

It happened from time to time, but to other drivers. He had even asked himself how he would have reacted in their place. Well, now he knew, faced by the bloodied heap of cloth and flesh his train had trashed. He had turned to stone, couldn't move.

He wanted to shout, swear at the body, furious that the bloody fool couldn't get it right, do it the proper way. It was as though the man had challenged him, coming at him like a matador at a bull. Made it personal.

The body wasn't severed; it still had a head, though battered almost featureless. When Lee ventured close he saw the man's eyes flicker open. No accusation, simply despair and fear.

Lee closed his own eyes. He had called in the incident as a collision. Now the signaller would need to know whether the man was dead.

As good as, surely. Every instinct told Lee to return to his train, rate the man a goner. He would be, by the time anyone came. He was so small and broken. How could life still flicker on?

But the dying man was watching. Behind the stranger's eyes another image began to merge in and take over. *Tim Egerton* looking out at him. This suffering man was Tim again, ravaged by conscience and guilt over some wrong bitterly regretted; troubled to death.

He had to stay by him. At the end, he'd not been there for Tim.

It could take only a few more seconds. Lee knelt alongside. 'My name's Lee,' he told him. 'What's yours?' He reached down and took a shattered hand into his own bigger palm.

A small bubble of blood seeped from the man's mouth. He coughed weakly and a flow started. Lee bent closer and thought he made out a word.

'Freddy?' Was that it?

'Fer...di...'

'Ferdy, then. It's all right, mate. I'll stay with you till the ambulance gets here.'

No one could arrive for at least twenty minutes, and he ought to talk to his passengers, reassure them, but he couldn't leave Ferdy to die alone. Not even after the eyes went vacant and the bleeding tailed off.

When they came, there was a small orange-clad army: men and women officious with laptops, mobile phones and clipboards. But, for all their self-importance, they didn't get to run the circus. It was a sudden death. The police were in charge.

After Lee's statement to the police, his manager led

him away. 'My car's up on the road nearby. The On-Call DSM will take over your train now and he'll get your keys back to you later. You won't be requiring them for a while anyway.

'However, I do need you to give me a detailed account of what happened. This is a potential crime scene now, so it's a lot more important than just rattling off an internal staff report. But no worries; we can go through it together. So, let's get it all down in writing before the full shock hits you.'

Hits, Lee thought. Yes, that's how it feels. I've been sort of mugged, a bit numb all over. He followed Bascombe through the thin stretch of hilly woodland and onto a quiet residential road. Looking up he saw a sky of innocent cobalt. He remembered – not so long back – thinking 'A perfect early autumn day; it's good to be alive.' A lifetime ago.

'His name was Ferdy,' he said. 'He wanted out of it, poor sod.'

They followed a time-honoured procedure. Lee was off-track for three days, reduced to light duties at the depot. He'd undergone the required tests for drugs and alcohol, providing a urine sample which was divided into two bottles, sealed, labelled, signed and dated; one specimen to be sent for analysis, and the other retained as back-up.

There must be a coroner's inquest sometime, and the idea gave him crawling caterpillars in his guts. He wasn't sure how he'd stand up to questioning in court. There was so much extraneous stuff that could come out if he got rattled. He mustn't think of it as Final Judgement Day.

He was offered, but refused, counselling, afraid it would imply failure and be another mark on his record. Then the union rep took him aside and advised him to book a few sessions.

'Listen, feller, you've got to play the game, just to cover your backside. Show willing. It can't do any harm and, more importantly, if you find at a later date that you can't handle driving any more, it shows you did your best to get over the trauma.'

He wasn't sure it would help, might even pull him apart again. In a strange way, this latest incident had melded with the whole Egerton experience. He couldn't separate them in his mind, and it made him afraid that any open talking to a shrink would bring out things best left hidden for Tim's sake, as well as his own.

As things fell out, three months after the fatality and with the inquest survived, he found himself experiencing a new peace which he wanted nothing to shake him out of. It was as though being with the unknown man at the last had absolved him of any residual guilt over Tim.

Only life isn't like that, he concluded. No guaranteed peace. It's a ruddy roller-coaster ride. This counselling course could be the next risk he had to work up to and crest; then to rush headlong down the other side, into possible disaster.

Life was actually about simple survival. You chug along and take what's coming. No one can tell what's waiting ahead.

He would complete the counselling, give them the answers they expected, and try to make it round the next bend.

At least for the present he was back on track.